Chosen

Cheryl Pryor

Arlington & Amelia

ISBN-13: 978-1886541306
ISBN-10: 1886541302

FOR

CRAIG BRACKETT

1

Kylie was a genius. Her IQ was off the charts. She didn't have that nerdy look of most geniuses. She was stunning with long blonde hair that reached her waist and piercing sapphire blue eyes with a flawless complexion and high cheekbones. Standing at 5'11" she could have easily found work as a fashion model. Both men and women turned for a second look when she walked by, but she was oblivious to her beauty.

She worked at a think tank that specialized in different areas of scientific/medical research. Kylie, one of the youngest on staff in her late twenties, was a geneticist who specialized in the study of DNA. If she had taken the time to study her own DNA she would have been quite shocked. Then again one would never have suspected her DNA was part human, part alien. Least of all Kylie.

Kylie was totally oblivious to the role the aliens played in her life.

The aliens would soon change that, after all she had been chosen.

Kylie was exhausted by the end of the day. Her work was more mental than physical, but all the same she was ready to call it quits for the day.

Amir Singh a forensic psychologist who worked at the desk next to Kylie walked in as she was wrapping up to leave for the day. Amir, a Sikh from India who wore a turban and sported an unruly beard had worked at the think tank for just under a year.

Amir and Kylie working side by side even though working in different fields had become friendly. Usually not one to open up much to other people she found Amir to be a good listener and not one to overstep the boundaries of friendship. But then he wasn't who he appeared to be and had his own agenda for becoming friends with Kylie.

Setting his backpack down on his workstation he said to Kylie, "I'm glad I caught you before you left. I've been informed that for the next two weeks you're to accompany me in the field." He searched in his backpack and pulled out a memo signed by their boss giving her the specifics.

"In the field for you means working on corpses and performing autopsies," Kylie said holding the memo barely glancing at it. "That's not really my thing. Why would I be requested to work with you? I work to save people. I have no desire to work with the dead."

Kylie handed Amir the memo back and said, "Let me make that as clear as I can, zero desire. Thanks, but no thanks."

"Be that as it may, that's your assignment for the next few weeks," Amir told her. "You'll be working alongside me."

"Lucky me. Well, I don't look forward to working with you in your area of expertise," Kylie said. "Anyway, I'm out of here. I'm going home and put my feet up. I'm not going to answer my phone or talk to anyone for the next 12 hours."

"Sounds like a plan," Amir said.

"Thanks to the great news you just laid on me I'll probably be dreaming of dead people and zombies tonight."

Amir threw his head back and laughed at Kylie. She may be a genius but she was certainly entertaining.

Amir watched her walk out. He knew this would be a tough assignment for her. Her parents had died a little over two years ago in a car accident where the young man who hit them was drunk and had walked away unscathed.

She had also lost a sister to leukemia when she was very young, so he knew the thought of viewing and working on corpses would not be something she would look forward to.

2

Kylie turning down the road leading to home was tired and due to fuming about her new assignment she didn't notice the car with darkened windows parked by the curb. It was rare to see a car parked on the street in her neighborhood. Normally she would have spotted the car immediately and taken notice, but not tonight.

As she pulled into her driveway she could see Coco in the window barking with joy at seeing Kylie. She couldn't help herself and broke out in a grin. She loved that dog more than she ever thought she could love an animal.

Coco gave her something to look forward to at the end of each day. It was nice to be greeted with such unconditional love after a tough day. Once she saw Coco's happy greeting all the tension and stress from work was forgotten.

She just thinks I saved her Kylie thought to herself, when in reality she's the one who saved me.

The very day after she had attended her parent's funeral she had been sitting on the steps of her front porch crying feeling more alone than she had ever felt in her life, when seemingly out of nowhere this little black chow retriever mix with floppy ears came up to her and sat in front of her just looking at her and wagging her tail. The dog actually looked like she was smiling at her. Kylie couldn't help but to smile back.

Kylie had half-heartedly looked for the dog's owner and had even put an ad under the found pets section of the newspaper, but after a week of searching unsuccessfully she decided to keep the dog. They had been best buddies ever since.

As Kylie and Coco greeted each other and played on the front lawn the person in the vehicle parked down the street was taking pictures.

Not even having made it inside her house yet her next door neighbor, an elderly woman who walked with the aid of a walker, stepped out onto her porch waving her TV remote at Kylie.

3

"Kylie, dear. It's doing it again."

"What's wrong?" Kylie called from her yard.

"It's my television remote. I must have pushed the wrong button," her neighbor answered. "I missed my soaps today. I've been waiting for you to get home to see if you could fix it for me. I just don't understand these new fangled electronics. Can you give me a hand?" Without waiting for a reply she turned her walker around and walked back inside her house.

"So much for not talking to anyone for the next 12 hours," Kylie thought to herself. "Peace, quiet, and solitude...not gonna happen."

Kylie walked over to her next door neighbor's house with Coco following at her heels. "Sure, Helen. Let me take a look."

Helen was often sitting in the window just waiting for Kylie to get home to fix or adjust something for her. Kylie didn't really mind. She knew her elderly neighbor was lonely and sometimes just looked for an excuse to have Kylie come over.

Helen standing just inside the door said, "Come inside dear, and I'll show you."

Kylie and Coco followed her inside. When she walked in the house Helen set the remote on an end table and said, "There's nothing wrong with my remote. I just had to show you something."

She walked over to a window and picked up a set of binoculars. She handed the binoculars to Kylie and pointed down the street and said, "See that car parked on the street. It's been there three days now. It gets there just before you get home from work and stays until your lights go off at night."

Kylie put the binoculars to her eyes and said, "The windows are dark. You can't see anything."

"Stand over to the side and look in at an angle." She pulled Kylie over to the side a little by her shirt sleeve. "He was taking pictures of you when you got out of the car. It was one of those cameras with a long lens. He's probably one of those perverts you hear about on TV."

"Are you sure he was taking pictures of me?" Kylie asked lowering the binoculars. "Maybe he's a realtor and getting ready to put a house on the market."

"No, dear. He was very interested in you," Helen reached in the drawer of an end table by the couch and pulled out a gun. "Here, take this and go down and ask him what the hell he's doing."

Kylie gingerly took the gun out of her elderly neighbor's hand and set it back inside the drawer. "There's no need for that, but I am going to go see what's going on."

"Come on, Coco." Kylie headed for the front door and noticed a shotgun leaning up against the wall. "Thank you for letting me know Helen, and please put these guns away. For your own safety, if nothing else."

"Now you be careful. I'll be watching you through my binoculars. Just wave if you need me and I'll come as fast as I can," Helen said.

"Armed to the teeth," she added after Kylie had gone down the porch steps.

Kylie marched down the street at a brisk pace with Coco at her heels. The person in the car seeing she was heading for him quickly backed the car all the way down the street and made a turn and took off before she could get the number of his license plate.

3

Even with Kylie's long legs she had a hard time keeping up with Amir's long stride. She was explaining as they walked, "You know I really don't want to do this. I don't see the point. I have no intention on going into the field of forensics, so why should I be forced to attend an autopsy?"

Amir stopped walking and Kylie almost bumped into him. "Kylie, I understand. Really, I do. Today, I'll just be observing with you. I'll be there right by your side. You'll be fine."

"But why do I have to do this? Why does the boss want me to work with you on this?" Kylie asked. "It doesn't make any sense."

Amir holding the door to the medical building open for Kylie to enter ahead of him answered, "I don't ask questions. I just do what I'm told."

"Well, that's never been my way," Kylie said.

"Obviously," Amir said exasperated with this entire topic of conversation. He knew exactly why Kylie had been assigned to this duty and it wasn't by her boss, but he didn't have the authority to enlighten her of that fact. Not only that, if she had known the truth she never would have believed him. She'd find out soon enough. And when she did....her whole world would change.

They entered the office of the medical examiner's office. A man in scrubs walked out of an office and said, "Amir, you're just in time."

"You must be Dr. Carmichael," he said turning to Kylie. "I'm Dr. Brackett, the forensic pathologist who will be performing the autopsy you'll be observing," he reached out to shake Kylie's hand.

"Kylie, please. It's nice to meet you," Kylie said.

"Call me Craig," the pathologist said smiling at Kylie.

Amir gave Kylie a look as they were walking once Dr. Brackett's back was turned. He leaned over and whispered to Kylie, "He never told me to call him Craig."

Kylie poked him in the ribs and told him to behave.

They followed Dr. Brackett into a room with large stainless

steel drawers. Kylie immediately began to shiver.

Dr. Brackett noticed and said, "This area is kept at 40 degrees Fahrenheit. It can be pretty chilly if you're not accustomed to it."

Kylie merely nodded her head. Her nerves were frayed just thinking about what lay ahead. The cold temperature was only part of why she was shaking.

Dr. Brackett grabbed a sweater out of his office and handed it to Kylie. Her hands were shaking as she put it on. Amir noticing reached over and helped her with the sweater.

They followed Dr. Brackett into another room where the floor was tiled and there were several large stainless steel tables with scales hanging overhead.

Kylie looking around noticed the surgical instruments nearby along with a few tools you wouldn't find in any operating room. She didn't want to give too much thought as to what those tools were used for.

Standing next to a large stainless steel sink was a woman wearing a white lab coat waiting for them. Dr. Brackett introduced the woman as Melissa and explained that she was the diener.

Melissa asked him if he was ready for the body and he told her to hold off for a few minutes.

"Are you going to be O.K.?" Dr. Brackett asked Kylie.

"This isn't my idea. I don't even know why I'm here. I'm a geneticist and have no interest in pursuing forensic pathology," Kylie explained.

It seemed she had been using the same argument with several people ever since she had discovered this assignment, but to no avail. As here she stood, about to witness some body that was a person who was alive a matter of days ago walking around enjoying life and now about to be sliced and diced.

"In an autopsy you can discover hereditary illnesses that can aid in discovering cures or treatments. You'll be surprised at all you can learn through an autopsy and how that knowledge can be applied in your field," Dr. Brackett explained.

Melissa said, "There's no shame if you get sick or pass out at your first autopsy. Believe me, you won't be the first to have done so. Some of our toughest med students have passed out before the autopsy even began."

"Just be sure you don't puke on my dead body or any body parts. Use the garbage can or go outside in the hall if you start feeling sick," Dr. Brackett said.

"And don't throw up in the sink," Melissa added. "That's where we wash body parts and we can't have that area contaminated."

"The smell of the formaldehyde is probably what's assaulting your senses now," Amir said as he put his hand on her back to reassure her. "If at any time during the autopsy it's too much for you, just let me know and we'll step outside."

Melissa reached in a cabinet and pulled out a bottle of Vicks Vaporub. Unscrewing the top she said, "Dip your finger in there and rub a little bit underneath your nose. The smells can get pretty intense. This will help."

Kylie smiled tenuously and said, "Thanks."

Dr. Brackett nodded for Melissa to bring in the body.

4

Kylie watched Amir dig into his food. "How can you eat after what we just saw?"

"You have to remember, I've been doing this for years and in all types of deaths. There isn't much I haven't seen at this point. You have to look at it as a job and keep it impersonal or it can eat at you," Amir answered.

Kylie picked up her fork but merely pushed the food around on her plate. She took one small bite and then set the fork back down. "When Melissa wheeled the gurney in the room with feet sticking out of the sheet and a toe tag on it's big toe, that just seemed so impersonal."

Amir said, "They're doing their job and trying to give the families of the deceased some answers and comfort."

Kylie answered, "I'll never get used to it, nor do I want to. How many more of these am I expected to observe?"

"Quite a few, I'm afraid. They'll get easier once you begin to look at it clinically and as a learning opportunity," Amir said. He thought to himself that if she thought this was tough just wait until she witnessed the autopsy on an alien, because that was exactly what she was being groomed to do.

That afternoon at least she was able to go home early as she wasn't expected back at the lab. She was going to go home and get Coco and go for a long walk. Fresh air was what she desperately needed.

Driving home she tried to put the sights she had seen out of her mind. And the smells...she wondered if she would ever get those smells out of her clothes.

As she got home and was getting out of her car the school bus pulled up at the end of the block. Gordon her six year old next door neighbor spotted her and came running down the street with his book bag dragging on the sidewalk beside him. "Kylie, wait for me."

Gordon was the son of her next door neighbors on the other side from where her elderly neighbor lived. He often found his way over to Kylie's spending time at her house. She didn't mind. He always had a sunny disposition and was better company than most.

After a long, hot shower and a change of clothes she grabbed Coco's leash and asked Gordon if he wanted to join them for a walk. Gordon set down his PlayStation gaming system he was playing and jumped up to join them.

Being out in the fresh air gave her a new perspective and listening to Gordon's constant chatter enabled her to put the events of the day behind her.

At the moment his main topic was NASCAR. His dad was a fan and he and Gordon never missed watching the races together. "Did you know I was named after Jeff Gordon?" he asked Kylie.

"No, I didn't know that." she answered. "Who's Jeff Gordon?"

"For real? You don't know who Jeff Gordon is?" he asked as he walked backwards down the sidewalk looking at Kylie. "He was my dad's favorite NASCAR driver. He doesn't race anymore. He was the best." Gordon made sound effects as though he was revving up an engine.

"And my baby sisters named after Danica Patrick. Only her middle name is Taylor after Taylor Swift 'cuz my mom made a deal with my dad. She's a race car driver too, Danica not Taylor Swift," Gordon explained barely coming up for air. "Do you like country music?"

Kylie tried not to laugh. "I'm more of a rock and roll fan than I am of country music."

This adorable little boy was certainly entertaining. He could change topics as fast as those race cars drove around the track. You never knew what he'd come up with next.

Gordon slowed down and stopped and waited patiently while Coco sniffed at something in the grass that had captured her attention.

Gordon spotted the frog as it hopped out of the grass trying to escape from Coco. He dropped Coco's leash and ran to try to catch it.

"Leave that frog alone if you're coming home with me," Kylie said bending over and picking up the leash he had dropped. "No frogs."

Gordon laughed and came back and started walking beside her reaching over to hold her hand. Kylie smiled down at him.

"Girls are afraid of frogs and spiders and snakes," he said. "If you're afraid, that's O.K. My dad said everybody's afraid of something."

"Is that right? And what are you afraid of?" Kylie asked him smiling down at him.

Gordon thought for just a minute. "Going to sleep at night and things coming out of my closet."

"You mean things like monsters," she said and raised her arms and started growling and chasing him around pretending to be a monster.

"Not monsters, aliens," he shouted as he ran from Kylie squealing in delight with Coco joining in the fun by barking and dancing around them. Kylie caught him and tickled him.

As they walked along the street Gordon talked about what they were learning in school, his new best friend, and a myriad of topics.

Kylie tuned his chatter out as she enjoyed the sunshine and being outdoors.

As they turned down their street heading towards home Kylie noticed the car that was there yesterday was back again but parked in a different spot. It was worrisome. Why would someone be watching her, if that was indeed what they were doing?

5

Kylie and Gordon spent the afternoon playing video games. She invited him to stay over and have dinner with her.

Gordon was sitting at her dining room table with paper and crayons Kylie had set him up with while she made them spaghetti squash topped with vegetables and salsa for dinner.

Kylie stood at the counter and chopped up the vegetables. Most kids turned their noses up at eating veggies, but Gordon seemed to be satisfied with whatever she fed him. She knew most meals he ate at home came out of a box, a bag, or container so when he ate at her house she tried to make sure he had something healthy.

Once the spaghetti squash came out of the oven she forked out the strands for the spaghetti and added the toppings. She came over to set the table and asked, "What are you drawing?"

Gordon happily held up the first picture he drew of a little boy who she assumed was Gordon playing baseball.

"That's really good," Kylie said. "What's this one of?" Kylie asked pointing at the other picture he had drawn.

"That's the alien spaceship and the aliens that come to get me," Gordon said.

"That's quite an imagination you have there," Kylie laughed as she looked at the picture of little gray aliens with big heads and big slanted eyes.

"Oh, no; they're real." Gordon said in all seriousness.

Kylie stood up to check on the timer for the bread in the oven. The bread was almost done so she started putting the spaghetti on the plates.

"I've seen them take you, too. Don't you remember?" Gordon asked.

While putting the food on the plates Kylie answered, "I don't think I'm likely to forget something like that if it ever happened."

"But, it did," Gordon insisted. "I saw you going into the

spaceship."

Kylie chuckled to herself thinking how the young had great imaginations.

There was a knock at the door and then Olivia, the woman who had been Kylie's mom's best friend, let herself in. "Something smells good."

Kylie called out, "We're in the kitchen. You can join us for dinner." She opened the oven door and took out a long loaf of cheesy onion bread. The smells immediately permeated the room with the scent of garlic and fresh baked bread.

"Yum, how could I resist," Olivia responded. "Hey, Gordon."

He immediately held up his artwork for her to admire while Kylie filled another plate and put silverware on the table for their additional guest.

Olivia's face drained of color when Gordon held up his picture of the aliens and their spacecraft. He excitedly explained to Olivia how they were visitors and sometimes came and took him and Kylie aboard their spaceship.

"Stick your art work on the fridge Gordon so we can eat," Kylie said. "We wouldn't want to get any food on your pictures and mess them up."

Gordon happily complied, grabbing magnets off the fridge and putting his drawings up for Kylie to keep.

Olivia looked at Kylie to see how she responded to what Gordon had said about seeing her on a spacecraft. She didn't seem to be bothered by what he said as she sliced the cheesy bread and continued talking while serving everyone.

Olivia could only assume her mother had never informed Kylie that she was one of a third generation who had indeed been chosen and taken by aliens. Evidently from what Gordon said, it was still happening.

6

"I'm certainly thankful those weeks are behind us and I don't ever have to attend another autopsy," Kylie said to Amir.

"Never again, huh?" Amir said. "You know what they say about never saying never."

"Nope, never again!" Kylie said. "I'm sticking to that." She bent over the paper that she was writing on her discoveries.

Once she returned to the lab she had been asked to write what she had learned to add to the extensive notes she had written after each autopsy.

After the initial autopsy to prepare her for what was to come she had been ordered to focus at each following autopsy on different parts of the body. In doing so it had been at least a little easier to look at in a more scientific manner.

"Kylie, we're going out to the new club down the street. Want to join us?" one of her co-workers asked.

Kylie barely looked up to answer her co-worker as she and two others were packing up and preparing to leave work.

"Thanks, but I have to finish up here," Kylie answered.

"I guess that's a no then," her co-worker said and shrugged. "Big surprise. Come join us later if you finish. We'll be there for awhile."

"All the more good looking guys for us to choose from then," her other co-worker said. "We don't get a second look when Kylie is with us. The guys all spot her and start drooling and we never get a second look after that."

Her friend laughed and said, "See what you're missing out on, Kylie? Men drooling all over you."

"I have a dog that does that. You all have fun," Kylie said.

After they had left and moved down the hall, Amir leaned back in his chair and stared at her. "Why don't you ever join the others when they ask you? You're too young not to have any social life," he looked at her waiting for an answer.

"I went with them once, but that's not for me." Kylie answered while writing furiously trying to finish the notes so she could leave for the night. "Why didn't you join them?"

Amir stood up to leave and said, "I think the turban intimidates them. In case you haven't noticed, they never ask me." Amir standing at 6'4" could come across as pretty intimidating if you didn't know him.

"Besides I'm a Sikh, and Sikhs don't drink alcoholic beverages," Amir said.

"I don't drink either, and I have no desire to hang around a bunch of people who have been drinking," Kylie said.

"Please, don't tell me that you're going to let one bad relationship ruin you..." Amir started to say before Kylie interrupted.

"Bad relationship?" Kylie said with sarcasm. "Yeah, I guess that's what you could call a bad relationship when the man you think you're going to spend the rest of your life with runs off with your best friend."

"Not all men are like that, Kylie. Most men would be honored to have you for..."

"No, thanks," Kylie said. "Look, I'm not a man-hater or anything like that. I just made a bad choice. I'm not anxious to repeat that experience."

"No," Amir said. "He made the bad choice, not you, by leaving you like that. And it doesn't say much for your best friend either."

"You're right about that," Kylie said. "Ex-best friend, ex-fiancé; they deserve each other."

"Don't you want to have a family? You're so good with children," Amir said.

"Yeah, I love kids and would have loved to have had a few, but it doesn't seem to be in my future," Kylie said.

"You're young yet," Amir said. "Don't let one rotten apple ruin your appetite."

"That's a new one," Kylie said. "I've never heard that expression before." She bent back over her paper work to see where she had left off. "Well, if I can't have children at least maybe

I can save a few."

Amir knew Kylie was referring to her goal to come up with a cure for childhood leukemia. That was what her sister had died from and he assumed what had led her to the field of medicine.

"Don't give up on men, Kylie. You're a lovely young woman with a good heart. I hope you'll find happiness one day," Amir said.

"It's really hard to trust again after something like that happens. I'm not saying it won't happen one day, but I really haven't met anyone else I'm even remotely attracted to."

"Nor will you hiding behind your microscope all the time," Amir said. "You need to get out once in awhile and give yourself a chance to meet someone."

Amir picked up his laptop and stuffed his research papers in his briefcase. He was quietly packing up all his belongings while they were talking and stuffing them in a backpack and his briefcase. You're a good woman and you've been a good friend. Take care, Kylie."

Kylie waved without looking up not even noticing that he had cleared out his desk or said she 'had been' a good friend as though it was something in the past.

Amir gave her a long, last look before walking out. His job here was finished.

Amir hadn't been gone for long when two men entered the room where she was working and closed the door behind them. At the sound of the door closing Kylie looked up and was surprised to see who was standing just inside the lab.

7

Kylie's boss who seldom came to the laboratory stood just inside the door of the lab with another man who even though not in uniform his stance gave him away as military. Kylie's guess from the way he held himself was that he was a high ranking officer. Her boss looked oddly ill at ease.

"Kylie, umm, excuse me... Dr. Carmichael, there's an important assignment that needs taken care of immediately," her boss said as he approached her work table.

Kylie picked up the paperwork she had been working on and put it inside a folder and set it off to the side of her desk.

The other man who had come in with her boss stepped forward and without any small talk got right to the point of his being there. "I have to make this perfectly clear before we proceed any further. This is classified top secret work you'll be doing and the item I leave with you cannot leave this room. You can not talk about what you are about to see or your work on this with anyone. I understand you have a top secret clearance so you understand the importance of what I'm saying?"

"Of course," Kylie answered while glancing at the clock on the wall. It was Friday night going on 6:00 P.M. and she was wondering when she was supposed to be working on this special assignment since she was officially off the clock.

The man caught her glance at the clock and said, "I realize it's late in the evening to be starting work on a project, but this needs to be taken care of immediately. Your dinner will be brought in. If there's anything you need taken care of, please do so before I turn the work over to you."

"How long do you think this will take? I have a dog at home that needs to be walked and fed," Kylie answered.

"Is there someone you can call to take care of the animal? If not, I'll send one of my men out to take care of the dog," the man responded. "You may want to make arrangements for the dog to be taken care of in the morning, too."

Kylie called Olivia, her mother's best friend, and arranged for her to stay over at her house to care for Coco. By the time she was through with the phone conversation a delivery had arrived that she assumed was her dinner.

"I'm sorry if you had plans, Kylie," her boss said. "If this weren't of utmost importance I wouldn't be asking you to take time out of your weekend."

"No apologies or explanations needed," the man said. "It's in the interest of your country, and I'm sure that has more precedence than whatever plans you may have had."

Kylie looked at him and merely nodded and said, "Of course, if it's that important. But, why me? Surely you have others that would come more highly recommended than me to do this work."

The man looked around at the state of the art laboratory and said, "Dr. Carmichael, your IQ speaks for itself. You certainly have the qualifications to do this work. You come very highly recommended. We want your perspective on this – a fresh set of eyes and viewpoint. We often use employees from your workplace on certain projects, some which eventually come to work for us. Perhaps one day you will, too."

"Who is *us*, if I may ask," Kylie asked as she unwrapped the delivery bag holding her dinner and peeked in. There was a cucumber, sprouts, and cream cheese sandwich on a toasted ciabatta bun, some kale chips, along with hummus and some carrot sticks and two bottles of green tea. Wondering how they could possibly know her dietary choice she closed the bag and set it aside.

"You understand you cannot leave this room other than to use the rest room while you're working," the man went on to explain choosing to ignore her question.

"Excuse me, but we haven't even been introduced." Kylie reached out her hand to shake his and smiled and said, "My name is Kylie Carmichael. What's your name?"

"My name is of no importance," he said turning away from her extended hand. "You will sign..."

"It may not be of importance to you, but it is common

courtesy. You've asked me to give up my Friday evening and work into the night doing who knows what, and you won't even introduce yourself?" Kylie said a bit ticked off. While not exactly rude, she didn't mince words.

Her boss stepped forward, "Kylie, please..."

The man looked over at her boss and put his hand out to stop him and said, 'You're right. For whatever it's worth, my name is Winston."

"First or last?" Kylie interrupted.

"First or last what?" the man asked exasperated with the conversation, unused to being questioned by anyone.

"Your name is Winston. Is it your first or your last name?" Kylie asked.

"Just call me Winston, if you must call me anything."

"See, that wasn't so hard," Kylie said with a smile. "Now, you're beginning to seem human. Well, almost anyway. If that were only your true name I might feel we might be getting somewhere, but I noticed you looked at the package of cigarettes poking out of my bosses' breast pocket before answering me and amazingly enough they just happen to be Winston cigarettes. I would say what a coincidence, only I'm not prone to believe in coincidences."

Her boss covered his laugh with a cough and turned away to hide a smile. He had warned him that the best way to approach Kylie was with complete honesty, not deceit. She saw through people in no time.

The man sighed and ran his hand through the little bit of hair he had. "You're beginning to sound like my daughter."

"Aah, so he is human," Kylie said with a smile.

"No more interruptions. This is serious business," the man said firmly, clearly becoming frustrated with where this conversation was going. He had somehow lost control of the situation, something he was unaccustomed to.

He waited half expecting her to interrupt him again but Kylie merely nodded her head for him to continue. She had made her point, no reason to push it.

"You will be asked to sign a waiver stating you understand you are not to discuss this work or your findings with anyone other than me or anyone I clear – even your boss. If you do not follow this you can be and will be imprisoned for treason."

At this point he turned and dismissed her boss. As her boss stepped out of the room Kylie looked up at the doorway where she could see that there were two armed guards standing by the door. Another man stood between them holding a lock box.

8

"Let me make this clear. You will not leave this room and no one else will enter. The building will be guarded until your work is complete," he said.

He knew he was sounding a bit peevish, even to himself. This young lady had clearly pushed his buttons. He thought to himself that he was glad Alan wasn't here to witness this. Alan had warned him in how to approach Kylie, and somewhere along the way it had gone all wrong.

He looked at Kylie intently to see if she was paying close attention to what he was saying. After reassuring himself that he had her undivided attention he continued.

"You will be given an item to study and see if you can discover what it is or it's origin. It is entirely possible that even after hours of study you will not have an answer, but I would like you to take extensive notes on any findings you have or any questions or concerns and turn those over to me when you're finished.

When you feel you can do no more you can notify one of the guards and I'll return, and only then will you be able to leave," Winston said. He then pulled out the waiver for her to sign.

She hesitated before she accepted the paperwork and quickly scanned it before signing.

She had to wonder what she was about to get into. Once you knew something you could never un-learn it, and from how he had described this work she thought it was probably something she would have rather not known about.

"Dr. Carmichael, we aren't the enemy here. This is of vital importance that could have a bearing on our national security. The reason we have chosen you is we have respect for your intelligence and have faith that you can be an asset in this matter."

After handing over the signed paperwork she leaned back in her chair and said, "Understood. I guess I'm supposed to be flattered. Let's get to work then."

Winston motioned for the man to enter the room who had the lock box. He left it in the care of Winston and the man and the armed guards then left the room.

"I have no instructions other than to take extensive notes on your findings, discoveries, or any thoughts or questions you have. No thoughts or findings are too small or irrelevant. Please make note of everything."

As he prepared to leave he said, "I must confiscate your telephone until this is completed. Hand it over please with no further discussion."

After confiscating her phone he explained that there would be armed guards keeping everyone else out and keeping her in until the work was complete. He then left the key to the lock box in her care and left the room.

She listened to him walk down the hall and only after the doors at the end of the hall banged closed did she pull the locked box towards her.

Kylie inserted the key and slowly opened the lock box with trepidation.

Once the lid of the lock box was open she took a deep breath and peered inside.

Peering inside the lock box she gazed at the item inside and said, "All that for this little thing."

9

She had been given no clue of what to expect to find inside the box, only that it was of Top Secret/Sensitive clearance. She had been threatened with being charged with treason if she so much as talked about what she discovered inside the box.

She reached inside to remove the specimen on it's glass microscopic slide covered with a glass coverslip.

She wondered why the slide and coverslip were sealed which was most unusual. Never before had she received a specimen sealed between the slide and the coverslip such as this one.

She didn't like the fact that it was sealed. It would prohibit her work somewhat. She would have liked to have run a DNA test on it to give her some insight as to it's origin.

Not knowing what she was dealing with she donned a mask and latex gloves before proceeding any further. Even contained under glass she wasn't taking any chances.

Kylie held the slide up in the light. Her first inclination was it had the look of human skin, but then again not.

The color was off, the specimen being almost a gray with a bluish tint to it. So, definitely not human skin unless whoever this came off of suffered from methemoglobinemia, an inherited or congenital condition or a condition sometimes caused from exposure to toxins or dehydration.

She couldn't completely rule that out, but that usually turned the skin very blue where this was more of a hint of blue. Still, she made note of it. Like the man said, keep extensive notes.

She turned the slide at an angle and noticed some sort of microscopic suction cups attached to it that were so minute they would have gone unobserved by most.

There were other differences she discovered as well that threw her off from her first thought of human skin. By first glancing at it she would have sworn it was skin of some sort or some sort of outer covering.

As she examined it more closely she decided it definitely did not have the appearance of human skin as she had first assumed. So, not human then.

She rolled her chair over to her work center and slid the slide under the microscope. Peering into the microscopic lens she began adjusting the dials back and forth very slowly to bring it into focus and enhance the image.

The enhanced image of the specimen showed it to be mesh-like, unlike human skin, but more like that of a lizard. She continued peering into the microscope and looked at it from all angles.

Her total focus was on this two inch piece of specimen and the puzzle at hand of just what it was.

She had been so involved with the work that she didn't hear two sets of footsteps softly approaching down the hall and entering the room next to where she worked, silently closing the door behind them.

The two men had entered the adjoining room with a one-way mirror and set themselves up knowing they would most likely be there for hours.

One of the men took a seat in the back of the room and picked up Kylie's phone. He began scrolling through her contacts list on her phone and making note of them. When he finished he set her phone off to the side.

The other man pulled up a chair by the one-way mirror and watched her every move. The man sitting in the shadows of the back of the room spoke in hushed tones to the man watching her.

"The thing that's going to trouble her, even if she considers the possibility of where this came from, is it's something outside her realm of thinking. She's one of those 'I have to see it before I believe it' type of people."

The other man answered, "Well, it's certain she hasn't seen anything like this before. The fact being that it's not of this earth. I doubt she's had the opportunity to come across any aliens in her lifetime."

"Well, that's about to change, isn't it?" the man in the shadows said.

All signs of peevishness at being asked to stay and do this job had left her the moment she set eyes on the specimen in question. Her curiosity now had the best of her. She loved a challenge and this certainly fit into that category.

The hours passed and she was completely unaware of the time or the fact that she had worked nonstop for almost 16 hours. She had taken time out only to drink one bottle of green tea and to take a few bites out of her sandwich while she continued studying the specimen before her.

She locked the specimen in the lock box and took the key with her removing the mask and gloves as she got up to take a bathroom break.

Entering the hallway she glanced to the end of the hall as she approached the bathroom door. She could see through the glass in the doorway a guard standing watch. There was another armed guard at the door at the other end of the hall. No one was getting in or out, that was certain.

Just what was the importance of this two inch specimen she had been given for observation and study? All she really knew is it took one of the highest Top Secret clearances to work with it and a threat of her life or imprisonment if she so much as breathed a word of what she had seen. It was hard for her to imagine that the two inch specimen she was studying would have that sort of importance.

She had been amazed to learn they had upped her clearance level to enable her to work with it. To up one's clearance level took pulling strings.

She threw some water on her face and vigorously wiped her face off with paper towels trying to wake herself up. Before heading back to work she made a fresh pot of coffee, something she normally avoided.

As the room filled with the scent of fresh coffee brewing she quickly scanned a few of her notes and got back to work. This time she omitted donning the mask and gloves. The gloves hindered her writing and the mask was hot. The specimen was after all contained, so she felt safe handling it.

She looked at the clock surprised to see how the hours had passed. The coffee in the pot remained untouched, forgotten as she continued to work. She rubbed the back of her neck. She felt stiff from being bent over a microscope for hours on end.

"Damn, I wish Amir were here," she said as she slid her chair back from the table. "He would be able to answer a few questions I have," she said out loud to an empty room.

She got up and paced as she thought, only to return to her desk moments later to lean over it and scribble a few more notes before she continued her pacing.

Not only were the men in the next room watching her every move, but they could hear her as clearly as if she were in the room with them.

"Who is she talking to? There's no one in the room with her," the man asked his companion who sat off to the side taking notes. "Are you sure she's mentally stable? You know sometimes geniuses are a bit off."

The man sitting in the back of the room let out a little chuckle. "There's nothing off about Kylie, I assure you. She talks to herself all the time when she's working. She likes to think out loud is how she explains it. Seems to work for her," he shrugged and smiled. "Believe me, she's not off. She's one of the most brilliant people I've ever come across. Probably has a higher IQ than you. No, not probably; most definitely."

The man standing at the one-way mirror gave him a dark look and said, "It's strange. Talking to an empty room. Seems a bit deranged, if you ask me. And why does she say she wishes you were there?"

The man Kylie knew as Amir answered, "She knows I work with corpses, and she has obviously at least figured out somewhat of what she is working with. It's the discrepancies that have her baffled," he explained to the major who was watching Kylie.

"How much longer do you think she'll work at it?" the man asked.

Amir answered, "She's not a quitter. You might as well get comfortable." Amir grabbed a pillow off the sofa he was sitting on and adjusted the pillow behind his head. He kicked his shoes off and put his feet up on the chair in front of him and closed his eyes.

After working straight for over 19 hours Kylie rubbed her eyes. "Just going to rest for a minute or two," she thought as she laid her head on her desk. She jerked as she started to doze and when doing so her elbow knocked the slide off the desk and onto the floor where the glass shattered.

Kylie reached down to pick up the pieces. As she reached for some of the broken glass a sliver of it cut her finger and a stream of blood ran down her finger.

"Ouch!" She pulled the sliver of glass out of her finger and tried to staunch the blood with a paper towel.

She looked around the floor for the specimen and finding it reached down and picked it up. As she did so it wrapped itself around her finger and adhered itself to her.

If she hadn't seen it happen herself, she wouldn't have believed it. It was wrapped tightly around her finger without so much as a sign of a wrinkle or tell-tale line. The bleeding immediately stopped and there was no longer any trace of a cut.

Kylie was amazed when she saw how the specimen had stuck to her finger like a second skin. She tried shaking it off her finger and then tried removing it manually. She not only couldn't get it to budge, but it had clung to her finger to the point where you couldn't tell where her skin began and the specimen ended – it had merged seamlessly.

To be sure what she thought had just happened had indeed happened she put her finger under the microscope. It was only then that she noticed the little suction cups on the end of her finger.

She got up and walked over to a work station and picked up a scalpel and tried cutting it off. When that didn't work she really began to panic.

That's when the two men entered the room.

10

Winston walked over and picked up her hand examining it very closely. He had been standing at the one-way mirror when the incident occurred so he was well aware of what happened. He had never expected it or seen anything like it.

Kylie looked up at the other man who had entered the room with Winston. She did a double take. "Amir?"

Amir, without his turban which she had *never* seen him without stood quietly. He merely nodded at Kylie.

"Amir, you're not supposed to be here," Kylie said in a panic to her co-worker.

Winston still holding her hand examining her finger closely said, "He's with me."

Kylie rapidly began explaining to Winston what had occurred not yet realizing he was well aware of everything that had gone on inside the room.

"Others have worked with this specimen, but nothing like this ever happened," Winston said more to himself than to anyone.

"I knocked the slide off onto the floor by mistake and the slide broke. When I reached for the specimen it wrapped itself around my finger," Kylie was explaining.

"But where? I can't see a thing," Winston said not so gently turning her hand in all directions.

Amir stepped forward and said, "Put her finger under the microscope and enlarge the view. Perhaps then you can see it to remove it."

"Believe me, I've tried everything," Kylie said in a panic. "Even under the microscope you can't see where it ends and my skin begins. It seems to have merged with my skin. The only way you can even tell it's there is from the little suction cup things from the ends."

Kylie asked Winston, "Is he supposed to see this? You told me no one was allowed in or out of the building. I wasn't supposed to talk about this to anyone with the threat of death or imprisonment, yet how is it that he's here?"

"He works with me," Winston said.

"He what!?" Kylie said pulling her hand back. "Would you explain that, please."

"I'll explain later, Kylie," Amir said in a quiet tone. He knew once he explained there would be trouble from Kylie.

Winston said, "I've got to make a call. We can't have you walking around with that on your finger."

He stepped out of the room and she could hear him talking on the phone to someone, but she couldn't hear what he was saying.

"What's going on, Amir? What does he mean you work for him? And why aren't you wearing your turban? You always wear it." Kylie asked her friend and co-worker.

Amir let out a long sigh and walked over and sat at his old desk. "Kylie, let me explain and please let me finish before you interrupt me."

"I work for... well; it doesn't matter, but let's just say I work for the government. I was sent here to get to know you and to watch your work and see if you..."

"What?! You were sent here to spy on me? Is that what you're saying?" Kylie asked, even angrier now that he was explaining.

"Well, if that's how you want to put it yes, I guess that's..." Amir said.

"Well, let's call a spade a spade. Don't try to sugarcoat it. If you were sent here to get to know me and watch me then yeah, I'd say you were spying on me," Kylie said now standing up and pacing. "And I thought you were my friend!"

Amir sat back in his chair frustrated. He knew this day would come when he would have to try to explain the situation and he knew it wasn't going to be easy. With Kylie everything was either black or white, there was no gray. Trust was a big issue for her. It was important if they were going to work together in the future that she get past this and not hold a grudge.

"Am I allowed to ask why?" Kylie said with her arms folded across her chest staring at Amir. "And what's the deal with the turban? Was that some sort of disguise? Seriously, you went to..."

"Your work and your intelligence has been noted by higher

ups and you are highly respected. The people I work with are considering you for a career opportunity, but it's a highly sensitive job..."

"Did they even bother to see if I was interested in this job," Kylie said. "Because I'll tell you, I'm quite happy where I'm at and there's no way I would ever work for someone who's so devious, so underhanded. Especially the government!"

"Kylie, listen please," Amir said. "It's important to me that you understand. During the time I've gotten to know you I not only respected you as a colleague but as a friend..."

"Friends don't spy on each other," Kylie said. "And you didn't answer me about the turban. Were you a spy in disguise? What's going on?"

"Yes, it was a disguise," Amir said quietly. "I'm sorry I had to go to those lengths. It wasn't my idea."

Winston walked back into the room. "Dr. Carmichael, you're not a child so stop acting like one. In some situations it's necessary to know more about a person before you know if they can be trusted."

"Oh, that's rich," Kylie laughed. "You want to spy on me to see if you can trust me, but how do you think I could ever trust you after this revelation."

Winston said, "Sit down. When Kylie just glared at him he said, "Please. Let me explain."

Kylie sat, but she wasn't any less angry.

"The work we do is of the highest security clearance in the nation. You're an intelligent human being, but just because a person is intelligent doesn't necessarily mean they're honorable. You know we couldn't just hire someone off the street before we knew if they could be trusted with national secrets." Winston paused a moment to let that sink in.

After a moment Winston continued, "This wasn't Alan's idea. He called in many times wanting to bring you into the loop. The idea of deceiving you in any way didn't sit well with him."

"Well, I should hope not," Kylie said a little quieter. She sat back in her seat, then immediately sat forward. "Wait, you just called him Alan. So, not only was he in disguise, but Amir isn't even his name?"

"No," Amir answered himself. "My name is Alan Christenson."

One of the guards escorted a woman in with a doctor's bag. Once she was in the room the guard turned around and went back to his post.

"Hello, Major. I understand you're in need of my help. The woman smiled at Kylie and extended her hand and said, "Hello. I'm Dr...."

"No names, please," Winston interrupted.

"Very well then," the doctor said. "Let's see if we can't remove that specimen from your finger."

"Please do," Kylie said and held out her hand for the doctor to examine.

The doctor did tell Kylie she was a surgeon. She worked on Kylie's hand for a solid hour but to no avail.

"I don't know what to tell you, Major. But the specimen appears to be on to stay," the doctor said.

"We can't have her walking around with that on her finger. Can you at least cut off the suction cups so it appears to be an ordinary finger?" Winston asked.

"I've tried and they aren't coming off. I couldn't even make a cut in them. I've cut into all types of body organs, skin, muscle, tissue, and everything else with no problem; but this, it was like the scalpel just bounced off it," the doctor put her surgical tools back into her bag.

"There's nothing else I can do," the doctor said. Perhaps eventually it will wear off like an old Band-Aid, but as of now you can't even tell it's there. If only I could do as good a job in surgery."

Kylie rubbed her hand. Between the doctor, the major, and her trying to get it off her hand was sore.

"Can you at least put some kind of bandage on it so no one will notice the suction cups?" the major asked.

"She can't walk around with her finger bandaged for who knows how long," the doctor said in response to the major's question. "No one is going to notice. The suction cups seem to have withdrawn into the skin somewhat. You won't even feel them if someone is holding her hand. I don't think you need to worry about a bandage. It would just draw more attention."

The doctor picked up her bag and said, "Sorry I couldn't have been of more help, but you knew what you were working with. You knew it was a risk."

As the doctor walked out of the room Kylie looked at him and asked, "Just what *was* I working with?"

"I could tell you but then I'd have to kill you," the major said in an uncharacteristic joke which didn't go over very well.

"What! You think this is funny?" Kylie asked. "I think you owe me at least an answer to what this is wrapped around my finger since it now seems to be a part of me."

The evening Kylie was pulling an all-nighter at work was the night the aliens came.

Olivia had stayed over night to care for Coco. She was sleeping in the guest room when she was woken up from a deep sleep. The room filled with bright colored lights. It was the middle of the night, yet the room was as light as though it were the middle of the day.

As Olivia opened her eyes she could see the rotating lights coming in through the bedroom window. She let out a groan.

She knew what the lights meant. She was one of the chosen ones and *'they'* were coming for her. She had been through this before. This wasn't her first rodeo, or in this case, alien abduction.

She watched with dread as two aliens about three to four feet in height with large heads on skinny necks stepped out of the closet. It always astounded her how they walked through walls. It defied physics.

The aliens stared at her with their large, slanted eyes until they knew they had her attention. They stood at the end of the bed and without uttering a word motioned for her to follow.

They escorted Olivia out the front door and to their spacecraft. The spacecraft hovered in the street in front of Kylie's house with swirling bright lights.

There was no point fighting them, she knew who would win. They always did. She stepped towards the beam of light.

The next thing Olivia remembered was when she woke up the following morning to the smells of Kylie cooking bacon.

As Olivia rolled over and looked at the bedside clock she saw it was close to noon.

Olivia forced herself to get out of bed. What she really wanted to do was roll over and pull the covers over her head. She did not want to have to face Kylie. Not after what had occurred last night.

Olivia was pulling her shorts on when she noticed bruises on her legs. Bruises that were shaped like hand prints. She reached in her purse and grabbed some make-up and put it over the bruises trying to conceal them.

"I feel like crap," Olivia said to herself. She ran her fingers through her hair and headed towards the kitchen where she knew she would find Kylie.

Olivia stood in the doorway for a minute trying to get up the strength to walk in the kitchen. She was exhausted and felt like she was getting sick. She was feeling achy and feverish, typical of how she felt after an abduction.

Kylie looked up and saw Olivia leaning against the door frame and said, "Good thing I got home when I did. You overslept and Coco desperately needed to go out."

Kylie turned back around to turn the bacon over. "Are you alright? You look like you aren't feeling good?"

Olivia came into the kitchen and reached for a piece of toast that had popped up out of the toaster. Just as she reached for the toast the lights in the kitchen dimmed and sparks shot out of the toaster.

Kylie ran over and quickly unplugged the toaster. "I guess my toaster has gone kaput. At least I got some toast made first." She watched as the lights dimmed several times. "I should probably call in an electrician to check out the wiring in this house. It probably hasn't been replaced since the house was built."

"It's not the wiring," Olivia said quietly.

Olivia walked over and took a seat at the dining room table. Gordon had left behind his handheld gaming system and as Olivia sank down into a seat at the table the game came on by itself. You could hear the sounds of Skylanders Spyro's Adventure game playing.

Kylie hearing the game turned around and looked at Olivia in an odd manner.

Olivia had a spaced out look to her, as though her mind were a million miles away.

"What's going on, Olivia?" Kylie asked as she set a plate of scrambled egg whites on a bed of spinach with roasted tomatoes and mushrooms, turkey bacon, and toast spread with honey in front of her.

She brought her own plate over to the table and looked at Olivia waiting for an answer. She was tired. She had worked all night and into the morning with no sleep and she was short on patience at the moment.

Olivia picked up a fork and just pushed her eggs around on the plate. She set the fork down on the plate and said, "Do you really want to know, Kylie? *Really*?"

"Of course," Kylie answered.

"I don't know if you're ready for what I'm about to tell you," Olivia asked.

Kylie took a bite of eggs and listened intently as Olivia began telling the story of how she had met Kylie's mother. They had met at a UFO convention and the two women had met while attending a smaller meeting for those who claimed they had been abducted by aliens.

"My mother?" Kylie asked with a nervous laugh. "Surely, you don't expect me to believe that nonsense. My mother is the most down-to-earth person I ever met. She was a smart woman, not some flake."

"You mean, a flake like me?" Olivia asked.

"You know that's not what I meant," Kylie said.

"That's O.K. I knew that's the response you would have," Olivia said as she sat back and let out a sigh. "She should have told you about this herself. And who knows, maybe if she had more time on this earth she would have."

Kylie raised her voice, "Now that my mother isn't here to defend herself you're going to try to convince me that my mother has been taken by aliens? Is that where you're going with this conversation?"

"Didn't you ever wonder why we were such good friends?" Olivia asked. "We're as different as two people can be."

Olivia walked over to the sink and wet a paper towel and scrubbed off the foundation she had put on her legs to hide the bruises.

"Yeah, I have to admit that you and my mother were an odd combination. I never could figure out what you had in common, but you seemed to be good friends and that's all that really mattered."

"But we had *that* in common," Olivia said.

"What, that you were both abducted by little green men?" Kylie said with a smirk.

"They're not green."

Olivia pointed to the bruises on her legs. She tried to explain to Kylie that the aliens had come last night and left these marks on her legs.

Olivia sat back and let what she had told her sink in a little before she continued.

Kylie looked at the bruises but remained quiet, contemplating everything Olivia had just told her.

"That's not all, Ky," Olivia said gently reaching for Kylie's hand.

Kylie pulled her hand out of reach and just looked at Olivia like she was trying to figure her out.

Olivia continued, "You too have been chosen and abducted. As a matter of fact, so was your grandmother. As far as your mother knew you were the third generation."

Kylie got up and dumped the rest of her meal in the garbage having lost her appetite.

Thinking for a minute she turned around and leaned back against the kitchen sink. Waving her fork in the air at Olivia she said, "Look, I'm not saying I don't believe that it's not possible there's other life out there. There are so many planets and other solar systems out there, that yes, it makes sense that perhaps there is some form of life out there somewhere."

Olivia opened her mouth to say something.

Kylie held up her hand to stop her from saying more. "But no way, no how, will you *ever* convince me that they just happened to pick our planet of all the planets to visit and that alien abduction is real. Sorry, don't buy it. And then to try to tell me..."

Just then Gordon knocked on the door and seeing Kylie and Olivia let himself in. He had his backpack on his back and was dressed for school.

Excitedly he piped up talking a mile a minute, "Olivia, I saw you last night. I saw the lights and the spaceship through my window. I saw you get on the spaceship with the aliens."

Olivia looked at Kylie and didn't say a word.

Gordon's mother yelled from the driveway next door, "Gordon, your bus is coming. Hurry up! I am *not* driving you to school if you miss the bus again." Gordon left as quickly as he had come.

Kylie walked back to her bedroom and slammed and locked the door.

12

Monday morning when Kylie came into work she was called into her boss' office.

"Sit down, Kylie," her boss said as his secretary ushered her into the office.

Her boss said, "You'll be picked up in ten minutes in front of the building and taken for an interview on the top secret work you performed the other evening. Any questions?" her boss asked.

"Plenty," Kylie said.

"Actually I don't know anything, so that was a moot point asking if you had any questions. Don't return to the lab before you leave and do not discuss what you're doing with anyone. I believe they'll be waiting for you downstairs. Good luck," her boss said dismissing her.

As she stepped outside a black Suburban with blacked out windows immediately pulled up to the curb. A young man got out of the front passenger door and held open the back door. Without saying a word to her he motioned for her to get in.

Kylie got in the SUV and before she had her seat belt on they sped off.

On the drive Kylie had time to fume yet again about how she had been spied on by Amir, who wasn't really Amir, and wasn't even a turban wearing Sikh but some government guy who had been watching her for the last nine months or so. The more she thought about it the angrier she got.

Why go to the pretense of changing his name and disguising himself? It's not like she would have known the real, what was his name again; oh, yeah, Alan Christenson. If she ever saw him again, she was going to tell him exactly what she thought of his subterfuge.

The worst part is she had trusted him. She didn't trust many people and that's what hurt the most. She wondered if she'd ever see him again or if he would disappear now that he had served his purpose.

She had to wonder if he had anything to do with the guy in the car watching her house. If she saw him, she was definitely going to ask him about that too.

The SUV came to a stop and the passenger in the front seat jumped out and held the door open for her.

"Ma'am," he said, as he held the door open for her.

"Don't ma'am me," she said in a snippy tone. "For crying out loud, I'm younger than you. Why would you call me, ma'am?"

"Out of respect, ma'am," he said catching himself and trying not to smile. He held the door to the building open for her.

As she stepped in front of him and went in the building he couldn't help himself. He stole a look at those long legs that seemed endless. She was a beauty and a feisty one. A combination he found particularly enticing. He would be more than happy to escort her anywhere, anytime.

13

The interview wasn't anything about the top secret work she had done, but seemed more like an interview for a job. After filling out what seemed to be reams of paperwork and talking to four different people who asked her questions that seemed more like an IQ and a personality test she was told to please wait.

After sitting and waiting for about twenty minutes she was taken to yet another room and given a lie detector test. When the test was completed the man who ran the test packed his equipment up and before leaving told her someone would be right with her.

The next person she saw came and took her fingerprints. He tried four different times to get a print off the finger that the specimen had adhered to but was unsuccessful.

While unsuccessful in getting a print, even after looking at her finger he didn't seem to notice anything off. For that she was grateful. She didn't know how she would have explained that.

After attempting to get a print several times he left the room and stepped into the next room and made a call. After hanging up he returned to the room and said, "I guess we're done here. Someone will be here in a few minutes to take you to your next stop."

After a few minutes the last woman who had interviewed her came in and asked if she would mind waiting in the cafeteria where she could have lunch on them.

She escorted her to the cafeteria and told her she could have anything she wanted and to just give the chef her order and enjoy her lunch. They would get back to her in about half an hour to forty-five minutes.

Kylie went through the cafeteria line which was unlike any cafeteria she had experienced in most business offices. Here she was given her choice of sushi, a T-bone steak, lobster, or just about anything she desired.

Looking over the enticing choices in front of her she chose

roasted fennel and potato soup and a wild mushroom, spinach, and goat cheese tart.

She didn't realize how hungry she was until she dug into the tart. She would have loved to have had the recipe for it. It was unlike anything she had ever tasted with several kinds of mushrooms and a delicious goat cheese that was slightly tart but a great combination with the mushrooms.

It was late for lunch and there were few people besides her in the cafeteria so she was surprised when a few minutes later a young lady with platinum blonde hair with pink tips asked her if she could join her.

"Sure," Kylie said.

The girl set her things down across from her and said, "I'm going to get a mixed berry smoothie. They're addictive. Would you like one?"

Kylie having just taken a bite of her tart pointed at her bottle of green tea with her fork.

The girl left her purse behind with a dog eared book titled, 'The Alien Abduction Files.' The cover being worn flipped back a bit where Kylie could read the name written inside, Daphne Sowers.

Her handbag Kylie recognized as a *very pricey* Hermès crocodile handbag. It had the monogram DS, so that fit with the name in the book. Kylie knew that to be able to afford a Hermès handbag this girl wasn't just some ordinary underling of the company.

The young girl returned to the table with a smoothie and a bowl of black bean soup. As she sat down she said, "Thanks for letting me join you. I hate eating alone. My name is Mindy. What's yours?"

"Mindy?" Kylie asked. She was beginning to feel like this was a set up. "My name is Kylie, but I suppose you already know that."

"No, how would I know your name? I don't think I've ever seen you here before. Have you worked here long?" Mindy stirred her soup which was steaming hot and blew on it before taking a bite, evading Kylie's eyes.

While Mindy was eating her soup Kylie dropped her fork on

the floor and reached down to pick it up. While doing so she glanced over to see what the tattoo was on the girl's ankle that she had noticed while she was standing in line ordering her food. It was a tattoo of Daffy Duck and had Daffy Daphne printed beneath it.

Kylie having retrieved her fork set it aside on the table and took a bite of her soup ignoring the girl's question. She was mulling over in her mind just what was going on here.

Mindy picked up her book and opened it where a bookmark was set. After appearing to read a few pages she looked up at Kylie and said, "This book is definitely scary. If you believe what it says in here aliens come to visit earth and people are abducted. What do you think? Do you believe in aliens?"

Kylie looked at Mindy with an intensity that made her squirm. Kylie said, "My mother's crazy best friend does which isn't saying much, and the little boy who lives next door to me, but then he's only six so he's at an age where his imagination runs wild. Somehow, I doubt that's true with you."

"What do you mean?" Mindy asked.

"You come in here to a cafeteria that has all but cleared out leaving only you and me which makes me believe perhaps this is a continuation of my interview," Kylie said. "Am I correct?"

Mindy laughed nervously and said, "Look at me. Do I look like someone these people would trust to perform an interview?"

She was dressed in what was the current trend for young college age girls, the only difference being that Kylie recognized quality when she saw it. Between the handbag and the clothes she was wearing they would have cost Kylie a few month's salary and she made a pretty impressive salary.

"I think that's exactly the point," Kylie leaned forward and said. "To most perhaps you could have pulled this off, but I'm nobody's fool, Daphne."

Mindy looked stunned for a minute and then realized how she had come up with the name. "Oh, you must have seen the name inside the book. This is just a book I borrowed from a friend."

"That's why your purse is monogrammed with the initials DS, the same as the name inside the book. The Daffy Daphne on your ankle bears witness that your name is indeed Daphne."

'Mindy' leaned back in her chair realizing she had been busted, but was curious to hear what else she had to say. "Please, continue."

"Your blouse is a Carolina Herrera, your shoes Monolo Blahnik, and your handbag, which I recognize as a Hermès by the way, are all way too expensive for a normal office employee to be able to afford," Kylie finished.

"Wow! They told me you were smart, but I think even they're going to be surprised at just how ridiculously astute you are."

Daphne reached inside her purse and pulled out her phone and said, "I guess you got all that. Game's over; why don't you just come clean. I think she can handle it and would appreciate a little honesty."

A few minutes later the man who had passed himself off as Winston entered the cafeteria in full military dress with a chest full of medals. As he approached the table Daphne said, "Have a seat, Dad. You owe Kylie here an apology for this bullshit game you're playing."

"So we meet again, Winston," Kylie said with her arms folded with a defiant look on her face.

"Winston?" Daphne asked her dad.

Without missing a beat he said, "Mindy."

"Touché," Daphne said.

He looked at his daughter and said, "Care to join us? Ladies, follow me, please."

"Yeah, I think you could use some help with this one. You definitely got off on the wrong foot." Daphne said while getting up leaving her food behind, but reaching back and snatching her smoothie and taking it with her.

As he escorted the women from the cafeteria Kylie noticed his name tag said Brannan, *not* Winston. She left the room with a smug smile on her face for catching him at his game.

14

Kylie was told to take the next three days off and by then they would get back to her. She decided to take advantage of the few rare days off she had and go visit the Archers.

Coco was following closely at her heels as she packed knowing they would soon be going somewhere in the car. Coco followed Kylie out to the yard while she put her bike on the bike rack.

Kylie noticed the car that had been parked down the street for the last week wasn't there, but in it's place there was a dark colored van with dark window tint. She decided not to worry about it and just enjoy her time off.

She was inside packing her suitcase when Olivia stopped by. She seemed nervous as she stood there watching Kylie pack. Kylie ignored her and grabbed the bag of dog food and poured some in a plastic container. She collected Coco's dog food, water bowl, and leash and set them next to her suitcase.

Olivia took Gordon's picture of the aliens and spaceship off the refrigerator and was holding it while she watched Kylie grab items to take on her trip. Olivia looked like she had something to say but didn't know how to start the conversation. She nervously asked, "Are you still mad at me?"

"I want to be, but you know me. I can't stay mad at anyone," Kylie said.

She went to her closet and grabbed a few tops with Olivia following closely behind.

"Thanks, Kylie. My intentions weren't to upset you," Olivia said.

"Let's just drop it," Kylie turned around with a few tops in her hands and about tripped over Olivia who was right behind her.

"Between you and Coco... You're both following me around right on my heels."

Olivia stepped back to give her a little space, but when Kylie walked out of the room she followed her out.

"I'm not mad, but be assured I do *not* want to talk about it anymore," Kylie said.

"Where are you going?" Olivia asked pointing at the suitcase. "I didn't know you had plans to go off anywhere."

Kylie looked up as she folded the tops and fit them in the small suitcase. "It was last minute plans. I got some time off so I thought I would go visit some friends and go hiking and biking."

"Oh...what friends would that be?" Olivia asked dreading the answer she thought she already knew.

Kylie sat on the floor and looked up at Olivia. "Look, I don't want an argument. I'm going to go stay with the Archers for a few days."

Olivia walked into the kitchen and put Gordon's picture back up on the fridge that she hadn't realized she was still holding. "I don't understand you, Ky. How could you be friends with them? They're..."

Kylie interrupted holding her hand up for Olivia to stop. "I know what you're going to say. You've said it a dozen times before, and I really don't want to hear it. They're good friends, besides what happened is no fault of theirs."

"It was their son who killed your parents," Olivia said raising her voice. "While he was drunk! Your mom and dad weren't as fortunate as he was. He walked away with no injuries while your parents paid with their lives."

Kylie was furious. "You think I don't know that." She paced around the room fuming. "I wouldn't exactly say he walked away with no injuries. There's such a thing as mental..."

Olivia said, "Oh, please. Don't even go there. And then to go to court and defend him so he walks with barely a slap on the wrist. How could you do that?"

Kylie fell back into a living room chair. "He was young. He made a mistake. Haven't you ever made a mistake in your life?"

"Plenty of them," Olivia said. "But I didn't kill anyone doing it."

"That's enough," Kylie said. "They're good friends and have been there for me when I needed someone."

"Of course they were. You kept their son out of jail," Olivia said.

After wiping a tear away she said, "I thought I was here for you. Your mother was my best friend. I've tried to step in and try to help fill the void a little."

Kylie got up and walked over and put her arms around Olivia and said, "Yes, you've been wonderful. You've been a great help. But you have to understand, it does me no good to hold a grudge. He's learned a hard lesson and hasn't touched a drop of alcohol since. He's gone on to have a good career, something he never would have been able to do if he were in jail."

"He should have thought about that before he got behind the wheel while drunk," Olivia said.

"I agree," Kylie said. "It was bad judgment on his part. The Archers have been very good to me and I enjoy their company. Coco and I are going to go stay with them for a few days. I hope you can understand. Even if you don't, I'm going. I need some down time."

"He won't even have anything to do with you. Has he ever apologized to you?" Olivia asked.

"Not that it's any of your business, but yes he has. He wrote a letter. And you're right; he won't face me. It's something that's been hard for him to live with too. The fact that he took two lives isn't something easy to live with."

Coco lay on the floor with her head on her paws and watched them, following their discussion with her eyes. When Kylie picked up her suitcase to take out to the car Coco followed her out. Kylie opened the trunk and Coco attempted to jump in the car but had a hard time.

"You must be getting old girl, or I'm feeding you too much," Kylie said as she lifted her up and placed her in the backseat of the car.

Kylie went back in to get Coco's things and to lock the house up. Olivia gave her a hug and got in her car and drove off looking dejected.

Kylie came around to the driver's side of the car and before she could get in the car Helen from next door called her over to the porch.

"Did you notice the white car is gone but there's a van there?" Helen whispered.

Kylie said, "I don't think you have to whisper. I don't think they can hear you from down the street."

"Maybe they have one of those listening devices you see them use on TV on those detective shows. They've been watching you pack up your car so they know you're going somewhere," Helen said.

"That's fine. Maybe they'll go away then. I'm going to be away for a few days. You keep an eye on the house for me, O.K.?" Kylie said this more to get Helen off the subject than because she was worried about anything.

"You know I will," Helen said.

"You have my number if you need me," Kylie called out as she got in her car before driving off.

As Kylie drove past the van she gave a wave to whoever was inside to let them know she knew they were watching her.

"Hang on, Coco," she said as she stepped on the gas and sped around the corner.

No sooner had she turned the corner than the van pulled up in a nearby driveway and quickly turned around to follow her. By the time they rounded the corner she was out of sight and they never were able to find out where she was going.

15

It was almost a four hour drive from her home in Phoenix to the Archer's. At about the half way point Kylie went through a drive through to pick up lunch for her and Coco. She found a nice area for them to have a picnic.

Kylie got a salad for herself along with a grilled chicken sandwich and bought a burger and fries for Coco. Kylie broke up the burger into bite sizes for her while Coco watched patiently with drool running from her mouth in anticipation of this unexpected treat.

After gulping the burger down Coco devoured the fries. Kylie pulled her chicken out of the bun and fed Coco her bun too. She broke the chicken into small pieces and added them to her salad. About halfway through this seeing that Coco was watching her intently she gave in and gave the rest of the chicken to Coco who seemed to enjoy it more than she would have.

After their meal Kylie walked Coco around before they got back in the car to give her a chance to exercise a bit before the last leg of their journey.

Kylie was a bit concerned as she had noticed that Coco had seemed a bit listless lately, but she seemed to be enjoying the trip and was definitely eating good.

Kylie made a mental note to take her in for a check up at the vets when they got back home. She thought the fresh air at the cabin and going hiking would be good for her. She had been cooped up a lot lately with the long hours Kylie had been working.

As they pulled up at the Archers home Pilar and Philip came out to greet them, happy to see her. They had become as close as family.

Coco made sure she got her share of attention before wandering off to explore.

Kylie told few people about her friendship with the Archers. She feared most people would have the same reaction as Olivia had to her befriending the family of the man who had killed her parents in a DUI accident.

Pilar was a part time OB/GYN doctor working her way towards retirement. Her husband Philip was an accountant and they lived off the grid.

They had built themselves a beautiful log cabin home near Kingman, Arizona surrounded by peace and quiet with a memorable landscape. Kylie always felt at peace when she visited and relished her time in the outdoors.

16

Kylie was sitting in the Archer's living room talking to them about the revelations that Olivia had told her about her being a third generation in her family that had been chosen and abducted by aliens.

Both Pilar and Philip were highly educated and she expected them to laugh and scoff at what she had told them, but instead was completely surprised when Pilar said, "It makes sense that we aren't alone in this universe. Why should we think we're the only ones?"

"Don't you think that's a bit far-fetched to believe that aliens come to visit earth? To me it seems like one of those stories such as Sasquatch that only nut cases believe in," Kylie said.

"It's a pretty big world," Philip said. "I've heard where some of the astronauts and pilots have admitted to seeing spacecraft. I've often wondered why it isn't more commonly accepted."

Pilar interjected, "I think it would be if it weren't for the government cover-up and for people made to feel ridiculed when they admit to believing in UFOs and aliens."

"There are literally thousands of other planets and probably many more than that. For sure there are many yet undiscovered and many of those in other solar systems. Many of those planets could be similar to earth and in that case the idea of life on some of those planets could be a very real prospect," Philip said. "It's really not such a far-fetched idea as you think. It would be harder to believe we were the only life source on all the planets."

"It's hard for me to even consider that aliens could be real," Kylie said. "I think I'd have to see it to believe it. For Olivia to try to convince me that not only my mother but I have been abducted though is totally ridiculous."

"Why is that?" Pilar asked. "Many people have reported such a thing as having happened to them. Questioned about it they all gave similar reports as to what they saw and experienced."

"But that's the point. I don't remember anything. Don't you think I would have remembered something like that? How could you ever forget it?" Kylie asked.

"Perhaps it was too much for you to accept at the time and you blocked it out," Philip said.

"I think my mother would have said something to me, especially if it were true that I had been abducted," Kylie said.

"Maybe she was waiting until she thought you were ready to accept it," Philip said.

"How can you believe in something there's no proof of?" Kylie asked.

"Do you believe in God?" Pilar asked.

"Yes, of course," Kylie answered, "but you can hardly compare aliens to God."

"What I'm saying," Pilar said. "You believe in God yet you've never seen Him."

Kylie was stunned that they so casually accepted that it could be possible. It isn't anything she had ever given credence to or even much thought of in the past. Lately it seemed it was all she could think about.

The Archers often joined Kylie when she went hiking at Monolith Garden Trail. Her favorite time to hike there was in the spring with the wildflowers blooming and the awe-inspiring scenery. She knew many looked at the landscape as desolate, but she loved it.

Kylie usually hiked the entire six plus mile trails, but Pilar and Philip would often veer off to go birding or to indulge in their new found hobby of photography. There was a large boulder in a shaded area where they would arrange to meet and in the meantime it gave Kylie some quiet time.

When Kylie returned to what she called 'their little rock' Philip reached down at the edge of the boulder and picked up what looked like a film canister and said, "We had just left you a note that we were going to head back. Pilar has some work she needs to tend to. We weren't sure if you would find the note though."

Kylie made note of where he had left the canister with the note and said, "No, probably not. It's pretty much out of sight, but I'll remember to look there in the future."

The day before she had to head home Kylie decided to take Coco and go mountain biking to get a last bit of exercise and fresh air. They had only gone about two miles when Coco laid down in the middle of the trail and wouldn't budge.

"Are you being lazy, Coco? Do we need to stop and take a rest?" Coco thumped her tail at Kylie but she didn't even lift her head.

Kylie took a bottle of water out of her backpack and pulled out Coco's fold-up water bowl and tried giving her a drink thinking she had become overheated.

Coco seemed to have a hard time lifting her head to drink out of the bowl so Kylie poured some water in the palm of her hand and she licked a bit of that up and put her head back down.

Kylie was worried as she had never seen Coco give up on a hike before. She reached over and rubbed her head. Coco licked her hand. Sitting above Coco's head when Kylie looked down as Coco was panting she noticed a large cauliflower shaped growth on her tongue.

Kylie gently pried open Coco's mouth enough to get a good look at the growth on her tongue and then laid Coco's head in her lap. In the middle of the trail Kylie began sobbing so hard her entire body rocked back and forth.

17

"How could I have not noticed that before?" Kylie said aloud, berating herself. Kylie knew immediately when she saw it that Coco had a tumor. From the looks of it, it was a tumor that had been growing for quite some time or was growing very rapidly.

Kylie rocked the dog in her arms sobbing so hard that some hikers heard her and came over and asked if they could help. They thought perhaps the dog had been bitten by a rattle snake.

One of the hikers helped her make a sling out of a jacket Kylie had in her backpack. They gently placed Coco inside the sling so Kylie could carry her back to the car.

One of the hikers walked her bike back to her car for her so Kylie could walk Coco without jostling her too much.

As she pulled into the Archer's driveway she saw Pilar and Philip sitting on the porch in their porch swing sipping a glass of wine and enjoying the view.

Kylie put her head down on the steering wheel crying. She had thought she had cried herself out, but she would never run out of tears for this little dog.

She reached over and put her hand on Coco's head to give her comfort. She knew her tears were upsetting her.

Coco had given her such unconditional love these last few years when she came into her life. What was she going to do? She couldn't let the poor dog suffer, but the thought of living without her was more than she could bear.

The Archers had taken them inside the cabin. Coco had gotten a second wind and was wanting to follow Kylie around, but she had her lay quietly next to her on the couch.

Pilar had an office set up in the cabin and she had taken some blood work and was checking it now. Kylie didn't need to wait for the results, she knew exactly what was wrong. She knew Pilar did too.

She had been so preoccupied with her own life that she had missed all the signs. How long had the growth been there?

The Archers quietly discussed with her the best thing to do for Coco. Kylie decided she would play it by ear and keep a keen eye on her. She wouldn't let her suffer. When it got to that point she would do the right thing regardless of how difficult it was. She knew that time wouldn't be far off.

18

The company that had interviewed her called Kylie into her boss' office when she returned to work. Evidently her boss had worked with them in the past as he seemed familiar with the procedure.

He left his office as Winston, who she now knew as Major Brannan, came in and made himself at home at her boss' desk. He explained that they would really like her to come work with them.

She listened but said she couldn't commit to anything at the moment. There were personal things going on in her life and she couldn't consider a major change in her life at this time.

The major named a price for her salary that astounded her. He informed her she would be given a place to live, a place of her choice out of the many pieces of property the company owned, all expenses paid; but she would have to move just outside of Las Vegas.

When she asked what was involved in the job he told her that he couldn't really go into detail right then as she would first have to sign a non-disclosure contract and take an oath of secrecy that would remain in effect until her death.

When she was reluctant to commit he assured her she would be working in her field in DNA but at times would be expected to assist others in other areas.

Kylie listened and nodded her head when he said they would get back to her within a week or two. He said she wouldn't have to move immediately, but they did need an answer one way or the other by then.

After they left Kylie was still sitting in the chair when her boss walked back in.

"I guess you'll be leaving us," he said as he pulled his chair out and sat at his desk. "We hate losing you, but ...."

"I need some time off," Kylie said in a monotone voice. "Something has come up. I'm going to need some time off and I'm not sure how long."

"Sure," her boss said. "Everything O.K.?"

Kylie got up and just walked out.

19

Kylie spent the next two and a half weeks giving Coco all the love and attention she so richly deserved.

She had planned to take Gordon to a ball game but instead gave the tickets to his father to take him. It was good that Gordon was spending more time with his family so he wouldn't miss her too much when she left. She had decided to accept the job in Vegas.

It was now at the point where she had to grind up Coco's food in the blender and give her little bits at a time hand feeding her. The tumor on her tongue had grown to a point where it was causing her difficulties in swallowing, eating, and drinking. Her stomach was distended and Kylie knew the end was near.

Instead of following at Kylie's heels she would raise her head and watch her, but if she was out of sight for too long Coco would get up to see where she was.

You could see the pain in Coco's eyes. These days it seemed to be a constant look. It was a look that broke Kylie's heart.

Kylie knew that time had come when she had to say good-bye. She had an appointment the next day at the vets to have Coco put to sleep. She wasn't sleeping just thinking about it and had placed a soft cushion for Coco to lay on next to her.

Kylie laid awake through the night just gently petting Coco and telling her how much she loved her. Through her tears she explained why she was making the decision she had. She wanted Coco to understand she didn't want her to suffer and that she was loved so much and would be missed something terrible. She would never forget her. Coco may not have understood the words she was saying, but it helped Kylie to explain it to her anyway.

Just as dawn was beginning to break Kylie fell asleep and slept for about two hours. The first thing she noticed when she woke up was a small puddle of blood under Coco's mouth. She was awake and watching Kylie not taking her eyes off her.

Coco was in pain and struggling even to lift her head. She told herself she had to let go and stop being selfish. She had to think of Coco and do what was best for her. She could put it off no longer.

She gave her one last car ride which perked Coco up. She got up and looked out the window and wagged her tail. There was nothing she loved more than a ride in the car. Unfortunately, this would be her last.

Kylie pulled up in her driveway an hour later with Coco's body wrapped in a blanket by her side. She saw Gordon's father working on his car in the garage. She called him over and asked him if he could help her dig a hole to bury her in.

She was crying so hard he could barely understand her. She told him she wanted to bury her underneath the tree in her backyard so she would be in the shade. It had been her favorite place to lay when they were outside.

She sat on the stoop cradling the body of Coco in her arms as Gordon's father dug the hole for her grave. After she gave her beloved dog a final kiss on the top of Coco's head and buried her face in Coco's fur sobbing she gently placed her in a box lined with a blanket that her neighbor had been kind enough to put together to place her in.

She watched as he covered her grave with dirt. When he was finished he walked over and put the shovel up and came over and held Kylie in his arms while she sobbed her heart out.

"I lose everything I love," Kylie cried. "Everything I have ever loved has been taken from me."

20

Kylie had taken a few days to go up to Vegas to look for a place to live with Daphne's help, Major Brannan's daughter. Daphne showed her around and Kylie had been given her choice of several houses or a condo from the company she was going to work for.

She chose a small but spacious three bedroom home in Henderson, about fifteen or sixteen miles outside of Vegas.

Henderson was situated in the Mojave Desert. The neighborhood she was moving into was called Green Valley which Kylie found amusing as there was nothing green about the area. There wasn't even grass for a yard. In place of grass there was gravel or crushed rock which suited her just fine...less upkeep that way is the way she saw it.

Having lived in Phoenix she was used to the heat and hot, dry desert climate. The heat didn't bother her except those days that reached or climbed over 100 degrees.

Having returned home only the day before from house hunting she was surprised when she got a call from Major Brannan asking if it would be possible for her to make the move within the next day or two. He explained that something had come up and they would be needing her sooner than they originally thought. The sooner the better.

They worked out the details on the phone and he offered to pay for a moving company to come pack up her belongings so she wouldn't be delayed any longer than necessary.

With the pain of having lost Coco still fresh she thought it would be a good thing to go ahead and make the move. A change of scenery would be good for her.

Daphne, Major Brannan's daughter, lived just a few blocks away in a condo. Daphne had tried to convince Kylie to pick a condo where she lived, but Kylie didn't think that condo life was for her.

Daphne had barged into her life with all the subtlety of a hurricane. She was now helping her unpack and get things in place. She had taken Kylie shopping and picked out a few things Kylie would never have thought would look good together.

Just as Daphne's personality seemed to brighten a room so did her decorating style. The colors brightened the place up and at the same time gave a homey, comfortable look to the place. As Daphne said, "Now the place pops. The room has energy." Kylie had to agree.

Kylie surprisingly admitted to herself that she was enjoying the kooky girl's company. She was without pretense, she said what she thought and Kylie found that refreshing.

They made plans to go see Cirque de Soleil at the Bellagio, or at least Daphne made plans for them to go and see a little bit of Vegas before Kylie officially started work.

She had initially balked at paying well over $200 for an evening of entertainment until Daphne reminded her of the exorbitant salary she would now be receiving. She convinced her she could afford to splurge a little. Besides she told her, once she began work she would have little time to spend her money.

Daphne walked in that evening to pick her up. When Daphne saw Kylie her mouth dropped open. Daphne had told her the restaurant they would be going to and the show were places that were dressy. Kylie had chosen a little black dress that was form fitting and some high heels that added substantially to her already tall height.

"Wow!" Daphne said. "When they see you, they'll think I'm your little sister. You look amazing," Daphne whistled.

"Is this O.K.?" Kylie said smoothing down the dress.

"It's a head turner for sure," Daphne answered. "And those legs seem to never end. You certainly got handed everything on a silver platter when God was handing out looks and brains. You've got it all."

"You look nice too, Daphne," Kylie said while putting in some silver, dangly earrings.

"Yeah, I'm cute like the kid next door and you're knock-'em-dead stunning. Oh well, it is what it is," Daphne said.

Kylie went to grab a little black clutch and when she walked back in the room Daphne was standing peeking outside her side window.

Hearing Kylie she turned around and said, "Now I know why you picked this house over the condo. You've been holding out on me. Who's that great big pile of deliciousness that lives next door?"

"I don't know. I've never seen anybody over there. Why don't you go introduce yourself if he's that good looking," Kylie teased.

"Yeah, right. The minute you walk out the door and he lays eyes on you he'll look right through me. Come on, we have dinner reservations so we better get a move on."

As they walked out the door Daphne made sure she made enough noise to get Kylie's neighbor's attention. Like she said, he never gave her a second glance, but the moment he saw Kylie he did a double take and never took his eyes off her even watching her as they pulled out of the driveway.

21

Daphne teased her about her neighbor on the drive to the restaurant. The two of them having known each other such a short time were amazingly comfortable in each other's company.

It had been awhile since Kylie had a close friend. It was nice having someone to do things with and to talk to. Daphne was certainly upbeat and entertaining. She was fun to be with.

Driving down the Vegas Strip Kylie was like a kid in a candy store looking in all directions and pointing things out that grabbed her attention. Kylie, not really one to be attracted to the glitz and glamour of Vegas, found herself pleasantly surprised at how much she was enjoying herself.

The casinos were amazing and the streets and casinos were lit up like Christmas. There were lots of dazzling lights everywhere in every direction as far as the eye could see.

They drove up to the Bellagio and Kylie was impressed with the beautiful fountain and was totally unprepared for what she saw once they entered the casino. It was noisy and crowded but the action drew your attention, and she couldn't get enough of the sights.

"I could just sit here and people watch for hours," she said to Daphne.

After looking around for a short time Daphne reminded her of their reservations and they headed to the Picasso, a French and Spanish influenced restaurant inside the Bellagio run by a famous chef.

When the servers brought the food out Kylie looked at it and said it almost looked too pretty to eat.

They feasted on foie gras as the appetizer with veal as the main dish. It was rich food for Kylie and she barely tasted the food with her attention drawn to the views of the fountain and the original Picasso artwork decorating the walls.

"You're not in Kansas anymore, Dorothy," Daphne said

referring to Dorothy from the *'Wizard of Oz'*.

Daphne picked up the tab saying, "It's worth it to me just to watch your reaction to all this. I've lived here so long the magic has sort of diminished for me, but watching you take it all in like a little kid makes it a fun experience."

They headed to watch the show. Kylie was completely mesmerized by all the action in every corner of the huge theater.

The show was spectacular, unlike anything she had ever experienced. She had to admit she enjoyed herself and the show was well worth the price of the ticket.

As they drove out of the parking lot and were driving back home Kylie couldn't get over the difference of the city once they left the Strip. The Strip was bright, colorful, and well kind of tacky in a high priced way; but once you drove off the Strip everything was brown and plain. Kylie was on sensory overload.

They stopped in at a grocery store so Daphne could pick up a few things on the way home. There were even slot machines in the grocery store.

"It's 1:00 in the morning. I can't believe how many people are out grocery shopping," Kylie said.

"This city comes alive at night. A lot of people that live here work nights. Besides, it's too hot to come out in the day," Daphne said.

On the drive home Kylie asked Daphne about what to expect the following day as she had only been told she would be signing documents and given information on her new job.

"I don't even know where I'm going to be working," Kylie said. "Or even who I'm working for. What's the name of the company? Everything has been so secretive."

"Have you ever heard of Area 51? Well, of course you have," Daphne said answering her own question. "Everyone has heard of Area 51, the nation's most secretive military facility. Well, that's where you'll be working. But of course we aren't to call it Area 51, but that's exactly what it is."

22

"Area 51? Seriously?" Kylie asked. "I thought that was a secret government facility where..."

Daphne interrupted, "Everything, and I mean *everything* is a big secret of what happens at Area 51. Everything you've ever heard about it...well; it's true."

Kylie asked puzzled, "What could they possibly be doing at Area 51 that they would need my field of expertise for?"

Daphne answered as she turned onto the street where Kylie lived. "That I can't answer."

"Can't or won't?" Kylie asked noticing how Daphne had answered her question.

"You'll find out soon enough everything you need to know. I'll be picking you up tomorrow and taking you to complete the paperwork and orientation. From there I'll take you and show you around where you'll be working. I'll introduce you to a few people before you get started," Daphne continued all while ignoring Kylie's question.

Kylie looked nervous. She didn't know what to think now that she had been enlightened to her new place of employment.

"You'll be asked to sign a secrecy oath and given a security clearance. You have a bunch of paperwork to fill out. Basically you'll be asked to waive your constitutional rights and after that, well; life as you have known it will never be the same."

Kylie didn't say anything else. She was thinking about what Daphne had just told her.

"We're here," Daphne said as she pulled into Kylie's driveway. "I'll be back to pick you up at 9:00 AM."

Kylie sat in the car with the door open. "What do you mean, give up my constitutional rights? I don't like the sound of that."

"You didn't think that humongous salary you were offered would come without strings, did you?" Daphne asked.

Kylie looked like she wanted to ask more questions but before she could Daphne told her, "Look, that's really all I can tell you. Tomorrow you'll be informed of everything. And besides, I'll be around to look after you."

As Kylie stepped out of the car Daphne said, "Just a word of warning...Just assume your phones are monitored and your house is bugged. I'm not paranoid, it's just a fact of life when you become an employee of Area 51. It's for national security purposes. And, never ever tell anyone where you work or what you do – ever, *for the rest of your life.* You'll be given a cover story of what you do for a living in case anyone ever asks."

At that Daphne backed out and pulled away waving to Kylie who was still standing in her driveway with that deer in the headlights look on her face wondering what in the world she had gotten herself into.

Money wasn't everything. It really wasn't even all that important to her. But her privacy, that was.

Kylie wondered if she had just sold her soul to the devil.

23

As Kylie finally finished with orientation and after completing her paperwork she had serious doubts about what she had committed herself to. It was too late to back out now. Once she had signed the nondisclosure paperwork and been briefed there was no turning back.

Daphne had been sitting out in the lobby reading a romance novel while she waited for Kylie.

Two men and the woman who had conducted the orientation and gave Kylie her credentials to enter the workplace came out of the room. Kylie followed in their wake and when Daphne saw her she got up to greet her.

Kylie walked over and glanced at the book Daphne was reading and said, "No more books about aliens?"

Daphne glanced at the cover of the book she was holding and seemingly embarrassed stuffed it inside her handbag. "That's the only romance I'm experiencing these days."

"What now?" Kylie asked Daphne. "I have a serious headache. All that paperwork and orientation was a bit overwhelming." She rubbed her temples as Daphne dug in her handbag and pulled out a bottle of aspirin.

Kylie walked over and bought a bottle of water out of the vending machine and swallowed the aspirin.

"We have a little time to kill before we catch our ride. Come on, we'll go grab a quick bite to eat."

Kylie followed her out and they got in Daphne's car and drove to a small diner.

On the drive Kylie asked Daphne, "What's the deal with everyone giving fake names? So far, everyone I've met that's connected with this work originally gave me a fake name...including you."

"Yeah, that was a bust," Daphne laughed. "You were on to me in no time. I didn't know my dad did the same thing."

"And Amir," Kylie said.

"Who?" Daphne asked her as they pulled into the parking lot of a diner.

"Sorry, I forgot. You know him as Alan Christenson, but I worked with him for almost a year and knew him as Amir Singh."

"I guess the reason for that is if they decide you aren't right for the position the less you know the better," Daphne said.

As they got out of the car Daphne reminded her not to discuss anything about work while they were out in public where they could be overheard. Kylie nodded that she understood. It seemed her life had turned into one big secret after another these days.

As they entered the diner Kylie was overwhelmed by the smell of grease. Daphne joined in singing along with Steve Perry of Journey blaring from the jukebox their hit song *Don't Stop Believin* and playing the air guitar as she looked around for a place to sit.

A waitress looked up as they walked in and smiled and called out to them, "Have a seat anywhere you like, ladies. I'll be right with you."

Daphne made her way to a back booth that seemed to be held together with duct tape with some of the stuffing protruding. Kylie noticed at least the place appeared to be clean, and from the looks of the crowd she assumed the food must be good.

Kylie rarely ate junk food and she assumed the only thing they would have to offer at a diner was high fat and fried foods. She looked at the menu and discovered she was right. The only thing even remotely healthy, and it was a far stretch to call it a healthy choice, was an iceberg lettuce salad with blue cheese and bacon crumbles.

Daphne ordered a cheeseburger with onion rings and a large double chocolate milkshake. Daphne was a little bitty-thing, standing about 5'2" and barely weighing 100 pounds but that girl could put the food away.

Kylie not seeing a healthy choice to choose from went with the country fried steak and loaded mashed potatoes. She found much to her surprise that it was really tasty.

After finishing their meal and checking her watch Daphne said, "Time to go to work."

Kylie had no idea where this place was where she would be working so sat back as Daphne drove and enjoyed the sights as bleak as they were.

Once you were out of the downtown area of Vegas everything became brown and dead looking, all the glitz and glamour left miles behind. In contrast to the casino area everything else was quite a let down.

Daphne pulled into McCarran International Airport but instead of following the signs for the airport's main terminal she took a separate road where they had to stop to show their ID's to guards before they could pass any further.

If anyone would have noticed the road they had turned down they would have assumed it was a turn off road for employees or equipment, but the road led to a separate terminal that few people were ever allowed to enter. The only ones that made it past the check points were employees of Area 51.

Daphne had informed her that Area 51 was sometimes referred to as Dreamland or Groom Lake. Daphne's father had worked there for as long as she could remember and she herself had worked there for several years.

They boarded a 737 jet that had a red stripe down the side but no markings of any other kind as to identify the airlines or any insignia. The windows inside the plane were blacked out.

As Daphne led the way down the aisle of the plane Kylie noticed dozens of people already on board. No one made eye contact with each other or acknowledged each other's presence in any way.

As Kylie buckled herself into her seat she leaned over and whispered in Daphne's ear, "Do we fly into work everyday?"

"Yeah, there's no driving into Area 51. This is how you'll get to work from now on," Daphne answered. "It's a short flight. It's only about 75 to 80 miles from here."

"Isn't the blacked out windows and all this secrecy a bit much," Kylie whispered during the flight to Daphne. "After all, for anyone who really cares I'm sure all they have to do is go to Google Earth and find out exactly where Area 51 is located."

"Ssh!" Daphne said holding her pointing finger to her lips.

"The bigwigs all think Area 51 is still a big secret to the rest of the world. No, I'm just kidding, but they do take extreme precautions that no one gets too close. It's hidden away within a ring of mountain ranges with restricted fly over space and you have to have a top secret clearance to get anywhere near the place. Even then you only see the area you work in."

"But I've heard that conspiracy theorists come up here to make videos for YouTube," Kylie said.

"Oh, yeah; there's a whole club of them. Some of them come up every year. I've actually met some of them and they're pretty nice people. Some of those conspiracy theories they talk about aren't too far from the truth," Daphne said.

"Did you tell them anything?" Kylie asked. "I'm sure they wanted to know what happens at Area 51."

"Girl, did you not just go through orientation where they swore you to secrecy upon your death or imprisonment? Believe me, they weren't kidding. No, the people I met had no idea I have any connection with Area 51."

"So these people come up here and try to get in?" Kylie asked out of curiosity.

"They know they'll never get in," Daphne told her. "They just like to see how far they can push it and brag to their friends and people who watch them on YouTube how they were at Area 51. They don't get too far. There's fences with signs that warn that anyone who crosses that point will be met with deadly force."

Kylie sat back in her seat and thought about this a minute. "They wouldn't actually do that, would they?"

"Yep, sure would," Daphne answered. "They take their security very seriously. Before people ever get close to that point security drives around to be seen and let the people know they're being watched to intimidate them. After that if anyone pushes it security calls the local law and they're arrested."

Daphne leaned closer to Kylie and whispered, "In answer to your question, yes, they most definitely would shoot them if they passed a certain point. What's behind Area 51 is of the highest national security and is one of if not the most secure and secret government facilities in the United States."

24

The jet was landing at that point and Kylie was anxious to see this place for herself. After exiting the plane they then entered a bus that also had blacked out windows that they rode in for about another fifteen or twenty minutes down what felt like an unpaved bumpy dirt road before arriving at a hangar built into a mountain.

At this point they were directed through a portal of sorts and depending on where you had clearance to access is where you were then directed.

Kylie was disappointed to see that as they exited the bus there was no opportunity to see what was out there. She figured if this was the procedure she probably never would see what the place looked like. Even though she now worked at Area 51, as far as what the place looked like from the outside would remain a mystery to her.

As they entered the building their ID's were checked. They were scanned and searched to be sure they weren't carrying weapons of any kind or secreted away any cameras.

After they passed through the check-in area Daphne explained that you were only allowed inside the building and in the area where you worked. The rest was off limits. Your pass would only permit you to go in the areas you needed to be in.

"How big is this place?" Kylie asked.

"It's three times the size of Rhode Island and over twice as large as the state of Delaware," Daphne answered as they walked down a tunnel.

"Wow, that's pretty impressive," Kylie responded.

Daphne gave her a short tour of areas she would need to know how to get to and told her it would get easier over time.

After having a chance to look over her work area which was quite impressive Daphne received a call and said, "Come on. We've been summoned to the principal's office."

25

Daphne stopped outside an office door and knocked. Before Kylie had a chance to catch her breath they were told to enter. At the desk sat Major Brannan, Daphne's father.

Sitting quietly beside the Major's desk sat Amir. Only he wasn't Amir, he was Alan. He was now clean shaven, minus the turban, and looking like a completely different person.

He nodded at her and simply said, "Kylie."

"Was your work station up to your standards and satisfaction," Major Brannan asked Kylie drawing her attention away from Alan.

"Yes, sir," she answered. "The equipment is state of the art. When do you want me to start?"

"I'm glad you asked," Major Brannan said. "Initially we were just going to have Daphne show you around today. I know you already went through orientation, but I'm afraid our time table has been accelerated which we had no control over. Do you think you're up to putting in a few hours today?"

"What's going on?" Daphne asked before Kylie had a chance to respond.

"Later," her father said pointing at one of the seats by his desk for her to take a seat. "Well?" he asked Kylie.

"Sure, that shouldn't be a problem," Kylie said.

"Go with Alan then. He'll show you where you need to go. You'll be working with him on this," Major Brannan said.

Major Brannan said to Alan, "I'll call down and let them know to be ready."

Kylie followed Alan out and before the door closed behind her she heard Daphne questioning her father. She couldn't hear his response, but she definitely heard Daphne raising her voice clearly upset by the response she had received from her father.

Alan was quiet for most of the walk to wherever they were headed. He seemed to be deep in thought as they stepped inside an elevator and went down several floors in silence.

Alan continued down a long hall before stopping outside a door that was guarded with armed guards. Their passes were checked before they were allowed to enter.

Alan said, "Kylie, look. I'm really sorry that you're being asked to do this with no forewarning. This wasn't the way things were planned, but something happened to expedite matters and this is something we couldn't put off."

Kylie said, "Understood. Do you want to tell me what we're doing?"

"It would take too long to explain, and I really wouldn't even know where to begin," Alan said. "Besides, they're already waiting for us. I promise though, when this is over you'll be fully briefed."

He then led the way into a white room where someone was waiting to help them dress in a hazmat suit. They were told to first remove all their clothing.

The room and the suit she was given to wear reminded her of when as a student she had a stint working at a communicable and infectious diseases lab.

She looked around for a room to change in when she was told by the assistant there was no time for that. She turned her back to Alan as he did her while she stepped out of her clothes and into the suit which covered her from her neck to the tops of her feet. She was given a pair of hazmat boots to complete the outfit.

An assistant collected their clothing, bagged them up, and took their items to another room.

The same assistant who helped her into the suit then stepped forward and put two pairs of thick latex gloves on her and then covered her hair tucking all loose strands in. The only part of her exposed was her face. Amir and Kylie both were handed full face shields to wear.

"Ready?" Alan asked who was already suited up.

She nodded and he opened the door to what appeared to be an operating room. As she entered the room the thought crossed her mind that knowing the work Alan did, she assumed she now knew why she had been assigned to attend autopsies with him previously. That seemed a lifetime ago.

She remembered telling Alan that she would never attend

another autopsy again, yet here she was. By all appearances she was about to do exactly that.

She looked around for the dead body and sure enough someone who she assumed was the diener was pushing a gurney into the room, a room that already held more than half a dozen people who were waiting.

Included in the group was an X-ray technician, a forensic photographer, the diener, and a few people who were there to observe the proceedings.

A horrible stench filled the room as they approached with the gurney. Kylie couldn't help herself and brought her hand up to cover her nose. She quickly put on her face shield hoping that would help cover the stench. It didn't.

The smell that permeated the room was unlike anything she could even begin to describe. This was worse even than the autopsy they had performed on a body that had drowned and been in the water for days before being discovered.

The assistants stepped back to allow Alan and Kylie up front. It was only then that she noticed the size of the body on the gurney.

The body under the sheet appeared to be that of a child.

26

Before they had the chance to remove the covering from the body Alan looked at her. She could see he had a concerned look and thought it was due to the fact that they were about to do an autopsy on a child, something in the past she was able to forgo.

She looked at Alan with frightened eyes. He said to her in a firm voice, "Try not to think of the world as you have always known it. Have an open mind and remember all you learned when you attended the autopsies with me in the past."

He gave her a moment to gather herself.

"Ready?" Alan asked.

Kylie took a few deep breaths and nodded. Alan reached over and put his hand on her back giving her support.

The diener removed the covering of the body.

Kylie fainted.

The body was put back in the freezer since they had yet to begin the autopsy. Alan had Kylie brought into an adjoining room and someone gave her smelling salts to bring her around.

Once she came to she glared at Alan. "What was that? Seriously?"

Alan said, "I'm sorry you weren't warned ahead of time. There was just really no time to explain, nor is there now." He began pacing. "But to be brief, we currently have aliens in captivity here. This one...."

"Aliens?" Kylie said. "That's an alien? You mean not of this earth?"

Alan nodded. "One of them has been doing poorly and passed away yesterday. We thought we would have had more time to introduce you to the fact that we have aliens here. We at this time have two of them here to study. Well, one live one and this one we are about to do an autopsy on."

Alan paused and then said, "Originally there were three. We found one dead at the scene that was burned so badly we really weren't able to glean any information from it's autopsy. The only part of the body that hadn't been badly burned was part of an arm and a hand which had become severed from the body during the crash."

Kylie began to hyperventilate. Alan pushed her head down between her knees. After a moment she raised her head. "And you couldn't have warned me beforehand? How did you think I would react?"

Alan said, "It wasn't supposed to happen like this, but as you could smell the body is rapidly decomposing. It's decomposing at a much faster rate than a human body would. It's decomposing now as we sit here talking. There's really no time to wait."

He stood over her waiting to see what she would do. He wouldn't have blamed her if she walked out of the room and kept walking. But he knew this was no time for drama or hysterics.

"We really don't have time for this discussion right now. I promise later I will answer any and all questions you have. But right now, you have to be the professional you are and get the job done. As time is passing the body is decomposing," Alan said.

Kylie thought for a moment. "And I have to be involved in this...autopsy of an alien?"

Alan said, "Yes, we really need you to be there."

"O.K., then. There's a lot of people waiting and I don't want to be the one holding things up," Kylie said.

Someone came in to aid both Alan and Kylie in changing into new clean, sterile suits before they entered back into the autopsy room.

As they were being suited up Alan said, "Thanks for understanding. I know this is difficult for you. The others here have at least had time to process this and knew about the aliens beforehand."

"I didn't expect this," Kylie said. "Though with the reputation of Area 51 I guess I shouldn't have been surprised. I just wish someone would have warned me ahead of time. This is a helluva way to find out our world has been invaded by tiny, green men."

"Not green, but duly noted. There just wasn't time," Alan said. "Try to remember the other autopsies we performed when we focused on different parts of the body in great detail. I need you to do the same thing here. Don't think of it as anything but a body. We need to go over each body part extensively and learn as much as possible."

"O.K.," Kylie said.

"The difference is we only have one chance at this. Take as long as you need for each part and when you think you've learned all you can we'll continue," Alan explained.

As Alan held the door open for her he said, "Just speak your thoughts aloud. Omit nothing. Nothing is irrelevant. Make note of everything that even crosses your mind. Everything will be recorded automatically and photographed."

27

The body was retrieved from the refrigerated section of the room and brought to the autopsy table. The head was placed at an elevated area of the table. Seeing that alien head looking at you was unnerving.

Kylie took a moment to look at the alien's body, terrified at having learned that they truly did exist. But this wasn't the time or place to contemplate what that could mean. She had to get her head in the game.

"Ready?" Alan asked her.

Once they began their work all other thoughts ceased to exist. She made note of the time they began. It was 3:42 P.M.

The diener who was assisting Alan and Kylie in the autopsy had placed all the necessary tools needed on a table within reach. This autopsy would be performed by Alan and Kylie with the others assisting as needed.

Kylie looked the tools over to see that everything needed was there. Included were electrical saws, scalpels, spreaders, loppers, knives, sponges, needles and thread.

She gave Alan who was to be the forensic pathologist in charge the nod that she was ready to proceed.

They began with a detailed inspection of the body. The fact that the autopsy was being recorded they spoke of every move they made and of everything they saw. They knew the importance of this for posterity's sake and for current and future study.

They took an excessive amount of time considering this may be the only opportunity to study an alien in detail; both body, organs, and their functions.

As they were making their inspection Kylie said, "The body, or alien, is very human like, to the point that it must be related to humans in some way."

The alien was weighed at approximately 40 pounds and measured at 50 and ¾ inches.

Each outer part of the body was inspected inch by inch. It was noted that the body was decomposing in an accelerated manner. She could see for herself why they couldn't wait any longer to get this done or the tissue samples and DNA would be compromised.

"Might as well start at the top," Alan said.

The head was noted as being somewhat pear shaped in appearance and over-sized in accordance to the body size or in comparison to human heads. There was no hair or hair follicles. The bones of the head were pliable.

Kylie could hear one of the observers retching behind her and then quickly leaving the room. The smell was making many of the observers sick to their stomachs.

Kylie tried not to shiver as she touched the alien. The skin had a slimy feel to it even through the thick gloves.

Working their way down they next described the forehead as high and broad. The eyes were extremely large and almond shaped. There was no visible eyelid, eyebrows, or eyelashes. There was a notable absence of hair anywhere on the body.

The nose was nothing more than a small protrusion.

The mouth was an area they inspected for a considerable amount of time. One of the questions Alan had been given beforehand was to try to discover how the aliens ate and what their diet consisted of.

The mouth was little more than a slit with no lips. Kylie pried the mouth open where they found the tongue to be atrophied. The oral cavity was narrow and only a few inches deep with a membrane in the rear of the oral cavity.

Alan angled the head so the light would shine inside the mouth. "There's no opening for food to be ingested into any sort of digestive tract," Kylie observed and said into the recorder. She mentioned the fact that the mouth couldn't function as a means of ingesting food or be used as a means of communicating with each other.

Alan verbalized a question into the recorder of whether evolution had anything to do with the atrophied tongue and membrane in the back of the mouth. Did they at one time speak and eat like humans but changed over time. Otherwise, what was the purpose for the tongue even being there or the mouth for that matter.

"There are no teeth nor does it appear there ever has been," Kylie mentioned while Alan was still examining the mouth.

They stopped long enough for an X-Ray technician to take X-rays of the cranial bone structure.

While the technician did their work Alan said to Kylie, "They haven't communicated with us in any way since they've been here. We aren't aware of how they communicate even with each other. It isn't known if they choose not to communicate with us or are unable to. It could merely be an issue with a language barrier but we have no way of knowing."

The technician informed them that he was finished taking his X-rays of the cranial area and moved his equipment out of the way. He remained close by for when they next needed him.

The diener stepped forward and made a mold of the inside of the mouth where teeth would have normally been.

When they completed their work Alan resumed his place and turned the alien's head slightly to get a better presentation of the side of the head where he could examine one of the ears. There were no outer lobes. Again, it was little more than a slit in the body.

They spent little time on the chin and neck merely noting that the chin was small and pointed and the neck was slender.

Alan explaining to Kylie and recording the information for posterity said, "The skin in the body we are examining is grayish in color but seems to be partially due to the decomposition. Initially the skin tone of this being was described more as bluish-gray. I've been told that other alien beings that have been captured in the past, both dead and alive, have been described some as tan, brown, a pale white, and some as pinkish-gray."

Kylie looked up startled as he mentioned other aliens that had been captured. She started to say something, but Alan quickly shook his head and mouthed silently to her, "Later."

"The one we currently have in captivity that arrived at the same time as this one is pinkish-gray in color."

Alan looked at Kylie and asked, "How would you describe the

texture of the skin?"

One of the assistants stepped forward and was leaning over her shoulder trying to get a closer look before Alan waved her back.

"The skin appears to be elastic like. It seems to have the texture of a reptile." She reached over and pulled a hanging magnification piece over to where she could closely examine the skin of the alien. "Under magnification it appears mesh-like and extremely strong, durable."

"We are now examining the arms," Alan said into the recorder, "which are long and slender reaching to just above the knees."

Kylie lifted one of the hands to examine and noted there were four fingers and no thumb. There was a webbing between the fingers. Examining the fingers she spotted something that looked familiar. She pointed to the tiny suction cups on the tips of the fingers.

She looked at Alan and pointed at her own finger with a questioning look. He nodded.

The specimen she had examined in the lab where she had previously worked was apparently the skin from an alien finger. She could only assume it came from the one found dead at the scene – which was now firmly attached to her own finger.

28

Daphne paced inside her father's office. "How much longer are they going to be?"

Her father, Major Brannan, sighed deeply. "As long as it takes. Will you quit looking at your watch every two minutes. It's really annoying."

Daphne said, "They've been in there for over four hours now. Just how long does an autopsy take?"

"Usually about two or three hours but this is a different case," Major Brannan said.

"Gee, ya think?" Daphne said putting her hands on her hips and glaring at her father.

"They have one chance at this. It's important they learn whatever they can while they have this invaluable opportunity, even if it takes all night. So get comfortable or go home."

"Her first day of work before she's even been briefed about the aliens and she's made to do an autopsy on one," Daphne said. "You really should have talked to her before this, like maybe let her know that she's walking around with part of an alien wrapped around her finger."

Her father just glared at her.

Daphne plopped down in a chair and crossed her legs, rapidly swinging her leg and crossed her arms across her chest. Her body language was a dead give-away on exactly how she felt about this whole ordeal.

Alan stepped back and motioned for the diener and asked her to open the body. Alan and Kylie stepped back to give her room to work.

The diener stepped forward with a scalpel meticulously cutting a Y-shape into the body starting at both sides of the collarbone extending down to the bottom of the torso.

As the body was opened Kylie had to turn her head as the fetid smell filled the room, even worse than before. Several of the assistants took a big step back trying to give themselves some space from the horrible odor. There was no getting away from it.

The skin of the alien was pulled apart on each side where the cuts had been made. The chest area was opened exposing the entire chest cavity. At this point the organs were usually removed, but Alan told the diener to hold off.

The photographer was motioned forward and spent a good bit of time taking numerous photos of every position possible.

Alan and Kylie examined the different organs and their placement in the body extensively before allowing the diener to step forward to remove and weigh the organs.

Razor thin slices were cut into the different organs in a few different areas for closer microscopic examinations to be done at a later time. Kylie would be assisting with that work also, but for now she was glad to let the diener take over and remove the slices of organs and seal them in uncontaminated containers.

The last thing to be done was to examine the brain. The diener cut the scalp across the back of the head from ear to ear. She then began gently peeling the face away from the skull. For this Kylie turned her head. It wasn't a pretty sight.

The face was folded down and laid inside out on the chest area.

The diener picked up an electrical saw and she proceeded to cut the skull open from one side of the head to the other.

Kylie turned away wincing at the sound of the saw hitting bone. Regardless of how many autopsies she had attended it was a sound that was like fingernails on a chalkboard to her.

The last step was for the diener to take a hammer and chisel and pop the skull open similar to how one opens a coconut. As the two parts were aggressively pried apart there was a sucking sound. The parts of the skull were set aside and the brain was exposed for them to examine.

Parts of the brain would be examined in more detail under the microscope later. The brain was removed and weighed. Several cuts were made and removed and preserved for Kylie and those who would be working with her to study the alien's body parts.

At this point Kylie noted the time. It was now 8:54 P.M. The autopsy had taken a little over five hours to complete. An extraordinarily long time for an autopsy, but considering this was a new species they were examining perhaps it really wasn't that long.

Alan and Kylie walked out, their part completed. The diener stayed behind and bagged up the body and removed it. Her part wouldn't be complete until the area was cleaned up and sterilized.

An assistant was there to remove the hazmat suits from Alan and Kylie. Alan turned his back to Kylie and she could hear him stepping out of his hazmat suit.

Kylie with help from the assistant quickly shed her hazmat suit and headed for the shower room. She wanted that awful smelling suit off of her and any trace of the alien washed off her as quickly as possible.

Alan before leaving the room to head to the men's showers told the assistant, "Burn these suits. You'll never get this smell out."

"Yes, Dr. Christenson," she said as she gathered up the hazmat suits. "Gladly." The assistant got the dry heaves just carrying the suits out to dispose of them.

Kylie washed with lye soap to try to remove the stench from her body. She washed her entire body several times and still felt her nostrils were full of the smell of the rotting alien.

It had been a long night, and an eye-opening one for Kylie. In the shower tears ran down her face as she leaned her head against the wall thinking about what Olivia had told her about being one of the chosen ones and being abducted by these creatures. For what purpose she didn't even want to think about. Sometimes your imagination was worse than the reality - *and then sometimes not.*

29

As exhausted as Kylie was she tossed and turned throughout the night not able to get the thought out of her mind that aliens were real. After laying awake for some time she decided she might as well just get up. She decided to go for a run to clear her mind before she had to get ready for work.

She sat on the steps by her front door lacing up her running shoes and tied her long hair into a pony tail. She looked down the street and noticed the only lights on in the homes on her street were hers and those of her neighbor next door.

When she began her run it was still dark out with only the street lights to light her way, but it was a time that she found peaceful to run.

She had been running for about half a mile when she spotted another runner a little ways ahead of her. She slowed down a little so she didn't catch up to him. She was out to exercise, not to socialize.

About ten minutes later he stopped and bent over to tie his shoe. She passed him and politely said hello and kept running.

After she made a turn in the road ahead he caught up to her and jogged up beside her and introduced himself. She recognized him immediately as her next door neighbor.

Whether she felt like company or not he jogged beside her. She was soon surprised to realize she was enjoying his company. He matched her stride and still was able to keep up a conversation.

By the time they parted at the end of her driveway five miles later she felt completely at ease with him and had enjoyed running with him. During their conversation they discovered they had many things in common.

They both loved the outdoors and tentatively made plans to go jogging in the mornings together and go hiking one day. He had invited her to go kayaking with him when they both had the same day off. Kayaking was something she had never tried before but sounded like fun.

"T.C. Tanner," Kylie said his name out loud with a smile on her face as she walked into her house. "Even his name is sexy," she said to herself as she thought of those long, tan legs of his and that sexy smile. "Yep, I think I'm going to enjoy living in Vegas."

On the flight into work Daphne peered into Kylie's face and said, "That's not the face I expected to see today."

"What do you mean?" Kylie asked.

"I figured after what happened yesterday you would be all stressed out and have a million questions. You actually look, how should I describe this," Daphne said with a slight hesitation while she thought about it, "as though you just had great sex. Yep, that's the look," Daphne said sitting back in her seat with a satisfied smirk on her face.

Kylie said, "No, not great sex."

"What then? Don't hold back on me," Daphne pried. "Remember, I'm a snoop."

"You are at that," Kylie laughed.

After a little persuasion from Daphne she said, "You remember my next door neighbor?"

"How could I forget? Oh my God, don't tell me!" Daphne said fanning herself with her hand as though just the thought of him was making her hot. "No, wait; do tell me, and don't leave anything out." She leaned forward to not miss a word.

Daphne walked Kylie to her lab since she was still learning her way around and said she would be by later and depending on their schedules perhaps have lunch.

Kylie was just getting her lab coat on when Alan walked in and told her they had a meeting to attend on yesterday's autopsy. As they walked to the meeting he gave her a brief heads-up on who would be there and what to expect.

Even being forewarned she was still shocked at all the medals on the chests of the men sitting at the table for the meeting.

It seemed as though most of the people in attendance were top brass in the military. The Air Force, Navy, and the Army seemed to have representatives at the meeting. She assumed the Marines were included, too.

There were a few women sitting around the table, some in military dress and one or two that had been introduced as doctors. One she recognized as the surgeon that had tried to remove the specimen from her finger, which she now knew to be skin from an alien.

Deep in discussion when they arrived many of them hadn't noticed her and Alan come in. The topic being discussed was the alien.

It seemed they all had their own opinions, informed or not, on the aliens and why they had come to earth, how they got here, and how many aliens there may be out there. They were all questions Kylie had contemplated herself during her long sleepless night.

30

Alan led Kylie to a seat and pulled another chair over so he could sit next to her. He knew she was probably feeling a bit overwhelmed. The room was filled to capacity with higher-ups.

Major Brannan stood and addressed the group, "Ladies, gentlemen...you have all been briefed on the events from yesterday, but let me introduce to you Dr. Alan Christenson the forensic pathologist and Dr. Kylie Carmichael a geneticist who is our newest addition to the group. They are the two that performed the autopsy yesterday."

After a short discussion the lights were dimmed and video was shown of parts of the autopsy. Due to the lengthiness of the time of the autopsy only certain parts were shown.

When the lights came back on the room erupted in people talking about what they had just seen. There were lots of questions to be answered.

Once the questions began Kylie lost all inhibitions she had previously felt. She knew her subject well and could easily explain the questions those in attendance had.

One of the women doctors asked about what was discovered as far as what the aliens ate or drank and how they did so since there was a membrane at the back of the mouth.

"It wasn't discovered how or if food or water are taken since there was no digestive system or GI tract. There was no intestinal or alimentary canal or even a rectal area discovered during the autopsy," Kylie answered.

Those revelations seemed to raise even more questions. Questions began being shouted out by those in attendance.

"Are they living beings or are they machines of some kind?" was one of the questions tossed out.

"How can they survive without nourishment?" asked a man who identified himself to the group as Lieutenant Colonel Ward.

Before more questions could be tossed out Alan continued

where Kylie had left off on the topic of nourishment. "Actually, we were unable to come up with a definitive answer on the question of food intake. We don't know if they eat or if they do what they eat or how often. That's something we were unable to determine."

Kylie added, "We did question whether it was through the inner layer of fatty tissue on how they nourished themselves. The tissue is unlike that of humans. It was permeable and contained the chemicals of the lymphatic system which was far more developed than that of our own."

Most of the people in the room didn't understand the workings of the human body, let alone that of an alien. They politely listened, but it was few who completely understood everything they were describing.

"Have you been able to communicate with the aliens?" Lieutenant Colonel Ward asked the major. His question was more in line with the area the military was interested in and for good reason. They were most interested in their purpose on coming to earth.

"No, as of this time we have been unable to communicate with them in any way, and when the second one was alive they didn't seem to communicate in any verbal manner to each other either," Major Brannan answered.

One of the men with a chest full of metals asked, "What are their intentions? Do you think they are here to harm us or to attempt to take over our planet?"

Major Brannan interrupted him and said, "We seem to be getting off track, gentlemen. This meeting is only to be on what was discovered from the autopsy and where we need to go from this point on. Those questions can not be answered presently and some of those here don't have the security clearance for that discussion."

"Understood," the colonel said. "But I want to have a discussion with you privately before I leave here today."

The colonel's question had left the others feeling a bit uncomfortable.

After a brief pause a man whose name she didn't catch asked Kylie, "Was the alien a male or female?"

"Actually there was no genitalia and no apparent reproductive system that we discovered. Through our examination we were unable to determine how or if they reproduce," Kylie answered.

The colonel said, "It seems there's quite a lot the two of you were unable to determine."

Major Brannan spoke up, "More has been determined than left without an answer. We're learning as we go. We actually discovered much more than we expected to and we look at the results as a successful mission."

The colonel nodded but frowned and appeared to be deep in thought.

"What stands out most in your mind of what you discovered from the autopsy?" one of the doctors asked Kylie directly.

"You mean other than the fact that there are aliens here on earth?" Kylie said with a nervous laugh.

Major Brannan interrupted, "Dr. Carmichael has just recently joined us and we didn't have the luxury of time on our hands. She went into this autopsy completely unaware that we had aliens held here in captivity."

"That must have been quite the eye-opener," one of the men in civilian dress said with a sympathetic smile towards Kylie.

"It was, most definitely; but back to the question of what most stands out from what we learned. I would have to say that I was most impressed by the similarities between the aliens and ourselves. There appeared to be more similarities than there were differences."

"Interesting," someone at the table said as they made some notes on a notepad.

"While there were many similarities there were differences, too. Their organs and skin composition were different from our own. Their heart and lungs were much larger than what you would find in a human body," Kylie said.

Alan explained about the skin and how the bones were thinner but appeared to be fibrous and more resilient.

One of the Air Force officers made the comment it would be interesting to speak to someone in the field of aerospace and see if that would be a factor in aiding the aliens in their space travel.

At that point Alan then turned the questions on the heart and lungs over to Kylie who explained that the larger heart the alien had meant a slower metabolism and how their lungs were over-sized in comparison to their body size.

After the meeting the discussion continued where they were all most interested in the alien that was still surviving. Any questions on this matter were ones Kylie was unable to answer and at this point she left the meeting and returned to her lab. She was anxious to look over the samples taken during the autopsy and study them further.

31

Kylie was working in the lab with Alan and another pathologist examining specimens the histology department had prepared on slides for them. They also had a microbiologist working with them looking over different specimens and discussing their findings.

Daphne walked in and pulled up a stool and listened for a minute.

They were discussing the fact that they had been amazed to discover that the aliens had no blood, only a milky like substance that passed through the circulatory system. They were deep into a discussion on it's possible functions.

It seemed to them the more they studied the samples taken the more questions they had. They certainly couldn't do research and see what others had found or in textbooks.

"We have nothing to compare it to," Kylie said a bit exasperated.

"You can always wait for the other one to die and compare the two," Daphne piped in.

They all turned around and looked appalled at what she said.

"Hey, lighten up. I'm just kidding. You guys are way too intense. I was just joking."

"I'm sorry, Daphne. Did you need something?" Kylie asked.

"I just came in to let you know that after lunch I'm going to be introducing you to somebody," Daphne said.

"O.K., that's fine," Kylie said as she grabbed another slide and peered back through the microscopic lens.

Daphne started walking out the door but stopped before she exited and said, "In case you're wondering who it is, it's the surviving alien."

Then she walked out the door.

32

Daphne had lunch delivered for the two of them brought to her office as she knew Kylie would have questions before she was taken to see the alien. It wasn't exactly a subject that could be discussed around others.

While the cafeteria would be filled with other workers from Area 51, the workers only know "what they need to know."

Many of the workers at Area 51 would be shocked to learn there actually are aliens and alien spacecraft within their walls. They believed those facts to be only in the minds of conspiracy theorists as that information had nothing to do with the work they did. They weren't enlightened to the fact that an alien was currently living several floors below where they worked on a daily basis.

Daphne was eating her lunch while Kylie simply stared at hers. "I have to be in the same room with the alien?" she asked.

Daphne said, "Don't worry. There have been half a dozen people who have been in the room with him-her-it, whatever the heck it is; and he appears to be harmless. Let's just call it a he to keep it simple. He's never made any aggressive moves in the past."

"I'm really nervous about this. Scared to death really," Kylie said.

"Scared like as in riding Kingda Ka roller coaster at Six Flags?" Daphne asked trying to lighten the mood.

"Roller coasters I can handle, aliens not so much," Kylie said.

"It's the fear of the unknown that's scaring you," Daphne said. "That's normal, and as a psychologist I should know." She ate one of her chicken wings and watched Kylie.

"What am I supposed to do in there?" Kylie asked.

"Today you are there to observe only," Daphne said. "There's a room next door where several people will be watching through a one-way mirror, and there are guards who constantly monitor his actions. There are cameras and microphones throughout the room. There's no need to worry. You'll be protected and watched at all times."

After a moment Daphne asked, "Do you have any questions?"

"No, I'd rather not think anymore about it." Kylie picked up a sandwich she had ordered and bit into it. No point in obsessing about it she decided. It was going to happen and there wasn't a thing she could do about it.

"Just remember, we're in control here," Daphne said. "He's locked in tighter than Ft. Knox. There's no way he can get out or do anything to hurt anybody."

Kylie looked up startled at this comment.

"He doesn't seem inclined to be harmful from what I've observed and I spend time with him everyday," Daphne reassured her. "Once you get over the fear of being in the room with an alien, you'll look at it through the eyes of a scientist and realize what a unique opportunity it is.

"An opportunity I'd just as soon do without," Kylie said putting her sandwich down.

"How many people can say, 'I spent the day with an alien'." Daphne thought about what she had just said and quickly added, "Not that you can tell anybody that, of course."

33

Major Brannan called Daphne and told her they were ready for her and Kylie and to proceed to the alien's room.

They weren't expected to do anything today other than to tell him who Kylie was and what her role would be with him in the future. They didn't know if he would understand them or not, but it would give him a chance to see Kylie and see how he responded to a new face coming in.

When the aliens had first been brought in they had thought they were both dead. They had crashed and were lying next to the spacecraft. They found another alien inside the spacecraft who had been badly burned and perished before they arrived.

As the other two aliens were being examined they began to regain consciousness and were rapidly brought to the room they were in now where they could be confined with no means of escape.

In the past they had kept actual visitors to the room to a bare minimum in case of diseases passed from the aliens to them or vice versa.

They still weren't exactly sure what had caused the death of the other alien, whether it was damages due to the crash or not able to acclimate to the earth's atmosphere. They didn't want to chance losing the other one also with such a valuable opportunity to study a live alien.

They hoped at the very least to learn where they came from and what their purpose was for coming to our planet.

Daphne as a psychologist had been meeting with him daily to study him and to try to instigate some type of communication, but to date had been unsuccessful in that endeavor.

Daphne and Kylie took an elevator down to a lower floor. When they stepped off the elevator Kylie immediately noticed the difference from this area than from where she worked. There were thick steel doors locked and guarded by armed guards at the end of the hall. Several more armed guards were intermittently placed along the corridor.

Their passes were checked even though Daphne's presence was a daily occurrence. They were allowed through and turning the corner they could see Major Brannan down a few doors holding a door open and speaking to someone.

Walking down the hall they passed a room that was open. As they walked past Kylie peered in and saw a communication room of sorts. Monitors completely filled one wall with four armed men watching the monitors intently.

As they approached Major Brannan she saw several people were inside the room where he was standing. The people were all staring at the one-way mirror with some writing notes as they observed. She could barely make out part of the body of the alien through the glass.

Seeing the alien Kylie began to breath rapidly. Daphne reached back to steady her.

The door they were about to enter had armed guards on each side of the door.

Daphne said to Kylie before they stepped into the room, "Don't let him sense that you're afraid. You're going to have to be working with him on a daily basis and you don't want him to know you're nervous around him. Just remember, he hasn't reacted in a defensive or aggressive manner in any way and isn't likely to start doing so now."

Kylie was standing behind Daphne when they first entered the room. The alien barely looked up to take notice that he was no longer alone.

He went from taking no notice of the two women to jerking his head up and staring intently at Kylie. His large, black eyes staring at her unnerved her.

Before anyone realized what was happening he rushed over to Daphne and pushed her aside grabbing Kylie's hand within his own. The hand he grabbed was the one with the alien finger part attached to hers. He looked into her eyes with an expression of intense pain and bereavement.

When he pushed Daphne aside and grabbed her Kylie was petrified. In a moment's time that fear passed and she knew he meant her no harm. She didn't know how she knew it but she felt it.

Kylie felt as though she could understand what he was feeling. She remembered that this finger held part of the finger of the alien that had been on the spacecraft with him that had died in the crash. Could he possibly know that?

Since then he had lost his only other companion, the only other of his kind on the planet – well, no maybe not; she remembered what Alan had said during the autopsy about other aliens. Her mind was racing with these thoughts.

She sensed his deep feeling of loss for his fellow alien. She couldn't explain it, but she could definitely feel his grief.

Guards rushed into the room with their weapons aimed at the alien while other guards grabbed the women and pulled them backwards out of the room to safety before slamming the door shut and re-locking it.

Major Brannan rushed from the adjoining room along with two others she didn't recognize and yelled, "What the hell just happened there?"

Kylie said, "I don't believe he meant to hurt Daphne. Somehow I believe he was aware of," she looked around and noticed the other people and didn't know how much she could share and continued tentatively, "you know." She held up her finger so Major Brannan would know what she was talking about.

"How would he know?" He paced in front of the door. He contemplated what she said for just a moment then said, "Let's go look at the film of what just happened."

They went into the communications room and watched the film several different times. He reversed it and watched it in slow motion over and over.

"I believe you're right," Major Brannan said to Kylie.

"Are you both willing to try to go in again?" the major asked.

They both agreed and were led back into the room. While the alien seemed to totally ignore Daphne he focused intently on Kylie.

Daphne nudged her and said in a soft voice, "Talk to him and see if he responds."

"My name is Kylie," she spoke calmly to him. "We're not here to hurt you or harm you in any way. I wanted to introduce myself."

She paused to see if he would react in anyway. He simply watched her every move.

She wasn't sure what happened next, but he seemed to speak to her without actually saying anything.

'I know who you are. You're one of the chosen. I know you mean no harm and neither do I,' the alien somehow sent this message to her.

She rubbed her arms and noticed the hairs on her arms were standing on end.

She had been a huge Star Trek fan, a Trekkie, and the closest she could come to describing what had just happened was when Spock would mind meld with someone – minus the touch in this case.

She understood what he was thinking. How was that even possible? Mental telepathy?

What did he mean 'he knew who she was' and that 'she was one of the chosen'?

34

The more she thought about the alien communicating to her, however that was possible; she decided to keep this information to herself, at least for the time being.

She wanted to process the information. What did it mean? Why had no one else up to this point been able to communicate with him verbally or otherwise? Why her?

Whether she wanted to admit it or not, she knew the reason it bothered her so much was because of what Olivia had told her about her, her mother, and her grandmother being abducted by aliens. She had even used the same wording as the alien, that they had been chosen.

Daphne dropped by her house that evening with take-out. Kylie didn't know how to broach the subject, but there was something she desperately wanted to verify.

"Are you going to eat that last egg roll?" Daphne asked pointing her chopsticks at the remaining eggroll.

"No, go ahead," Kylie said.

While Daphne took a bite of the egg roll Kylie said, "I know you told me that no one has been able to communicate with the alien, but I was wondering about that."

Daphne motioned for her to be quiet in a discreet manner and loudly changed the subject banging the plates and leftover dishes. "Come on, let's get these dishes cleaned up and go walk off this dinner."

Kylie was confused by her behavior but just thought maybe Daphne wanted to leave work at work and not talk about it.

They collected the plates and rinsed them off and stacked them in the dishwasher. Daphne said, "Come on. You can walk me part way home."

After they were outside and on the street Daphne reminded

her, "Don't *ever* forget that there is a 99.9% chance that your phone and your house is bugged. There are certain things you definitely should not talk about where there is any chance you can be overheard, and believe me any alien talk is definitely at the top of the list of things not to be discussed where there may be listening devices."

Kylie looked shocked, "You mean they may have bugged my house?"

"Most definitely," warned Daphne. "Don't forget you're a rookie. They need to be sure they can trust you. Make sure there's no pillow talk between you and a lover."

"Oh, my God. You mean they would even listen in..."

"I don't know," Daphne said. "Just saying..."

"I signed a nondisclosure agreement. I know how to keep my mouth shut," Kylie said indignantly. "I wouldn't violate that."

"I know, but whoever may be monitoring you may report you anyway. When in doubt just save it for another time. Anytime you have questions and we are away from work go outside to talk and leave your phone behind. Be careful even in your car."

"That just really pisses me off," Kylie said. "They don't own me. I deserve privacy in my own home."

Daphne said, "Of course they own you. You've been bought and paid for and once you were brought into the loop there was no backing out. And don't forget that's a company home you're living in, so they had plenty of time to put in surveillance. Sorry, that's just the way it is."

They walked towards Daphne's condo while Kylie processed what Daphne had said.

"This is a matter of national security we're talking about," Daphne reminded her. "For crying out loud, you know things even the President of the United States isn't aware of. They have to keep a lid on this information, and they'll do whatever they have to to assure that the information isn't leaked to anyone without a "need to know," and believe me, those are precious few."

"The President of the United States doesn't know we have an alien here?" Kylie asked.

"Are you kidding?" Daphne laughed. "If he did I'm sure the

whole world would have heard about it from one of his tweets by now. No seriously, there are very few people who are aware of our resident alien. You just happen to be one of those precious few."

Daphne let Kylie think about it as they walked and when she started to calm down she asked, "What were you going to ask me about our alien friend?"

"Has no one been able to communicate with him in any way whatsoever?" Kylie asked.

"Nope," Daphne answered. "There are times when he seems to understand what we're saying, but if so he doesn't really let on or even attempt to communicate in any way to us."

"I was just wondering," Kylie said. This was something she was *definitely* going to keep to herself for the time being.

35

Kylie was so exhausted that night she knew she wouldn't have any trouble sleeping.

She felt she hadn't been sleeping anytime at all when she was woken up by the light in her room. She rolled over and groaned and said, "It can't be morning already."

She looked at the clock on the table by her bed and saw it was 3:20 A.M.

She thought maybe her next door neighbor T.C. had a motion detector light on the side of his house since her bedroom was lit up as bright as daylight.

She pulled the covers over her head and rolled over. She laid there for a minute or two and had the eerie feeling she was being watched. She pushed the covers down and saw two aliens standing at the end of her bed watching her.

She tried to scream but was frozen in fear.

One of the aliens reached for her hand and looked over the finger that had the alien fingertip attached to it. He motioned for her to come.

"No way in hell," she thought to herself but strangely found herself following him against her will.

She was led outside where a crescent shaped spacecraft was hovering with rotating colored lights.

"How is no one seeing this?" she thought to herself. "Why haven't the lights woken any of my neighbors up?"

The alien motioned for Kylie to step into the light that shone from the craft. The next thing she knew she was aboard the spacecraft and being led down a hallway.

The hallway appeared oval shaped that had a ring of familiarity to it. She began to recall bits and pieces of past experiences aboard other space craft.

I could picture myself aboard a craft as a young girl with my mother crying in the background trying to stop them from taking me. Obviously her attempts had been unsuccessful.

I remember thinking when Olivia told me I had been abducted I thought she was insane, but now I believed I was the one who was crazy. How could any of this be real?

I was led into a white, brightly lit room which was empty other than a stainless steel table situated in the center of the room. The alien who had brought me here motioned for me to get on the table.

Did I really have a choice at this point I wondered to myself.

Fearing perhaps they had learned of the dead alien and the other alien we had in captivity I thought perhaps they planned to harm me in retaliation.

Again the alien motioned for me to get on the table and when I did he gently pushed me to a prone position. At this point another being entered the room. He, I say he only because the alien appeared to be male in his mannerisms and his brusqueness, but otherwise there was no indication whether it was a male or female.

The alien who brought me aboard the spacecraft watched as another alien entered the room. He appeared to be the type that tolerated no nonsense and lacked compassion. The alien I thought of as my escort seemed kinder.

A small table arose from the floor and he took my hand and secured it to the table. The other alien reached for an instrument from somewhere behind him.

I remember feeling terrified wondering what their intentions were. At this time yet another alien came forward and placed his hands on my face which calmed me immediately. Why, I don't know. I would normally have been repulsed by those hands touching me in any manner.

I remember nothing else. The next thing I remember is when I woke in the morning.

I woke to the sound of AC/DC belting out the song *Thunderstruck* from my bedside alarm clock. I rolled over and checked the time which reminded me of my dream.

"My God, what a nightmare!" I laid in bed for a few minutes going over in my mind the dream I had the night before.

I reached over to turn off my alarm clock and that's when I saw it.

36

Kylie paced outside Major Brannan's office waiting for him to return. "How was she ever going to explain this to him?" she wondered. "He'll think I'm certifiable and want to have me committed to an insane asylum."

"Kylie," Major Brannan walked up to her. "My secretary paged me saying you needed to see me." He opened his office door and motioned for her to precede him.

He went around and sat at his desk and motioned for her to have a seat. He waited a minute and when she appeared to be distracted he said, "Was there something you wanted to talk about?"

She reached into her lab coat and pulled out a cylinder metal tube and placed it on his desk.

He looked at her inquisitively, but when she didn't come forward with any explanation he opened the case and shook out the contents. There was the alien skin from a fingertip he had brought her to examine when she first met him.

"It came off?" he asked putting it back into the cylinder case.

"Well, it's off as you can see," Kylie answered. "But you're not going to believe me when I tell you how it came to be in that case and off my finger. As you well know more than one person has tried to remove it in the past unsuccessfully."

When she began explaining what she had originally thought was a dream, he stopped her only long enough to tell his secretary that he was not to be disturbed for any reason whatsoever.

He then motioned for her to continue with her story and listened until the end without interruption.

By the time Kylie got to the part where she told him what Olivia had told him about being abducted in the past the tears were running down her face.

"I don't expect you to believe any of this. It's so far-fetched," Kylie said.

Major Brannan handed her his handkerchief and quietly said, "On the contrary. I believe every word. You forget I've been working with the knowledge of aliens coming to earth for over twenty years now. Yours isn't the first story I've heard of alien abduction."

"How could I not have remembered any of that...something so bizarre?" Kylie said, clearly upset by her previous night's experience.

"As a child some things are just too damaging or frightening to recall. You must have pushed the memories to the back of your mind."

"The autopsy and alien at Area 51..."

Major Brannan visibly winced when she said Area 51.

Kylie said, "The alien here and the autopsy were at least removed from me. It wasn't personal, do you know what I mean?" Kylie asked. "I guess that's why I could deal with it. This though is something else entirely."

"Perhaps that has something to do with why our resident alien responded to you in the way he did," Major Brannan said.

Kylie sat and twisted the handkerchief in her lap.

"I'm wondering though how the aliens knew about your finger," Major Brannan said while he picked up a pen and rolled it between his hands as he spoke. "They did nothing for the last month while it was on your finger, but once our alien saw it the same evening they came and removed it from your finger."

"That never even occurred to me," Kylie said.

"I wonder if somehow he's communicating with them. But how would that even be possible? He's several floors below ground. I just don't know..." Major Brannan seemed to be thinking out loud more than discussing it with Kylie.

Major Brannan sat and gave it some thought. He said, "It would really be helpful for us to know about your abductions. I believe we could learn a lot by that knowledge. Would you be willing to be hypnotized?"

37

She was given two days off as Alan had convinced Major Brannan that she could really use a few days to relax and settle into her new home. She had experienced some life-changing events over the past few days and Alan being the friend he was knew the time off was sorely needed.

Alan went so far as to escort her home since it was one of Daphne's days off. While driving her home from the airport he reminded her not to discuss these events with anyone.

Fed up and totally stressed out from the last few days she let loose a tirade which was totally out of character for her. "Do you people have to remind me of this every single day? I signed a non-disclosure agreement and I take that very seriously. Besides, anyone I told would never believe me anyway."

"Sorry, you're right," Alan said. "I just know that sometimes people need to talk about traumatic events they've experienced. In that case, please know that Daphne is not only your friend but a very good psychologist who definitely would believe you. If you need to talk, I know she would be there to listen."

As Kylie opened the car door to get out he put his hand on her arm to stop her. "I just want to say that even though I did pass myself off as someone else, which was not my idea..."

"I know, Alan," Kylie interrupted. "We've been through it already. It's O.K. I understand why you did it."

"Please, bear with me. The friendship I developed with you and respect I have for your work is real. While we are co-workers I hope you will think of me as your friend, too."

Kylie smiled and said, "I do think of you as a friend."

"Go get some rest, go shopping, get a massage, or whatever it is you women do when you're stressed out," Alan said.

"Maybe I'll eat a gallon of double chocolate ice cream," Kylie said with a smile, "and after dessert I just may eat an entire pizza by myself."

She waved and stood in her driveway as he backed out and drove off.

She was putting her key in the lock when she heard a car horn and looked up to see T.C. in his Land Rover at the curb in front of her house.

He rolled down his window and yelled out, "Are you off work today?"

"Yeah, I have the next two days off," Kylie said.

"Can I come over for a minute?" Alan asked. "I want to ask you something."

"Sure," Kylie said. She waited at the door while he drove his SUV to his house and walked over from next door.

"Please don't have seen the lights or the spacecraft last night and ask me about them," she said to herself. "Please."

"Are you O.K.? You look a bit stressed out?" T.C. asked following her inside.

"I'm fine," Kylie answered throwing her purse down in the chair as she walked in. She kicked her shoes off and said, "What did you want to ask me?"

"Since you have a few days off would you like to go kayaking like we talked about?"

Her face lit up at the thought. That's exactly what she needed.

"I'd love to," she answered. "I can be ready in ten minutes."

38

Kylie watched as T.C. put the kayaks on the racks of the roof of his SUV. She loved the outdoors but hadn't tried kayaking yet. She had always longed to give it a try so she was looking forward to their outing. Not only that, but T.C. was the first guy that had appealed to her in a long time.

On the road T.C. said, "We'll go to Black Canyon. That's a good place for you as a beginner. There aren't any rapids there. We'll leave that for another time when you have a little experience."

"Sounds good to me," Kylie smiled at the thought of future kayaking trips with him.

She normally would have steered clear from having a relationship with a next-door neighbor in case the relationship went sour, but she told herself she would only be depriving herself as it seemed as though they enjoyed the same things. The fact that he was drop dead gorgeous didn't hurt either.

"What are you thinking about?" T.C. asked noticing the smile on her face.

Kylie thought quick. No way was she going to tell him she was thinking about him. "When I moved here I wondered how much of a chance I would get to be outdoors. All everyone told me about is how hot it is in Vegas and how I wouldn't want to ever go outside. I'm looking forward to getting out today."

"We'll be in the water so we can cool off at anytime," T.C. said. "Be sure to use sunscreen though, or you will definitely feel it later. It's important to stay hydrated, but the heat shouldn't keep you from being outdoors when you love it."

"What does T.C. stand for?" Kylie asked. "If I may ask."

"My name is Timothy. The C is for my middle name Carter, my mom's maiden name," T.C. said. "Ever since I was a kid everyone has always called me T.C. and it's just kind of stuck."

"I like it. Timothy is a really nice name but T.C. seems to suit you."

"Most of my friends probably wouldn't even know who anyone was talking about if they asked them about Timothy Tanner. I've been T.C. for too long now to change it," T.C. said. "But you can call me T.C. or Timothy, whichever you prefer."

They drove a little further and asked each other about their families and where they grew up getting to know each other. Surprisingly enough Kylie realized she was doing most of the talking, something that was unusual for her. She was usually pretty close-mouthed about her personal business especially to people she didn't know very well. She definitely wanted to change that fact. She would very much like to get to know him better.

"So tell me about what to expect today since I've never gone kayaking," Kylie said.

"The Black Canyon is perfect for beginners and seasoned paddlers enjoy it too. It's a great place to learn and you'll love the scenery. Once paddling becomes natural to you you'll have a chance to enjoy the views. Sometime when we have a few days off and plan ahead we can camp out and there's lots of areas to hike."

"Thanks for asking me," Kylie said. "I can't think of a better way to spend my day off."

"Me neither," T.C. said. "Well, this is it." He said as he pulled in and parked.

As he brought the kayaks down from the roof rack and brought out the cooler he reached inside and handed her the bottle of sun screen. He couldn't take his eyes off her as she lathered the lotion on.

How could a woman look so seductive just by rubbing sun screen on? he wondered. When she got to her long legs he had to turn away or he knew he would embarrass himself by staring at her.

They carried the kayaks down to the water's edge where he gave her a life vest to put on. She put a ball cap on to keep the sun out of her eyes.

"Later we'll have our picnic lunch. There's a beautiful beach area where we can enjoy our food," he said. "Maybe even go for a little swim if you'd like."

"Sounds like my kind of day," she said as she watched him load the cooler into his kayak.

They found a perfect spot to launch the kayaks from the shore. He held her kayak for her and explained how to get in and get settled before he gently coaxed her kayak free from the shore and into the water. He got into his kayak and paddled over to her.

T.C. was a good instructor and before they ventured far from shore he gave her tips on how to paddle the basic strokes and how to right the kayak if she capsized. By the time they ventured out further in the water it didn't take her long to master the strokes of the paddles.

"You're a natural," T.C. said. "What do you think? Do you like it?"

"This is so peaceful," Kylie said. "I can't believe it took me this long to try this. I'm going to have to get me a kayak now."

T.C. laughed and said, "I'm glad you like it. You don't need to buy one though. The kayak you're in now was my brothers, but since he started his own business he rarely has time to go out with me anymore. You're welcome to use it anytime."

Within ten minutes of paddling Kylie was comfortable on the water and pointed out a bald eagle she spotted to T.C.

"What's that?" Kylie asked pointing into the water. "That's a pretty good sized fish."

"It's a striped bass," T.C. answered pulling his kayak up next to hers. "Do you like to fish?"

"No, too much sitting still for me," Kylie answered. "I like to be on the move. Look," she pointed up at the sky. "I believe that's a falcon."

"You seem to know a lot about birds. Is that something you enjoy?" he asked. He was interested in learning all about this woman who intrigued him.

"Friends of mine that go hiking with me in Arizona enjoy birding. They've taught me to recognize different birds. It's not something I set out to do specifically but I've found I enjoy watching them in their natural habitat."

They paddled a little ways further and pulled their kayaks up on land. T.C. pulled out a blanket for them to sit on and a small cooler packed with drinks and lunch.

"It's not much but I didn't have a lot of time to prepare. This was sort of a spur of the moment idea when I found out we both had the day off."

Kylie passed out the sandwiches and scooped up some cold pasta salad she had contributed to the lunch and said, "This is perfect. Great food, great company, a beautiful setting..."

After lunch they sat back and enjoyed the spectacular views. They watched others glide by in kayaks and canoes.

After a time they packed everything back up and took a short walk. As they were walking he reached down and held her hand. As he took her hand in his she looked up at him and smiled. That smile of hers was enough to make him bold enough to stop and kiss her. Not wanting to overstep his boundaries the first time they were out together he stopped with the one kiss.

They brought their kayaks back to where they had originally gone into the water but decided before heading home to take a swim.

He watched without trying to be too obvious as she pulled her top over her head and then stepped out of her shorts. She wore a neon orange bikini that revealed a spectacular body.

He watched as she walked to the edge of the water. She looked like a golden goddess. She bent over and ran the cool water over her arms and chest to cool off.

T.C. dove in. She swam out and joined him. The water was refreshing after being out in the scorching sun for most of the day.

After swimming for awhile they swam towards shore where they could touch the bottom. He reached out and pulled her into his arms and kissed her.

It took someone going by in a canoe to remind him they were out in public.

"I guess we better go in," he said reluctantly.

She smiled at him and said, "That's probably a good idea."

He took her by the hand and walked up to their things and handed her a towel.

He was physically attracted to her, but he also felt he wanted more with this beautiful woman.

Kylie watched while T.C. loaded the kayaks back on the SUV. She put the cooler and wet towels on the floor of the backseat. She got dry towels out and spread them on the seats as they were still wet from their swim.

On the drive home T.C. asked, "Did you enjoy kayaking?"

"I loved it," Kylie said. "I've always wanted to try and I'm so glad I did. You were a great teacher."

She put her head back and closed her eyes thinking about the day's events as they headed home.

"Thanks for asking me today," Kylie said. "It was exactly what I needed."

T.C. smiled as he drove along. He thought she had fallen asleep a few minutes later until she said, "That was the first time I ever saw the Hoover Dam. The sights today were amazing."

T.C. said, "I do my best to never waste a day off indoors when I can be outside enjoying nature and the fresh air. The best part of the day was being with you and getting to know you."

She looked at him and smiled and said, "I feel the same way."

T.C. said, "I guess you know I'm attracted to you. I'd really like to spend more time with you and get to know you better, Kylie."

Kylie looked over at him and smiled. When she saw the way he was looking at her she knew she had met someone special. "I'd like that too," she said.

In the past the thought of getting involved in a relationship would have made her back off, but with T.C. she felt like she could put her trust issues in the past. She hoped he wouldn't prove her wrong.

They were unloading the gear at his place when he asked, "I know you haven't been in Vegas long. Where do you work?"

"Damn," Kylie thought. "I do *not* want to lie to someone who I would like to have a relationship with. That's not who I am. I'm basically a very honest person."

She hesitated before answering and before she had a chance to respond to his question Daphne pulled up in her driveway.

T.C. looked over and said, "Looks like you have company. Go ahead. I'll get this."

"Are you sure?" Kylie said. "I should help you clean up."

"No, go ahead," T.C. said. "She's waiting."

As Kylie started to walk next door he said, "Kylie?"

"Yeah," she turned around to see what he wanted.

T.C. said, "Would you like to get together later and have dinner? I know you're probably tired from being out in the sun all day, but I thought we could call in for pizza or something. How does that sound?"

"Sounds good," she said. "I'd like that."

39

Daphne followed Kylie as she headed inside. "Looks like you enjoyed your day off."

"Ummm..,." Kylie responded. "Most definitely."

"So, is something brewing between the two of you?" Daphne asked while watching T.C. out the window as he carried one of the kayaks over his head. She stood there and watched admiring his muscles.

"I think so. I mean I certainly hope so," Kylie answered.

"That's awesome," Daphne said sincerely. "Good for you."

"So what made you stop by? Checking up on me to see if I was wallowing in self-pity?"

"No," Daphne said. "I came by to talk you into going out with me tonight. My treat."

"Oh, Daphne," Kylie said. "Thanks, but I really need to get a shower. We went kayaking and swimming and being out in the sun all day I'm worn out. T.C. is coming over later and we're going to just order in a pizza. Another time?"

"Sure," Daphne said. "No problem. I'll see you later."

She had been so full of the thoughts of the wonderful day she had that she hadn't noticed how unusually quiet her friend had been.

After Daphne left Kylie jumped in the shower. She noticed as she was getting dressed that her shoulders were red and a bit tender from too much sun. She smiled as she thought of the day she had spent with T.C. deciding a little burn was well worth it.

"I didn't know what you liked on your pizza, so thought I better wait and order once I asked you," T.C. said. He held up two bottles of cold drinks and said, "Sorry I don't have beer or wine, but if that's what you prefer I'll make a run to the store."

"As far as the pizza goes anything except meat. I don't like meat on my pizza," Kylie said. "Keep it somewhat healthy and pile on the veggies."

"Veggies it is," he said. "No anchovies then, I presume."

"Definitely not," she answered. "Cold drinks are fine. Or I have green tea in the fridge."

T.C. called and ordered the pizza and they sat and talked while they waited for the pizza to be delivered. Kylie felt as if she had known him for quite some time. They were very comfortable in each other's company. She was attracted to him and felt that feeling was reciprocated.

After eating they were sitting on the couch when he put his arm around her. She winced a bit as he laid his hand on her shoulder.

"I'm sorry," T.C. said backing off.

Kylie said, "My shoulders got sunburned today."

He moved her top off her shoulder and saw how red her shoulder was. He said, "Hold on."

He walked in the kitchen and grabbed a knife and walked outside and came back in with a leaf from an aloe a desert-like plant. He cut off the thorns, sliced the leaf in half from top to bottom, then gently pulled the shirt off from her shoulder and ran the aloe plant's gel like substance on her shoulder. "This plant has great healing effects. It's nature's best remedy for a burn."

"That feels wonderful. Thanks," Kylie said.

He reached over and gently ran his hand through her long silky hair watching it slip through his fingers. He set the plant down and gently took her in his arms and kissed her.

His gentle kisses quickly turned into hungry kisses that she returned. She responded to his kisses with a passion she hadn't felt in a long time.

He pulled back and looked at her with a questioning look. In answer to that look she faced him and came onto his lap straddling him and putting her arms around him lowering her head into his neck. Her breathing was rapid as he ran his hands over her body.

He reached under her top and when he received no resistance from her he pulled her top over her head and dropped it on the floor. He passionately kissed her while undoing her bra. She slipped it down her arms and off adding it to the pile of her clothes on the floor.

He gazed at her with longing. "You're so beautiful." He lifted her breasts and cupped them in his hands.

She moaned with desire at his touch. She climbed off his lap and stood taking him by the hand to lead him to the bedroom. Unable to wait any longer he scooped her up in his arms carrying her.

"Where?" he asked in a husky voice.

Entering the bedroom he lowered her onto the bed and looked down at this beautiful woman.

He pulled her jeans off as she lifted her hips to help him. She watched as he undid his own pants stepping out of them. He rapidly pulled off the rest of his clothing and stood and gazed down at her skimpy red silk underwear running his fingers inside and pulling them down and off.

She reached up and wrapped her arms around him pulling him towards her. Filled with desire she begged, "Please, make love to me."

He was more than ready to fulfill her request and was about to do just that when the doorbell rang.

"Ignore it," she said.

He wanted her as desperately as she wanted him. It took every bit of will power he had not to do exactly as she begged. He could just ignore the doorbell.

The doorbell continued ringing incessantly.

40

T.C. dropped his head to her forehead as the doorbell rang again and again. It took all the willpower he had to stop. "I don't think they're going away. It might be important. You better see who it is." He rolled over and laid on his side.

Kylie trying to regain her composure as she rapidly put on just enough clothes to be presentable walked out closing the door behind her.

She took a moment to catch her breath before opening the door. A very drunk Daphne was leaning heavily on the door. When Kylie opened the door Daphne would have fallen if Kylie hadn't caught her.

She led her inside and lowered her to the couch. "What's going on? What were you thinking driving drunk, Daphne? You could have been killed or killed some innocent person."

Kylie was not amused as Daphne looked at her, grinned, and fell back against the cushions of the couch and fell asleep.

"Maybe I better go," T.C. said coming into the room wearing just his jeans and carrying his shirt. "Unless you need some help here."

"She obviously can't drive home in this condition and she lives upstairs. There's no way I'm carrying her up the stairs."

"Why don't you just let her sleep it off in your guest room," T.C. said "That's probably the best solution."

"You're right. I don't think I have much of a choice," Kylie said. "Can you help me get her in there?"

Kylie tried to pull Daphne into a sitting position but she was total dead weight. T.C. scooped her up in his arms and asked, "Where do you want her?"

Kylie led the way. T.C. took Daphne's shoes off and pulled the covers over her.

Watching from the doorway Kylie said, "It looks like you've had experience with drunk women in the past."

"Not drunk women, my father," T.C. answered. "That's why I don't drink. I saw enough of how drinking affects people as I was growing up to never have touched a drop myself."

He turned the light out and walked into the living room with Kylie following.

"I'm furious she was out driving in that condition. My parents were killed by a drunk driver and I have no patience with people who think it's O.K. to drink and get behind the wheel of a car," Kylie said.

She had told him about the death of her parents earlier when he had asked about her family, so this wasn't a new revelation to him but he knew she felt strongly about this issue.

"Does she do this often?" he asked.

"I've only known her for a few months, but I would have to say no. I've never even seen her drink more than a glass of wine before," she answered. "It seems so out of character for her."

"If this isn't the norm for her there may be a reason behind it, not that I'm excusing it. You never know someone's story or what makes them make the choices they do," he said as he stood in the doorway.

He looked outside and turned back to Kylie and said, "If it makes you feel any better her car isn't out here so evidently she didn't drive here." He leaned against the door and said, "I should go."

He reached for Kylie and pulled her into his arms and gave her a tender kiss before leaving. He said, "Sorry about the interruption. Another time?"

She gave him a passionate kiss and as he pulled away he said, "I take it that means yes. That'll give me something to think about as I go home and take a very cold shower."

41

About 11:30 that evening Kylie's phone rang. She quickly grabbed the phone thinking it might be T.C. calling to wish her a good night, but as she looked at her caller ID she saw Major Brannan's name.

"Are you calling to tell me I can't have two days off after all?" Kylie asked.

There was a moment of silence before the Major said, "Sorry, it took me a moment to figure out what you were talking about. I'm sorry to call you at home and disturb you this late, but I was wondering if you knew where Daphne was."

Kylie noticed concern in his voice and said, "She's here."

"Thank goodness. I've been trying to reach her all night and couldn't get an answer. I even had them check the global positioning on her car and it showed as being at her condo. I went by but she wasn't there," the Major said.

"You sound concerned," Kylie said.

"Of course I'm concerned. This day every year, well let's just say it's very hard for her and in the past on this day in particular she has made some bad choices. I worry one day....I just worry. She's my daughter..." the Major said.

"What is it about this day?" Kylie asked in a gentle voice.

"She didn't say anything to you? I thought if she would talk to anyone about it that it would be you," the Major said.

"Let's just say when she showed up at my house she wasn't in any condition to talk," Kylie said.

"I see," the Major said. "Would you like me to come get her?"

"No, maybe there's a reason she came here," Kylie said. "As a friend though it would be easier for me to help her through whatever she's going through if I had an idea of what was going on."

The Major was very quiet and at first Kylie didn't think he would respond but then said, "She was married to a wonderful man. They were very much in love. They were both thrilled when they found out they were expecting a baby. On this day four years ago she was in the hospital and gave birth to a stillborn daughter."

"Oh, how awful," Kylie said softly hanging her head feeling empathy for her friend.

"She was having a hard time dealing with the death of her baby when she learned her husband blamed himself for the death of the child. Who knows why people blame themselves, but he wasn't to blame and neither was she. Sometimes these things just happen."

He sounded choked up as he continued, "He drove into the desert and put a bullet in his head. On the same day she lost both her child and her husband."

The tears ran down Kylie's face as she realized the pain her friend had been in the night before to get so drunk.

Kylie was feeling guilty for having turned her friend down when she asked her to go out with her that evening. "If only I had known," Kylie thought.

"I had been worried sick about Daphne handling the death of their child, not even realizing how her husband was dealing with the death himself," the Major said. He drew a deep breath. "Needless to say, this day every year she suffers something awful. I don't know what to do to help her get through this."

It was at that time that Daphne walked into the room. Kylie looked up and said into the phone, "I have to go. My friend who's staying over night just came in, and we're going to spend some time together."

"Thank you," the Major said quietly.

42

Kylie and Daphne sat at her kitchen table and talked and cried together. Daphne had opened up and poured her heart out about what had happened with losing her baby and her husband. It was a heartbreaking story.

The following morning they went to the store and purchased a few arrangements of flowers and drove out to the cemetery together and left flowers on the graves of Baby Emma and Daphne's husband.

As they walked back to Kylie's car Daphne wiped the tears from her face and said, "I have to go on. I have to get past this. I can't let it destroy me or give up on the hopes of a happy future."

"It's O.K. to mourn," Kylie said draping her arm around Daphne. "It was a terrible loss you suffered."

"For the longest time everywhere I would go I would look at babies and see Emma's face. As time went by whenever I saw a little girl I would say, 'that's about the age she would be now if only she would have lived', or 'that's what she would have been like at such and such an age'," Daphne said.

"I can't even imagine," Kylie said. "I'm so sorry."

"Thank you, Kylie," Daphne said. "You're the best friend I ever had. I owe you big time."

"You don't owe me, Daphne," Kylie said. "That's what friends are for. They're there when they're needed. They share your secrets, your joys, and your pain. Anytime you need me I promise I'll be there for you."

"Ditto," Daphne said.

43

The two days off had been enjoyable but it was time to get back to work and that meant facing the alien again.

The major was still trying to find out if there was any way the alien was contacting other aliens. He explained to Kylie and Daphne that even though they didn't know if he understood anything they said, he wanted them to try to ask him some questions. He especially wanted to know how the aliens who had abducted Kylie knew about the skin of the alien that had been on her finger.

Daphne and Kylie entered the room where the alien was kept. They stood inside the door. He nodded his head in greeting.

Daphne spoke to him in a louder than normal voice and slowly, much like someone does when they're speaking to a person from a foreign country who understands little English.

She and Daphne pulled out two chairs with a table between them and the alien. Kylie motioned for the alien to have a seat. He ignored her and remained standing.

Kylie held up her finger and asked him, "Do you remember when I was in here before and you noticed my finger?" He looked at her hand and looked at her finger intently as though he knew exactly what she was saying.

Daphne leaned over and whispered in Kylie's ear, "I think he understands you. Go on. You seem to be getting further than I ever have with him."

The alien watched Kylie closely.

Kylie said, "The funny thing is I didn't know what it was when I was first examining the skin from the fingertip of your friend." She paused a moment giving him time to respond.

When he didn't she continued, "I'm sorry for your friend's deaths. I'm sure that must be hard for you and make you feel very much alone."

The alien moved closer but she wasn't getting any kind of

message from him other than the fact that he seemed interested in what she was saying.

Then it hit her. It was a feeling of intense pain over the loss of his friends. It was as though he had opened himself up to her, allowing her to experience what he was feeling.

Kylie glanced over at Daphne to see if she was feeling the same thing, but she didn't appear to be. She seemed oblivious to what was happening.

Kylie explained to the alien how the finger tip came to be on her finger and how she and others had tried to remove it but were unsuccessful.

"Did you tell anyone about it?" she asked. She knew others were watching in the other room and on the monitors and she wasn't sure how much information she should divulge. She certainly wasn't going to inform the others she had been abducted by aliens.

'What I know they all know,' the alien said to her through what she could only assume was some sort of mental telepathy.

She was stunned to realize she was actually hearing his thoughts. She hoped the surprised look on her face when it happened hadn't given her away to the others. She nodded in a small gesture so she hoped the alien would understand that she was hearing his message but the others would be clueless to the fact that they were indeed communicating.

"Who is they?" she asked without thinking.

Daphne jerked her head towards her and looked at her oddly. She silently mouthed "They?" to her with a questioning look.

Kylie realized she better be careful or she would give herself away. She wasn't ready to share with anyone yet the fact that she was somehow communicating with the alien.

Kylie began speaking again as though she hadn't just asked a question that would make no sense to anyone except the alien. "We would like to be friends with you and your people. Can you tell me why you're here visiting us on our planet?"

To this she got no answer. She tried again. "It must be difficult to be so far from your own home and away from your own kind. Can you tell me where you're from?"

She didn't hold out any hope on getting answers but he began making motions on the table as though he were drawing something.

Daphne realizing what he was doing reached for a pen sticking out of her lab coat and handed it to him. She rummaged in her pockets looking for a piece of paper but didn't have any. She requested some paper to the observers in the other room and one of the guards brought in some printer paper.

Daphne pushed the paper towards the alien to use to write on. He looked at her and accepted the paper.

The alien had no thumb and seemed uncertain of how to hold the pen. He had observed Daphne many times writing notes so was somewhat familiar but had a hard time holding the pen and controlling it.

After practicing for a few minutes he held the pen tightly between his fingers and began making curved lines on the paper. Initially it looked like something a young child would scribble, but he quickly mastered using the pen.

Everything was quiet in the room while the alien spent quite some time drawing what indeed looked like planets and a solar system. He then pointed at one planet and threw his arms up in the air splaying his fingers mimicking something blowing up. He then pointed at and scratched out the planet he had previously drawn. He then drew pieces coming off the planet as though it had exploded.

Daphne's mouth hung open in disbelief.

"Thank you," Kylie said gently. "I'm sure that's a painful memory for you. Thank you for sharing it with us."

Daphne took the paper and pen from him and also thanked him.

They turned to go and Kylie could feel his question, "I'll be back to visit again tomorrow."

44

When Daphne and Kylie exited the room there were a handful of people standing out in the hall who had been observing through the one-way mirror. They appeared to be very excited at what they had just witnessed.

A colonel who Kylie had never seen before held his hand out to Daphne for the paper the alien had drawn on.

He looked it over and said, "We have to get someone right on this and find out where this planet is. Call Dr. Musgrove from NASA and have him flown in immediately."

"Was," Daphne said.

"What?" the colonel looked up at her.

"I take it from his hand motions and from what he drew that the planet no longer exists," Daphne said.

"That may be." the colonel said. "Even so, we need to identify the location."

The others were trying to peer over his shoulder to see what the alien had written on the paper. There was great excitement in the air realizing they had experienced a major breakthrough.

"Great job," Major Brannan said. "That was amazing work. He seemed to understand what you were saying."

45

Kylie stepped outside her front door to wait outside for Daphne to pick her up for work when she noticed T.C. in his driveway with the hood up on his Land Rover. It looked like he was having car trouble and was working on his car.

Kylie quietly walked over and put her arms around him from the back and reached over and kissed him on his neck. "Good morning T.C."

She heard a tool fall to the ground and he stood up and turned around and looked at her with a look of utter shock on his face. The shock was quickly replaced with a huge smile.

"Wait a minute," Kylie said taking a step backwards. "Who are you?"

"You just kissed me and called me T.C. What do you mean, who am I?" the guy said who looked exactly like T.C., but wasn't.

"You're not T.C.," Kylie said firmly.

"Who am I then?" he said wiping his oil smeared hands on a rag that had been in his back pocket.

T.C. then walked out of his house holding two drinks, spotted Kylie, smiled and said, "I see you've met my twin brother Taylor."

"You didn't tell me you had a twin, let alone an identical twin," Kylie admonished him.

"You're right. I did tell you I had a brother though," T.C. said.

"Before I even opened my mouth and said a word she knew right away it wasn't you," Taylor said. "Right after she kissed me."

"She kissed you?" T.C. asked.

"I did not," Kylie said indignity.

"Did too," Taylor said with a smile. "I never forget when I've been kissed by a beautiful woman."

"Knock it off Taylor," T.C. said coming over to kiss Kylie who was looking unnerved. "I apologize for not telling you I had a twin brother. I've been wanting to introduce the two of you."

"That was some introduction," Taylor said with a smile on his

125

face rubbing where she had kissed him.

"Wait a minute," T.C. said looking directly at his twin brother. "Did you say she knew you weren't me?"

"Yep, right away," Taylor said. "That's never happened before. No one can tell us apart, not even Mom and Dad."

"What are you talking about?" Kylie said. "Yeah, you look alike. I mean you're identical twins obviously, but it's easy to tell the two of you apart."

"No, not really," T.C. said with a big grin on his face. "How about that? She knew you weren't me."

"Never happened before," Taylor said. "She must be pretty special."

"Oh, she's special alright," T.C. said. "And now I won't have to worry about you pulling any twin pranks on her."

"You know you have to marry her now," Taylor said. "You always said if you met a girl that could tell us apart that's the girl you'd marry."

"Hello, I'm standing right here," Kylie said.

Kylie was relieved to see Daphne pull up right then. Kylie started to say something and figured it was best to just keep her mouth shut.

Daphne got out of her car and as she was walking over said, "Am I seeing double? Lord, if this is double vision please don't take it away from me. What do you think, Kylie? One for you and one for me?"

Taylor laughed a hard belly laugh. "Someone introduce me to this girl. I think I just met the woman of my dreams."

"Well, you're no nightmare either," Daphne said sticking her hand out and not waiting to be introduced did the honors herself.

Taylor took her hand but instead of shaking it pulled her into his arms and said, "She introduced herself to me with a kiss," Taylor nodded toward Kylie.

"I wouldn't want to let you down then," Daphne said reaching up to give him a kiss on the cheek. At the last second he turned his head and gave her a kiss on the lips.

Kylie standing next to T.C. smiled when he said, "They look like a perfect match to me."

46

There was a lot of excitement around the major's office. Evidently Dr. Musgrove from NASA had been able to give them some information but was unable to pinpoint the location of the planet the alien had drawn.

"How difficult can it be?" Lieutenant Colonel Ward asked impatiently. "Just how many planets are out there?"

Dr. Musgrove chuckled, "To give you a rough idea of the answer to that let me try to explain. There are approximately 300 billion stars in the Milky Way alone. So even if only one percent of those which would be a very low estimation had planets around them that would be what, 3 billion planets just in our galaxy alone."

"Surely you can narrow it down better than that," a colonel said who had sat quietly throughout the meeting up to that point. "Can you narrow that number down by estimating which of those planets could possibly have some form of life on them?"

Major Brannan asked, "Or even planets that even remotely resemble the planet or surrounding planets around it from this drawing."

"Wait a minute, gentlemen," Dr. Musgrove continued. "The numbers I gave you were for our galaxy only. There are over 100 billion galaxies in the observable universe. Who knows what's out there beyond that."

"We may be able to study it and over time come up with some observations, but at this time I'm afraid that's the best we can do," Dr. Musgrove was clearly as frustrated as they were.

He looked over the drawing again. "But with this picture and the information included in the drawing we should be able to narrow it down somewhat. It will take a considerable amount of time though."

To have been given any idea at all of where the aliens came from was beyond their wildest expectations. They had hopes that

Dr. Musgrove would have come in and named and pinpointed the location immediately, but things were rarely that easy.

"Send the girl back in and see what she can find out," Lieutenant Colonel Ward said.

Daphne who had walked in earlier during the meeting said, "She's not a girl. She's a geneticist and deserves respect from you gentlemen."

"You're absolutely right, Dr. Sowers," the colonel said standing. "Are you and Dr. Carmichael going back in to see the alien today?"

"I believe that's on the agenda for later today yes," Daphne said.

"Can we move that time frame up?" Lieutenant Colonel Ward interrupted. "I'd like to be there to observe."

"I believe Dr. Carmichael is currently meeting with a dental anthropologist going over the data from the dental mold they made during the autopsy," Daphne said. "So no; probably not."

Daphne secretly gloated. She couldn't stand Lieutenant Colonel Ward who was always trying to throw his weight around.

They met again that afternoon with the resident alien but were unable to get any more specifics on where his home planet was located.

Daphne had brought several sheets of printer paper in case he was willing to draw or write anything else while they talked. She didn't dare leave the pen behind as he could have used it as a weapon even though he was watched carefully and had shown no signs of aggression.

Daphne said, "Do you have a name? We can't go around calling you the alien all the time. What should we call you?"

They waited for a response. None was forthcoming.

"I'd say this day is a bust," Daphne said gathering her papers and pen and standing to leave.

"Wait," Kylie said. She looked directly at the alien and asked, "Is there anything you would like to know from us? We can learn about each other."

"Nothing," Daphne said after a few minutes.

Kylie looked quietly at the alien. Daphne watched her intently with an odd look on her face without saying anything, then sat back and quietly observed the two of them.

"I guess we'll just have to make up a name for you then if you won't tell us your name," Kylie said. She paused for only a brief moment. "How about Ari? Would that be acceptable to you if we called you Ari?"

He simply stared at Kylie as they turned to leave the room.

47

The hierarchy seemed disappointed that nothing had come from the meeting. They had hoped to glean some new knowledge. They remained behind to talk among themselves while Kylie and Daphne headed off to return to their work areas.

They would have been a lot more excited if they had known that the alien had indeed given Kylie a name, but she was unwilling at this time to disclose it to them. She had already decided when she did so it would be in a private meeting with Major Brannan.

Neither one of them said a word on the elevator, but as Kylie neared her office and was about to say good-bye to Daphne she pulled Kylie by her lab coat into the nearest bathroom.

"What are you doing?" Kylie asked.

"That's what I want to know," Daphne said. "He's talking to you, isn't he? Somehow he's communicating with you."

Kylie was shocked that Daphne had come to that conclusion.

Without admitting it or denying it she said, "You were in the room with me, did you hear him say anything?"

"Ari? Ari the alien?" Daphne said. "I suppose you just pulled that one out of the blue. No, don't try to deny it. Remember, I'm a psychologist and body language can be quite enlightening. I was watching the two of you, and there was definitely something going on. Spill it."

Kylie explained how Ari was communicating with her. She didn't understand it yet herself. Daphne thought about how for weeks since he had been in their custody dozens of people had attempted to communicate with him and nothing until now that Kylie had come. He immediately began communicating with her from their first meeting.

Kylie said, "Please don't say anything to anybody yet. I'm trying to sort this all out myself."

Chelsey, one of Kylie's assistants, walked in the bathroom and looked at the two of them, "Having a meeting? I can leave and come back later."

"We were just leaving," Daphne said grabbing Kylie's hand and pulling her out behind her.

When they exited the bathroom she said, "Come to my office *now*. Convince me why I should keep this quiet. You do realize this is huge?"

Daphne didn't know whether to be furious that her friend had kept this information to herself or excited by what this could mean.

"This changes everything. We really need to learn everything we can about them and why they're coming here," Daphne said as she closed the door behind her.

Inside her office she propped herself on the end of her desk and motioned for Kylie to have a seat. "Start talking. You know friendship goes two ways. I spilled my guts to you, the least you can do is trust me. If you have a reason to keep this quiet now is your chance to convince me."

"Alright, you're right," Kylie said. She sat back in the seat and said, "I don't know how to explain it. I can feel his moods and sometimes understand what he's thinking without him saying a thing."

"And what is he saying to you?"

"Well, for one his name or title or something is Bidaiari. I knew if I came out with that you would wonder how I came up with a jumble of letters like that so I took the last three letters and came up with Ari."

"What did he say?" Daphne said very interested in this conversation.

"Just that word Bidaiari, nothing else. But I got the impression they don't have names like we do. I don't know maybe it's the name of his planet or what he is or what the aliens are called. All I know is that's what he said," Kylie said. "Or didn't say. It's all very confusing."

"That's what he said without saying anything," Daphne said.

"I know it sounds crazy. It's like mental telepathy. Don't you sense it at all?" Kylie asked.

"No, can't say that I do, but then he seems to be very tuned into you. I watch his body language and he seems comfortable around you for some reason."

"Please don't say anything yet," Kylie begged. "I'll tell you everything, and I do intend to tell them, just not yet. I need some time to understand this myself and figure out why me."

"You do realize you are the only one who can communicate with an alien that we know of? You realize what this means? How can you ask me to keep something like this quiet? This is a chance of a lifetime to learn what we can about life from another planet," Daphne argued.

"I know," Kylie said. "Please, just give me a little time. Please."

Daphne stared at her friend. She sighed, "I don't know why I'm agreeing to this, but alright..."

"Thank you, Daphne," Kylie said relieved.

"Only a little time. This is too important to sit on," Daphne said.

48

In the following months Kylie and T.C. often double dated with Daphne and Taylor. Both couples had become pretty serious. Kylie and T.C. spent every minute together when they weren't working and Taylor had moved in with Daphne within a week of meeting each other.

Kylie remembered after the fact when she and T.C. had wound up in her bed that Daphne had warned her about the very real chance of listening devices throughout her house. She wasn't really convinced they were there, but she didn't want to take any chances.

She never gave T.C. a reason for it, but after that first night whenever they were intimate she made sure they ended up at his house. The last thing she wanted to worry about was someone listening in or even worse and discovering a video had been made that may end up on YouTube one day. Over time she forgot about the possibility of the listening devices.

They both had the weekend off and were planning a two day trip to Arizona so she could introduce him to her friends the Archers. He had already packed and brought his bag over to Kylie's place. He was going to stay overnight and they would leave before daylight and get an early start hiking at Monolith Garden Trail.

He was laying across her bed watching her pack her bag. He was enjoying the view as she bent over to place her things in her overnight bag. When she stepped out of her clothes and looked back at him with a devious smile and told him she was going to take a shower he took that as an invitation. He quickly shed his clothes and joined her.

They took turns washing each other and made love in the shower. When Kylie started shivering from the cold the hot water long before had run out, he wrapped her loosely in a towel and led her to the bed. They made love throughout the night getting very little sleep before they had to head out in the morning.

When she woke up she sat up in bed and said, "Oh, my God.

What were we thinking last night?"

T.C. gave her that sexy smile and said, "I don't think either one of us was thinking about much. What's the problem?"

He reached over and pulled the sheet down exposing her naked body. Looking at him it was evident he was ready to continue where they left off last night.

He moved over close beside her and reached for her. He nibbled on her lower lip and moved down to the hollow of her neck. He looked up to see if he was getting the desired response he was looking for. He definitely was, he could see it in her eyes.

He said, "I know we're getting a little bit of a late start but it was worth it, wasn't it? Is that really a problem?"

"Wait, it's not that," Kylie said breathlessly.

"What then?" he said gently running his finger from her chin to her breast.

"We didn't use anything. We keep the protection over at your house," Kylie said. "What if?"

"Oh, yeah," T.C. said. "Can't say that would have stopped me though. I don't think a freight train running through your living room could have stopped me last night."

"I wasn't thinking too clearly at the time either, but what if..." Kylie started to say.

"What? What if you get pregnant? Is that what you were going to say?" T.C. asked. He reached for her proving he was willing to risk that chance again.

"We both know that's a very real possibility," Kylie said. "We're both young and healthy and there was plenty of opportunity for that to have happened last night."

"O.K., I'll play the 'what if' game'," T.C. said. "It's simple. We'd get married. You know I'm going to marry you anyway and I want you to have my babies. You do want kids? That's not a problem, is it?"

"Of course I want kids," Kylie said. "But we haven't even talked about getting married."

"Guess I took it for granted that since we were in love, and we are in love, that getting married was just a matter of time," T.C. said. "I'm more action than talk. Doesn't mean I haven't given it a lot of thought." He ran his hand down her hip heading south.

She swatted his hand away. "I'm trying to have a serious conversation here, and you're not making it easy for me to concentrate."

"It isn't very easy to concentrate looking at your naked body, either," he said. "Not that I'm complaining, because I'm definitely not," he said.

"I don't want to *have* to get married," Kylie said. "That may seem old-fashioned today, but I wouldn't want that to be the reason I was getting married."

"Kylie, I'd marry you tomorrow. That's not a problem. Should I get down on one knee and ask you proper?"

Without waiting for an answer T.C. slid off the bed in all his glorious nakedness and got on one knee. He reached up and took her hand in his and said, "Kylie, I love you with all my heart and I will love you forever. You are the joy of my life. Will you marry me?"

"Seems kind of like a forced proposal to me," Kylie said laughing at the sight of him on one knee with his manhood in full exposure.

"Are you laughing at little T.C.?" he said looking down at himself.

"Not so little," Kylie said.

"He has a mind of his own," he said. "He can't seem to get near you without standing to full attention."

Kylie pulled the sheet up over herself laughing at him.

"Anyway, what were you saying about a forced proposal?" T.C. asked.

He got up and walked over to his overnight bag rummaging through it and said, "Let's try this again."

He got back on one knee and held out a ring box holding a brilliant diamond engagement ring.

Her hand flew to her chest and she started crying. "Are you serious?"

"Never been more serious in my life," he answered her.

"Yes, I'll marry you."

He stood up and slipped the ring on her finger and said, "I had planned to do this when we were out hiking at your favorite spot, but this seemed to be the appropriate time. Throw out the romantic plan and go with spontaneous."

Kylie held up her hand admiring her ring.

"Just promise me one thing," he said.

"What's that?" Kylie asked holding the ring up to the light watching it sparkle. "It's beautiful. It's perfect."

"So promise me," he repeated.

"Anything," she said. "What is it?"

"You don't tell our kids one day how I proposed to you."

Kylie laughed and stood on the bed, leaned over, and wrapped her arms around him. He lifted her into his arms and she wrapped those long legs around him and bent down and kissed him.

Kissing his bride-to-be he lowered her back down to the bed and joined her.

"Oh no," Kylie said. "We're late as it is."

Instead he said, "I'll drive fast, but there's something I have to do before we leave."

"What do you have to do?" she asked in a husky voice.

"You," he answered as he lowered himself on top of her.

He got no further argument from her.

49

The Archers were thrilled to see that Kylie and T.C. were obviously very much in love and to see the happy glow on her face. They were happy to see that she was in a good loving relationship.

The two couples cooked out that night under the stars. No sounds of traffic, sirens, or city life. The only sounds out here were the steaks sizzling on the grill and crickets in the background. Occasionally you would hear a coyote but that was it. It was as peaceful as you could get.

Over dinner they made plans for the following day to hike at Monolith Garden Trail and have lunch at a new restaurant in town afterwards.

They were relaxing after dinner when Kylie asked the Archers how Paul their son was doing.

"He's got a great job in California doing computer work. He's always been a genius at the computer and he's really happy with the work. He says it challenges him, keeps him busy and out of trouble," Pilar answered.

Philip took this as an opening and asked T.C. what he did for a living. T.C. was telling Philip how he had been an international pilot until last year when he changed jobs to fly for a private company flying intrastate.

Philip was not only Kylie's friend but her accountant and they discussed her portfolio for awhile. T.C. asked him if he could take him on as a client also.

"While you men carry on your business we'll clean up," Pilar said while gathering up the dirty dishes.

Kylie helped Pilar carry in the dishes while the men sat outside discussing business. In the kitchen Pilar asked Kylie if she had talked to T.C. about being abducted by aliens.

Kylie had confided everything to the Archers when she first learned about it herself and then told them about her experience that had happened in Vegas.

She only omitted the part about the finger surgery and the fact that there was an alien at Area 51. That was a subject that she couldn't speak of due to her confidentiality agreement. She couldn't even tell them where she worked.

The Archers were unaware that she was working with an alien at her new job. She was pretty sure even they would be shocked at that revelation regardless of how open-minded they were.

"How do you tell someone something like that?" Kylie asked setting her pile of dirty dishes in the sink. "He'll think I'm totally bonkers and think twice about marrying someone who he'll probably think of as a lunatic."

"How can you not tell him?" Pilar asked rinsing the dishes and then handing them to Kylie to stack in the dishwasher. "You're going to marry him. You can't start off your marriage with a huge secret like that between you."

"He would never understand. He's too level-headed," Kylie said. "Besides, I wouldn't know how to even begin to tell him something like that."

"You told us," Pilar reminded her. "We don't think you're crazy, why would he? He loves you."

"He may think twice about it after a bombshell like that," Kylie said. "There's a reason people who have been abducted keep it a secret. They don't receive much support, but they do get a lot of ridicule."

"Give him some credit," Pilar said. "I think you'll be surprised. He loves you very much. He's not likely to leave you...."

The men walked in then and the women dropped the conversation.

To change the subject Pilar opened a kitchen drawer and took out a key handing it to Kylie. "Here, we want you to have this. This is the key to the cabin we were telling you about earlier. You and T.C. are welcome to use it anytime."

"Thanks," Kylie said. "We'd definitely love to take you up on your offer."

Philip said, "It's pretty remote. It sits on ten acres on the Hualapi Indian Reservation and your nearest neighbor is about three miles away, but it's peaceful and a great get-away."

"Use it as if it's yours," Pilar said. "We just don't have much of a chance to go, but it's a place I know you would love."

The next day they were out on the trails having a wonderful time. Philip and Pilar wanted to go take some photographs on their own for awhile and made plans to meet back up at 'their rock' in about an hour.

"I can see why you love this place," T.C. said. "It's really nice getting out of the city."

"I'm looking forward to going to stay at their cabin," Kylie said. "The next time we have a few days off let's go."

"Sounds perfect to me," T.C. said.

Kylie got to the rock and set her backpack down looking around. "I thought they'd be here by now. We were a few minutes late ourselves."

She opened her pack and took out two bottles of water handing one to T.C. and keeping one for herself.

She just sat down and then thought to look under the rock where in the past she and the Archers had left messages for each other. Sure enough, there was a an old film canister with a note rolled up inside from Pilar.

Kylie reading the note said, "She was called in for an emergency C-section and had to leave right away for the hospital. She said Philip was going to drive her and said for us to go ahead without them."

She didn't mention the part of the note to T.C. where Pilar had reminded her about what she said last night. She knew what she meant. She wanted Kylie to tell T.C. about the alien abductions. She wasn't so sure he could handle it.

Kylie took a deep breath and thought she might as well get it over with. "You're going to think I've been out in the sun too long when you hear what I have to tell you," she began.

139

50

"He didn't even blink an eye," Kylie said in amazement to Daphne on the drive in to work.

Daphne looked over at her and said, "Why did you think he would doubt you? It's not like you're some kind of crazy person or conspiracy theorist. He knows you're smart and would never make something like that up."

"You can easily accept it now because you see an alien everyday, but how did you feel when you first learned about them?" Kylie asked.

Daphne paused, "Yeah, it took me awhile to accept it until I actually saw one. I didn't believe him at first even though it was my dad who told me about them. He's not exactly the kind of guy to joke around so I knew he was serious, but still it was hard to accept initially."

"See what I mean," Kylie said.

Daphne drove while deep in thought. "Maybe he's a believer. Maybe he already believed in aliens and UFO's and things like that."

"Does he come across as that type to you?" Kylie said.

"You don't have to be 'a type' to believe in the possibilities of other forms of life, Kylie. Don't be so close-minded."

"I thought he would burst out laughing at the very least," Kylie said. "Thinking I was kidding. Oh by the way, now that you're about to become my husband I thought you might want to know that I'm sometimes abducted by aliens. Not only that, I'm a third generation abductee so our kids will most likely be abducted too."

"Or what leave you? That's what you thought, didn't you? You thought he wouldn't be able to handle it and he'd dump you," Daphne said. "Well, he's still here and you're still wearing that big, beautiful diamond ring."

Kylie held up her hand looking at her ring. "Yeah, amazing. I am marrying the most understanding man in the world."

"Drop dead gorgeous too," Daphne said. They got out of the car heading into the lobby of the private airport to catch a flight into work.

"He's almost as good looking as his twin brother," Daphne said joking.

"What are you talking about? They're identical twins," Kylie said.

"Yeah, but they can't fool us can they?" Daphne said. "I couldn't believe Taylor tried the old switcheroo trick on me the other night trying to convince me he was T.C. He couldn't believe I didn't fall for it. He said you and I are the only ones who've ever been able to tell them apart," Daphne said.

"You seem really happy with Taylor," Kylie looked at her friend. She was happy for her that she had found someone to love again after the heartbreak of losing her husband and baby.

When they stood outside Major Brannan's office Kylie said, "I know he's going to be really angry I've kept this from him."

Daphne squeezed her hand and said, "You're right. He's going to hit the roof."

Kylie looked worried when Daphne said this.

"Don't worry. He'll settle down and realize what this could mean. If he gets too mad you can just threaten to quit. He'll realize you're the only one the alien is communicating with, so he'll treat you with kid gloves after that."

The door opened and Major Brannan stood in the door frowning at the two of them. "Are you going to just stand out in the hall chit-chatting or are you going to come in and tell me what this is all about?"

A little over an hour later Daphne had not only talked her father out of what she called his "little temper tantrum," but she had also convinced him to have Kylie go in to visit Bidaiari the alien on her own.

She and her father would observe through the one-way mirror

in the adjoining room as Kylie met with the alien. She thought perhaps Bidaiari would be more open to communicating if it was just him and Kylie in the room. After considering it her father agreed.

After Kylie and Daphne left the room Major Brannan sat back and thought about what this could mean. They now had the opportunity to communicate with the alien. This could answer some questions and hopefully prepare them if their intentions were hostile. He knew he had to make the call to tell his superiors. It wasn't something he could put off. He reached for the phone.

51

Kylie received a text while she and T.C. were sitting and enjoying a quiet evening staying home. While Kylie was reading the text T.C.'s phone buzzed in his pocket. He had received a text from his twin brother Taylor.

Kylie looked up at T.C. still holding the phone in her hand. "Daphne and Taylor want us to meet them at the Stratosphere on the Strip. Want to go or stay home?"

"I just got a text from Taylor saying, 'Don't even think about not showing up'."

His phone buzzed in his hand. "He just sent another text saying, 'Dress up.'"

Before he had a chance to put his phone back in his pocket another incoming text came through. T.C. laughed and said, "This one says, 'Don't text me back, just show up and hurry up'. I don't know what's going on, but I guess we should get ready and go."

He stood up and pulled Kylie up off the couch. "Go put on that slinky black dress you were wearing the first time I saw you. I'll get dressed and meet you back here in about fifteen minutes." He pulled her into his arms and gave her a kiss before sending her on her way to get ready.

"Kiss me like that again and we won't be going anywhere," Kylie threatened.

"I'll take a rain check," T.C. said. As he was heading out the door he said, "I have a long memory. I won't forget."

When he came back Kylie was wearing another dress than the one that he had requested but one that she was equally as beautiful in. T.C. was looking quite handsome himself all dressed up.

"Sorry," Kylie said. "Daphne texted me back and specifically told me not to wear black."

They walked next door to T.C.'s and got in his Land Rover. As he backed out of the driveway he said, "Those two sure are acting mysterious. I wonder what's going on. Do you know?"

"No, I'm clueless," Kylie said. "She had off today so I didn't see her, but she didn't say anything yesterday about any plans."

"Same with Taylor. He had off today too. I stopped by the garage on my way home from work but they told me he was taking a few days off."

"Whatever it is, Daphne's always been a spur of the moment person. A lot of times she gets comped tickets to a show at one of the casinos so maybe that's what it's all about," Kylie said.

"Sounds like fun," T.C. said. Neither one of them were big on spending time in the casinos, but occasionally in the past the four of them had seen some of Vegas' spectacular shows and really enjoyed themselves.

T.C. left his SUV with valet parking at the Stratosphere. As they walked in the casino Kylie spotted who she thought was Major Brannan stepping into an elevator. The elevator door closed before she could find out for sure if it was him or not.

They walked into the Air Bar, the city's highest bar, a strange place to meet since Daphne and Taylor knew neither Kylie or T.C. drank, but T.C. said the views alone were worth going there for.

They looked around for the couple and Kylie spotted Daphne hugging her father. She saw Kylie and T.C. and enthusiastically waved them over. She motioned for them to hurry. She was wearing the biggest grin on her face Kylie had ever seen.

As soon as they were within range Daphne screamed, "We're getting married!"

"Congratulations," Kylie said. "We'll be sisters-in-law. When's the wedding?"

"In less than an hour, come on. We need to get moving. I need to get changed. My dress is at the chapel," Daphne said.

"Seriously?" Kylie asked stunned.

Taylor walked over and hugged his brother and said, "We want you and Kylie to be our maid of honor and best man."

"Wow," T.C. said shaking his head. "You guys don't mess around."

Major Brannan was hugging his daughter. He pulled back and

could see the happiness in her eyes and said, "I'm happy for you, Daffy Daphne. I really am, but couldn't you have given me some warning? These types of surprises are tough on the old ticker."

Daphne hugged her father and said, "I love you, Dad. I'd be honored if you'd walk me down the aisle."

She saw her father fighting tears and to give him a moment to compose himself she turned and said to Kylie and T.C., "No time to waste guys. You took too long to get here. We need to get moving."

She told them to meet up at the Little White Wedding Chapel the most well-known wedding chapel in Vegas. It was famous for several celebrity weddings having taken place there.

Daphne and Taylor ran ahead. Kylie noticed the Major wiping tears from his eyes. She went over and put an arm around him and said, "I think she'll be alright. She's really happy and he's really good to her."

Choked up he could only nod. He cleared his throat and said, "I know. It's been a long time since I've seen her this happy. I just wish her mother was alive to see her today and enjoy this moment with her. I'll meet you all there, just give me a few minutes."

When Kylie knocked on the bride's room door at the chapel Daphne was already dressed and was struggling with a cute little pill-box hat with a short veil trying to pin it on.

"Daphne, you look so beautiful," Kylie said. "When did you have time to shop for a wedding dress?"

"This morning when we planned the whole thing. We went out and got our license, then shopped for rings, and a dress. Since I found a dress right away Taylor said, 'Why wait.' I couldn't agree more."

"You had a busy day." Kylie stepped up and helped adjust the veil. "I'm so happy for you." She hugged the bride.

There was a knock at the door. Kylie opened it a crack to see who it was and then opened it wider and said, "Come in and see your beautiful daughter. I'll just step outside and give the two of you a few minutes."

Her father had stopped at the florist in the casino and had them make up a bridal bouquet of white roses and orchids for his daughter. She was really moved that her father had done that for her.

She pretended not to notice her father tearing up as she brought the flowers up to her nose and took a deep breath of their fragrant smell.

A few minutes later the wedding march began playing and Kylie peeked her head in the door and said, "It's time."

52

It was the week after the wedding when Kylie and Daphne had arrived at the airport for their flight into work. An announcement was made that the flight was delayed but wouldn't be long.

Daphne had her back to the door talking to her friend when Kylie noticed a white Land Rover come tearing into the parking lot. The SUV parked quickly and a guy jumped out and ran through the parking lot towards another entrance to the airport. His face was obscured as he was putting on a pilot's jacket as he ran.

She stepped to the side to look again, but Daphne was blocking her view. "I swear that looked like T.C. That looked like his SUV so it caught my attention. I couldn't see his face, but it sure looked like him."

Daphne said, "They'd never let him in here. You know you have to pass through checkpoints and they've very strict about employees only."

"I thought for sure it was him," Kylie said. "Do other flights fly out of here? Maybe one of his flights was leaving from this airport."

The loudspeaker announced that their flight was now boarding so Kylie didn't say anything else about it. Before leaving the lobby she took a quick look around to make sure he wasn't there.

They were boarding the plane when the co-pilot opened the door to the cockpit. Daphne was kidding with him, "Is it because of you we're all running late to work today?"

"Not me," he said. He pointed at the pilot and said, "Our pilot had car trouble and was running late."

Daphne moved down the aisle, but Kylie before following her glanced into the cockpit and noticed T.C. sitting in the pilot's seat. Even with his back to her this time she knew beyond a shadow of a doubt it was him.

During the flight Daphne said, "You sure are quiet."

"Just thinking," Kylie said.

Daphne pulled a magazine out of her handbag and started flipping through it.

Is that why he so readily accepted it when she told him about being abducted by aliens? He worked for Area 51 as a pilot. Did he know what went on at Area 51? She was shocked by her discovery. Did he know she worked there?

"Daphne," Kylie said. Daphne looked up from her magazine. "I never gave it much thought before, but are the pilots who fly these flights into Area 51 employees?"

"Of course," Daphne said. "They're very carefully vetted. The pilots all have a very high security clearance. After all there may be times they see things in the hangars or in the air. "

"What do you mean?" Kylie asked her.

Daphne looked around and whispered, "Flying saucers. How do you think Ari and the other aliens came to earth? We got their flying saucer at the same time we got the aliens."

53

Kylie sat across from the alien, "How are you doing Bidaiari?"

He was opening up to her more and more and she felt he trusted her, as much as an alien can trust someone who is as foreign to him as he was to her.

She felt confusion from him to her question and tried to explain to him what the question, 'how are you doing' meant.

Sometimes it was hard to communicate, the fact being that they truly came from different worlds. He was often confused to what she was trying to ask him. Living in different worlds in this case was quite literal.

He was confused by humans and often conveyed a form of question to her such as, why do humans show teeth and wrinkle their eyes? It took her days to finally figure out he meant why do humans smile.

He was equally confused at laughter and some human emotions. Love was a foreign concept to him. He was very inquisitive about sex or as he called it 'breeding.'

Kylie had been shocked when he admitted that some aliens had sex with some of the humans that had been chosen, as he preferred to call it. She had been appalled at that bit of information and had asked if the sex had been consensual. He didn't seem to understand her question and after that evaded any further discussion on the matter. She couldn't imagine anyone agreeing to having sex with an alien, a thought that was repulsive to her.

They were both learning from each other. She was especially surprised to learn that the aliens had been visiting earth for over half a century.

The top brass from the military who were in the know about Bidaiari were encouraged by the progress she was making. They had high hopes that through Kylie they would learn more about the aliens and of their intentions.

Often there was an audience in the room with the one-way

mirror and other times it was only Daphne or Major Brannan who sat in the other room.

They had thought that their presence in the room was unknown to the alien, but once when he was tired of the questions she was asking she sensed he was disturbed by their presence.

At times when the room was filled he refused to interact at all and just turned his back to her and to the mirror. Another time he went as far as shutting down all the electronics, visual and audio. They didn't know how he was able to do it, but there was no doubt who was responsible for the action.

He seemed to sense the military had their own reasoning for being there and was a bit hostile at times in his attitude to the questions they wanted answered.

He seemed as curious about Kylie as they were about him. Today he portrayed the question to her, 'Why do you fear us?'

"I'm not afraid of you," Kylie answered truthfully. "At first I didn't know what to expect. An alien wasn't something I had ever considered to be real in the past."

'Why?' Bidaiari wanted to know. 'You've been visiting us since you were a little girl.'

Kylie quickly grew uncomfortable with this conversation. She wasn't sure if anyone had entered the other room to listen in and observe since she had started the interview with Bidaiari.

He noticed she kept glancing towards the mirror and he said, 'There's no one there but Daphne.'

She looked towards the mirror but there was no way you could see in. "How do you know who's in there? You can't see in."

'I would feel their presence. I would hear their thoughts.'

"As I hear your thoughts?" Kylie asked.

He ignored her question and after a moment Bidaiari again repeated, 'You have been visiting us for years, most all of your life. Why would you fear us? We mean you no harm.'

Kylie asked quietly, "Are you sure it's only Daphne next door?"

He gave her an affirmative answer so she said, "I'm not *visiting* you. Visiting is when friends voluntarily go to spend time with family or friends. I am taken against my will. I'm given no choice in the matter. Why do you take me? What is the reason behind it?"

'We study you, like you study me. While studying you we discovered problems with...' he reached out and touched the area where her heart was. 'We fixed your problem. You are now healthy.'

She was stunned. Had they been practicing medical procedures on her?

She had read reports of cattle mutilations and how advanced surgery had been performed on the cattle that was way beyond what was humanly possible.

The thought that they were also experimenting or doing surgery of any kind on humans had never crossed her mind.

She recalled when she was young her mother used to not let her run and play like the other children and carried her from room to room telling her not to exert herself.

She now remembered that after a time her mother had told her that she had been healed and she could now play like the other children.

She clearly remembered that. It was one of her earliest memories. She had hated being left behind so it was a vivid memory.

'Yes, that was when you were fixed,' Bidaiari transmitted his thoughts to her.

Oh, God, she thought. I forgot he could read my mind. She jumped up and went to the door. "Give me a minute."

She went outside where two armed guards were guarding the entrance to the door. She paced in the hall until Daphne came out and asked her if she was finished.

Kylie shook her head no and went back inside.

"What did they do to me?" she demanded an answer. "And how do you know this?"

'What one knows we all know,' Bidaiari projected his thoughts to her.

"What are you aliens some kind of machine or walking computer or something?" Kylie yelled.

Bidaiari gave her a sympathetic look. 'We fixed your problem and at the same time...' He paused seeming to have trouble portraying his thought or not wanting to.

"At the same time what?" Kylie asked.

'You are a carrier of our DNA. It was implanted in you. This is our way to ensure our species continues to survive. You carry superior genes due to alien DNA that is a part of you,' Bidaiari portrayed to her.

"What are you saying?" Kylie jumped up and banged her hand on the table leaning into Bidaiari's face with a threatening look. The guards started to rush in but she turned around and yelled for them to get out.

The guards backed out and she looked at Bidaiari with steel in her eyes. She said softly but very firmly, "I'm not a damn alien. I'm a human being with human parents."

'With our, or as you prefer to call it, alien DNA intermixed. Our DNA will grow stronger as your line of descendants continues. At some point the new beings from your lineage will resemble us more than humans. Their knowledge and abilities will be unprecedented. At that point...'

Kylie stormed out but before leaving the room she pointed at Bidaiari and yelled, "You let your aliens know to keep their hands off me."

Daphne was waiting out in the hall. She had a hard time keeping up with Kylie as she stormed to the elevator.

Before the elevator arrived Kylie put her hand to her mouth and ran for the nearest bathroom. She was violently ill heaving over the toilet when Daphne came in.

Daphne grabbed some paper towels and got them wet handing them to Kylie for her to wipe her face.

After a few moments Kylie said, "Let's get out of here."

In the elevator Daphne started to open her mouth to say something and Kylie said, "Don't say a word in here. I don't want anyone to hear anything about this."

They exited the elevator and Daphne said, "Come to my office."

"I'll be there in ten minutes. There's something I have to do first."

54

Kylie walked into the lab, took off her lab coat and had Chelsey her assistant draw her blood. She planned to run a complete work up on her blood and run a DNA test. She took the blood sample out of Chelsey's hand and said, "I'll test this myself."

She stormed back to the room where Bidaiari was and told him, "Stick out your arm." He sat at the table and did as she asked while looking at her with a pitiful look on his face.

Since aliens don't have blood she withdrew some of the lymphatic fluid. She also took a skin scraping and took a swab from inside his mouth. That would have to do, she had no other way to compare the results other than any DNA taken during the autopsy from the dead alien.

Before she left the room he conveyed his thoughts to her, 'This isn't necessary. You know what I've said is the truth.'

"I know no such thing. I'm not an alien," Kylie said, "not any part of me."

Bidaiari didn't respond.

"You'll have to work with Daphne in the future," Kylie said. "I'm not coming back. I want nothing more to do with you."

'That won't change the truth,' Bidaiari said.

Kylie went to open the door, but it wouldn't budge. She set her tray down with the lymphatic fluid and syringe. She was unable to open the door.

"Open the door," she banged on the door for the guards to open it.

The guards yelled from the other side, "It's stuck. We can't get it open. We'll call for help."

She looked at Bidaiari and asked, "Are you doing this?"

'You'll be back,' he sent the message to her. 'I'm too important for them to allow you to not come back. I won't speak with anyone else, but I will answer your questions. Those that I can.'

The next time she tried to open the door it opened with no

effort.

She dropped the samples off in her lab and headed to Daphne's office. She knew that his thought he projected to her about him being too important was true. The higher ups would never allow her to neglect continuing her work with the alien.

How could they? It may be their only opportunity to get answers.

She thought about what he told her about eventually the line would be more alien than human. Is this how they planned to take over? Was that their intention? If so, perhaps he had revealed more than he had intended.

55

Kylie was in Daphne's office crying over the revelations that Bidaiari had revealed to her.

"I have alien DNA in me," Kylie cried. "How could they do this to me? Why? Why would they do this?"

"Perhaps that's the answer as to why people are abducted," Daphne was thinking out loud. "We can't hold back on this information, Kylie. They have to be told. You realize..."

"Yes, I know," Kylie said. "Go ahead and call your father. He can tell the others what..."

"No need to call me," Major Brannan said stepping into her office and shutting the door behind him. "The men who monitor the alien called me. I've seen the video from your last two meetings with Bidaiari."

"Oh God," Kylie said. "I forgot about them. The next thing you know my face could be all over the National Enquirer with headlines like *'Woman From Area 51 Part Alien.'*"

"The men monitoring Bidaiari have a higher security clearance than the President of the United States," Major Brannan said. "Unlike the White House you never hear of a leak from Area 51, so don't worry about that."

"What did he mean by 'they fixed you'? Daphne asked.

"I'm not exactly sure," Kylie said, "but when I was young, about kindergarten age I think, I remember I was never allowed to go out and play with other children. I remember spending a lot of time in doctor's offices and then suddenly whatever the problem was appeared to have been cleared up. I'm not really sure what the issue was. My parents never discussed it with me."

"And now they're gone so you can't ask them. It might be a good idea to get your medical records," Daphne suggested. "That should tell us something."

"You know my sister died at age four of leukemia. It seems we were both flawed, suffering from major medical issues. Why did they fix me and not my sister?" Kylie was thinking out loud.

Major Brannan appeared nervous. "They've been known to have performed medical procedures on people they've abducted. It's all documented. It appears they're far more sophisticated in their medical knowledge than we are. What really concerns me is him talking about inserting alien DNA into humans."

"And the part where eventually the lineage will be more alien than human. Why would they do that? Why don't they just have alien babies?" Daphne asked.

"He said for their kind, their species to continue," Major Brannan answered while deep in thought.

"We were never able to determine how or if they reproduce," Kylie said. "During the autopsy we discovered the dead alien had no reproductive organs."

"Well, they came into existence somehow," Daphne said. She looked at her dad and asked, "What do you think? Do you think their plans are to co-exist with us here on earth?"

"Or something far more sinister," Major Brannan answered. "I don't know, but we need to find out as much as we can and sooner rather than later. With what he said to you about the offspring becoming more alien than human, that can't mean anything good."

Major Brannan looked at Kylie and said, "I'm sorry Kylie, but he was right. You will need to continue visiting him and find out as much as you can. We're going to need to step those questions up."

"I was afraid of that," Kylie said. "I wish someone else could do it."

"So far he hasn't opened up to anybody but you," Daphne said. "I'm willing to try again, but I was thinking..."

"Go on," Kylie said. "What?"

"Perhaps the reason you can communicate with him is because of the alien DNA in you," Daphne said.

Kylie looked stricken.

"Sorry," Daphne said.

"This is no time to walk on eggshells," Major Brannan said. "It is what it is, and this may be our one and only chance to glean any information from him to prepare to protect our nation if need be."

"From alien attack?" Daphne asked.

"Or takeover," Major Brannan said. "I know there are those in the military who feel their intentions are not favorable towards us. This information makes me lean towards that way of thinking myself."

"Isn't there a way to check to see if what he said is true?" Daphne said.

"I'll have my medical records sent," Kylie said.

"No, I mean the part where he said you have alien DNA. That would be along your line of work. Would there be a way to check that?"

"I've already had blood drawn and running tests. I'm not sure exactly what to look for, but I should know if there are any anomalies."

Major Brannan stood to leave. "I'm afraid this isn't something I can keep from my superiors." He looked uncomfortable when he said, "I would if I could, but this could have some major ramifications for us here on earth. This goes beyond national security. This could affect the entire planet."

"I understand," Kylie said.

Major Brannan stood to leave, "Let me know as soon as you have any test results. And Kylie, have them overnight those medical records."

56

T.C. was watching Kylie. She had been on edge, yet when he asked if there was anything wrong she assured him everything was fine.

When the doorbell rang she jumped.

"Relax, honey," T.C. said. "I'll get it."

FedEx was at the door with a package that needed a signature. When T.C. shut the door Kylie was there and practically ripped the package out of his hands.

"Is this what you've been waiting for?" T.C. asked.

Kylie opened it pulling out a thick folder held together with a large rubber band. She took it over to the table and began to read.

T.C. came and stood behind her massaging her shoulders. "What is it, hon? Something for work?"

"It's my medical records," Kylie said. "I just wanted to see them to verify something."

"Everything O.K.?" T.C. asked concerned.

"Yeah, no problem," Kylie said. "I was just wanting to look the records over to compare it to something I'm working on. A source of reference is all."

"O.K.," T.C. said. He didn't even pretend to understand her work on genetics. It was way over his head.

"It looks like you're going to be busy with that for awhile. I'm going to run my SUV over to Taylor's garage. It's been giving me problems again, and he said he'd have time to look at it this afternoon."

"Alright," she said without looking up.

"Call me if you need me," he said as he bent over to give her a kiss before leaving.

After T.C. was gone she began reading over her medical records starting from her birth. They were extensive medical records as it appeared she was born with a congenital heart defect.

Kylie sat back and took a breath. Why had her parents never

told her about this? She had chosen the medical field herself as a career. At some point you would have thought they would have said something to her. It didn't make any sense.

Kylie read notes from a pediatric cardiologist. She had suffered with Total Anomalous Pulmonary Venous Connection also known as TAPVC. Kylie was unfamiliar with this so opened her laptop to get more information.

She read *'Severe obstruction of the pulmonary veins tends to make infants breathe harder and look bluer due to having lower oxygen levels. Children were advised to limit their physical activities. This must be surgically repaired.'*

Kylie looked through her extensive medical records and found no record of any surgery.

What she did find was extremely troubling.

57

Kylie looked at the clock and realized T.C. had been gone for hours. She checked her phone but there were no messages.

She texted him, 'Everything O.K.?'

He texted back, 'Something strange, explain later.'

She decided to use this quiet time to continue reading the medical records. She had been troubled by a note she had found scribbled off to the side of the records and reread the note to be sure she had understood it correctly.

The handwritten note from her pediatric cardiologist read: *'Apparently the parents had the surgery done elsewhere which they denied doing. There is no longer any sign of the infant suffering from TAPVC or any other medical issues whatsoever. The child has gone from extremely ill to the perfect picture of health. Inexplicable is the fact that there is NO physical sign that the child had open heart or transplant surgery. This was so troubling to me I had lab work done to confirm this was indeed the same child. Still waiting for lab results at time of this memo. This is not a condition that goes away on it's own - other than perhaps a miracle.'*

There were no further records from this doctor and it appears that at this time her parents switched pediatricians.

The new pediatrician whose records began about nine months after she had last been seen by the pediatric cardiologist included in his notes that the child had been born and lived overseas up to this point and there were no medical records from birth to the age of five.

What was that all about? She was born in Florida and she knew for a fact her family had never lived overseas.

She thought back and realized that this was about the time that her parents had moved from St. Augustine, Florida to Phoenix, Arizona.

They had also severed all contact from family members on

both sides around the same time period. Something neither of her parents had ever been willing to discuss with her.

She had assumed in the past there was a falling out between the families. But now that she thought about it, how likely was that to happen from both sides and at the same time? How could a child turn their backs on the parents who had raised them, no longer having anything to do with them? She had been deprived of having a relationship with both sets of grandparents.

People had differences but they got over it and put it behind them. Her parents weren't the type to hold a grudge. It was so unlike them.

She didn't even know if she had any aunts or uncles or if her grandparents were still alive. If so, did they know where she was and chose not to stay in contact?

When she had asked about family in the past her mother had simply said it was too painful of a subject for her to discuss. End of subject.

What were they hiding? She was afraid she had a pretty good idea.

She delved back into the medical records and found a note from her original pediatric cardiologist dated almost three years after his first note. It read: *'After receiving the lab results and verifying this was indeed the same child I searched for over two years to find out what happened to the girl. By a fluke at a medical conference out west where I spoke on this troubling incident her current doctor from Arizona recognized her from the photos I showed and asked to meet with me. I have since then shared these medical records with him. He was quite troubled by the parents misleading him and was also unable to find out what happened to solve this medical issue. At this point I have turned all the medical records over to him and wash my hands of it all. Mystery remains unsolved to this day.'*

She went in the bathroom and looked in the mirror for any sign whatsoever of a surgical scar. Nothing. If she would have had open heart surgery there would have definitely been extensive scar tissue and visible signs. Even plastic surgery wouldn't have been able to completely conceal such a scar.

58

T.C. came in with something in his hand saying, "Look at this."

Kylie walked over and peered at it. "I don't know the first thing about car parts. Is that what that is?"

"It was definitely on my car but no, it's not a car part per se. While working on my car Taylor found it. It's a tracking device," T.C. said.

Kylie's head jerked up at that revelation. She grabbed T.C. by the hand and pulled him outside.

"Kylie, what are you doing?" T.C. asked confused by her odd behavior.

"Can we go somewhere to talk?" Kylie asked standing in her front yard. "Ow, damn these rocks are hot." Kylie started hopping from foot to foot and then jumped up onto her front porch which was in the shade.

"Sure. Can't we just talk at your house or mine?" T.C. asked.

"No, somewhere outside," Kylie insisted. She ran inside and grabbed some shoes and her house keys and got in his SUV.

They drove for about ten minutes in silence and pulled over to a park and got out. "Let's go sit over there," Kylie pointed to a park bench.

T.C. said, "What's going on, Kylie?"

"What exactly was that thing on your car?" she asked.

"Is that what this is about? You had me scared. I was starting to think you had a serious medical condition after seeing what came in the mail, or you were having second thoughts about us," T.C. said.

"No way. You're stuck with me Timothy Carter Tanner," Kylie said.

T.C. said, "Sounds good to me. As far as the thing from the car it was a GPS and a listening device. It could track me wherever I went and also listen to conversations going on inside my car.

After that Taylor..."

"Who do you suspect would do something like that? Why would someone want to track you or listen in to your conversations?" Kylie interrupted clearly troubled.

T.C. was quiet but was clearly thinking about what she asked.

After hesitating for only a brief moment he said, "Look, I don't want to lie to you. We're getting married, and I refuse to start our relationship with a lie between us. I don't see what the problem is with me telling you anyway."

"Go on," she prompted.

"You know I told you I was a pilot, but what I didn't tell you is..."

"You work for the people at Area 51. I know," Kylie interrupted.

He looked shocked. "How could you know that?"

"Because I work for them too," she said.

"What!" T.C. looked at her in amazement. "You told me you worked for a medical research company."

"The research I do is for the same people you work for," she started to explain.

"But how did you know that's who I worked for?" T.C. asked.

"I saw you the day you were running late for work," Kylie said. "I was in the lobby waiting for my flight when I saw you come into the parking lot. Then I saw you in the pilot's seat when the co-pilot opened the door."

"You knew?" he asked. "Wait a minute. All this time you've been flying in my plane and I didn't know it?"

"Yeah, but believe me. I've struggled with not telling you where I work and what I do also," she said.

T.C. came over and hugged her.

"The only reason I haven't said anything is I signed a non-disclosure agreement and I was threatened with my life if I ever revealed what I did," she said.

"I signed one of those too," he said. "They gave me a cover story of who I worked for, but when I saw something that was top secret at that point I was called in and given the talk. I guess it's at that point that they started tracking me and listening in."

After a second he looked up with a strange look on his face, "You don't think they have my house bugged, do you? I mean, if they would bug my car maybe they would bug my house, too."

"Daphne told me when I first started working for them to assume my home and phone were bugged. At first it really bothered me, especially when you and I, you know...when we got together," Kylie said hoping he hadn't noticed her slip of the tongue by mentioning Daphne.

"When we got together? Oh, you mean having sex. Oh man, that's sick," T.C. said. "I didn't sign on for my privacy to be invaded. For me it's a job, nothing else. Wait a minute. Did you say Daphne? Daphne works there, too?"

"Yes, she does. Maybe we could have someone come in and check to see if there are any listening devices or any video surveillance," Kylie said.

"I'll definitely do that right away," T.C. said. "I bet Taylor knows. That's how he knew where to find the thing when he was working on my car, because believe me where it was tucked away it would have been very unlikely for anyone to discover it."

"Wait here," he walked over to his SUV and opened his back door pulling out a bag.

T.C. walked back over to the bench and said, "Taylor gave me these prepaid phones. I didn't even think about it at the time but he already had these before he found the device. His and Daphne's numbers are programmed in and so are our numbers on each phone." He handed her a phone and kept the other one for himself.

"What good will that do us? They'll have listening devices on their phones so they'll still be able to know what we're saying," Kylie said while scrolling down and looking at the numbers that had been programmed into her phone.

"They also have a set of these phones," T.C. said. "Taylor must know about all of us working there and that's why he's taking these precautions. Their numbers that are programmed in are their prepaid phones, so they should be secure. Carry it with you at all times, but don't let anyone other than Daphne know that you have it."

"So, you must have seen a flying saucer," Kylie said casually hoping he would be thinking about the phone and answer.

"Not only did I see it, I got to try to fly it. Imagine putting that on my next resume. Yeah, it was really awesome." T.C. said. "And by the way, I know you were trying to trick me into answering that one, but no more secrets between us right?"

59

Kylie was studying her DNA checking the molecular structure of her DNA chains. She checked the genomes at specific locations where she had determined she may spot something that would stand out.

Alan had been sent by the higher-ups to assist her. He didn't say anything to her, but they feared if she found something 'alien' she may change the results rather than be truthful with them.

Alan wasn't concerned. He knew Kylie. Regardless of whatever facts were revealed, she would be forthcoming with whatever they discovered.

Kylie had taken a buccal smear, a procedure using a cotton swab to collect a sample of cells from the inside of her cheek. They had also tested her blood, skin, and hair looking for specific changes in chromosomes, DNA, or proteins that may prove the alien's disclosure to her as either positive or negative. At this point she just wanted to know the facts.

Alan examining the sample said, "It's not exactly that we know what we're looking for here. How do you determine the alteration of DNA from human to alien? We really have nothing to compare it to."

"If it's there I'll find it. I feel as though my future is at stake here. Have you found anything at all?" she asked.

"Perhaps," Alan answered while peering intently into his microscope adjusting the dials.

Kylie's head jerked up. "What?" She moved over to his microscope and shoved him out of the way to see for herself.

He had hoped to have more time to study what he was looking at before having to say anything. After all, he wasn't sure yet what exactly it was he had discovered.

"What is that? I totally missed that," she looked up at Alan and said, "You probably don't believe me. You probably thought I'd try to cover it up if I found something, didn't you?"

"No," he reassured her. "That's not who you are."

"Yeah, well; isn't that what this is about? To discover just who I am? Alien or human?"

"You are who you are, Kylie," Alan said. "The results won't change who you are."

Kylie said, "Are you kidding me? I don't know who you're trying to convince me or you, but you are so far off base. T.C. and I would like to have children. If it's true what Bidaiari said, there is no way in hell I'll take that chance. For all I know I could give birth to some freak alien human..."

"Well, look at you," Alan said. "You're not exactly a freak. You're a lovely human being, and any children you have will be also."

"Wish I could be sure of that," she said.

She gazed through the microscope and said, "Oh God, what is that? I've never seen anything like it before. I'm a geneticist. I should know what I'm looking at, but I can't identify it. Is it the alien DNA?"

Kylie began to cry. Alan set his work down and removed his gloves. "Come on, Kylie. Take a break. I know this is eating at you. We've been at this all day and haven't found anything definitive yet."

"I'm sorry. I don't know why I'm crying all the time anymore," Kylie said.

"Well, let's see; in the last year you've discovered aliens do exist, you've performed an autopsy on one, "befriended" another, discovered you've been abducted by them for most of your life, found yourself to be the only one that can communicate with aliens that we know of, and now discovered they did major surgery on you...", Alan said.

"And don't forget that I carry alien DNA in me. Then there's the fact that my family line is tainted and may one day produce little demon aliens who plan to take over our world," Kylie said.

Daphne was standing in the doorway listening and said, "Are we having a pity party here?"

"Aah, my compassionate, understanding best friend," Kylie said. "I always knew you would be a great source of comfort in my greatest hour of need."

"I'd like to be. Just trying to prepare you. You're both being summoned to a meeting. All the big-wigs have been called in, so expect this to be a tough one. I'm sure they're going to have lots of questions for you," Daphne said.

"Great. Just what I need right now," Kylie said.

"Go ahead. I'll put this away and clean up," Alan said.

"No such luck, Alan. Did you not hear me? You too are being summoned," Daphne said.

"Fifteen minutes, 3rd floor, room 315," Daphne said. "I'll save you both a seat."

60

The conference room where the meeting was being held was large enough to seat 20 to 30 people and was filled to capacity. Normally it was Major Brannan who sat at the head of the table, but this time she saw it was a face she didn't recognize.

Most of the questions were directed at Kylie, which was understandable since she was the only one the alien had communicated with up to this point.

Other questions and comments were made mainly to those in the military who seemed to have all types of opinions on the aliens and why they were coming to visit.

The man at the head of the desk hadn't introduced himself and no one called him by name, yet the others seemed to be aware of exactly who he was and treated him with utmost respect. Or was it from fear or intimidation, she wondered as she watched their body language.

Daphne whispered to Kylie that in case she didn't recognize him he was the head of the CIA. A government within a government if ever there was one she said. The shadow government.

Kylie looked at Daphne and said, "Thanks for the heads up."

Daphne leaned forward and whispered again, "The guy sitting on his left is head of Homeland Security and NSA is also represented here. They brought them all out of the shadows. I've never seen them all out in the open together like this before. You seem to be a great source of interest to them, Kylie."

The man at the head of the table said, "If you ladies are finished with your private conversation we'll continue our business."

He asked Kylie to tell of every alien abduction she could recall from the day of her childhood to the present and to describe everything in great detail.

She was asked to describe how the aliens came to her, how she entered the spaceship, if she could refuse to go with them, to describe the size and interior of the spaceship, how many aliens were on board, and what they did to her when she was on board.

Major Brannan handed him a print out of Kylie's recollections from those abductions and what they had learned when she had been hypnotized, but he merely pushed the paper back towards the major and said, "I've read it, but I'd like to hear it in her own words."

On a few occasions he would interrupt to ask for a little more detail, but for the most part he just listened.

When she finished he turned to the major and asked, "Is lunch to be delivered? We'll take a break now, and I don't want anyone to leave this room until we've concluded our business."

Major Brannan made the call to his secretary that they were ready for lunch. A large buffet was brought in. Those who had arrived to serve were all asked to leave for fear they may overhear talk.

Everyone got up to stretch their legs, talk to others about what had been discussed, or to fix a plate of food. By this time the meeting had already been going on for several hours.

The man sitting at the head of the table walked over to Kylie and said, "I know it's not easy for you to open up like this about something so personal. I hope you understand why it's necessary."

"I do, but thank you," she said.

He then turned and walked out of the room followed by the head of Homeland Security and NSA.

About 30 or 40 minutes later after everyone had eaten and the dishes had been removed the meeting continued.

The next thing discussed was the autopsy. She and Alan shared information on that procedure and their discoveries.

Hours had passed by the time they had finished discussing Bidaiari. The man heading the meeting interrupted her at this point and asked if they could refer to him as Ari the name she had originally called him and a much easier name to pronounce and remember.

He was most interested in how Ari communicated with her. At times the man just wanted facts and other times he asked her opinion on matters such as, why he thought only she could communicate with the alien.

She answered that he seemed to be able to convey his thoughts to those he desired and shut them out with anyone else. She told him she thought perhaps the reason he was open to communicating with her was due to her alien abductions.

"Not due to your carrying their DNA?" he asked.

She looked at Alan before answering, "That is yet to be determined."

"Fair enough," he answered. He looked down at his notes to be sure he hadn't forgotten anything he needed to discuss with her.

"I have a list of questions I would like you to ask Ari. I know they can't all be answered at once, but as soon as possible I would like you to get started on them. The major has the list so he will accompany you on these visits."

Kylie spoke up and said, "I have been more than open with all of you and have opened up completely my entire personal life. I have agreed to all your demands in the past, but now I have a demand of my own."

A brigadier general in the room started to interrupt, but the man at the head of the table held up his hand for him to be quiet. "Let her speak."

"I'm engaged to be married. My future husband is aware of my alien abductions, but not that I am currently working with an alien or of the possibility of my carrying alien DNA. I wish to inform him of this before we get married."

"Request denied," the man said. "Anything else?"

"Actually, it wasn't a request. I guess you could say I was being courteous in the fact that I was telling you beforehand what I'm going to do. And I will tell him."

He stared at her trying to intimidate her, but she was unfazed and a very determined woman. She stared back at him. He was the first to break eye contact.

"He's a pilot here and an employee and has also signed a non-disclosure agreement. I insist he knows this information before our marriage which is only weeks away."

"And if I still refuse?" the man asked.

"I will hand in my resignation effective immediately and you can get someone else to get Ari to answer your questions," Kylie said matching his stare.

"Granted. But be assured, both you and he will be held to the terms of the nondisclosure agreement and may not discuss this with anyone else. You may tell him, but first we will need to have him come in to sign a new waiver and up his security clearance."

The major cleared his throat and said, "His clearance is the same as hers, and he has signed the document to which you've referred to. This won't be a complete surprise to him. He's one of the pilots who's attempted to fly the spaceship we have at this location."

"Well then, I guess you may proceed with your disclosure. Good luck."

"Thank you, sir," Kylie said. "There is one more thing. I want all the surveillance, both audio and video, removed from our homes and our vehicles."

"I don't see why not. There's no one else we have to worry about you telling is there? Any other demands?" His answer confirmed that they had indeed been under surveillance even though neither T.C. or Taylor were ever able to find any evidence of hidden surveillance equipment.

When she shook her head no, he looked around the room and said, "Does anybody have anything else to add before we're dismissed, and if so please make it relevant. This meeting has gone on long enough," he said.

"I just want to add one thing," Lieutenant Colonel Ward said. "It might be wise for Dr. Carmichael and her future husband to get fixed or sterilized, refrain from having children."

A roar erupted from the room at this statement.

"Hear me out," Lieutenant Colonel Ward said. He waited for the people in the room to quiet down before continuing. "It could be dangerous for them to have offspring. It hasn't been proven or disproved whether or not she carries alien DNA. The aliens may be planning something sinister..."

The man at the end of the table bellowed, "You're out of line. That's quite enough. This meeting is adjourned."

61

The room had cleared out with the exception of Lieutenant Colonel Ward, Colonel Hazard, Daphne, and Major Brannan.

The group was standing at the back of the room where Lieutenant Colonel Ward was giving an argument for why he thought it best to not only have Kylie "fixed" so she couldn't have children, but to try to round up all other people who had reported that they too had been abducted and have them all sterilized.

Daphne was seething and about to explode when her father very discreetly motioned for her to keep quiet. She had a very difficult time following his order.

Colonel Hazard waited for Lieutenant Colonel Ward to leave before saying to Major Brannan. "I disagree with what he said, but what a coup it would be if she were to have the alien's child for us to study. Is that even possible?"

Daphne gave him a look like she thought he was insane to even think such a thing. "Considering they aren't having sex and he or it has no sexual organs, I would say chances are slim on that one," Daphne said.

The colonel said, "What Ari told her about human–alien babies overtime evolving into more alien than human, this would give us a head start on studying the children with alien DNA to see how they evolve. She would be providing a service for her country. Dr. Carmichael would be our best chance of that happening. This alien seems to trust her and he says she already carries the alien DNA. If she were to have his child..."

"And why would you even think she would even consider something so absurd? It's not enough what she's doing for us now? She has to have sex with aliens and give us alien babies too?"

"Ms Tanner," the colonel said.

"It's Doctor," Daphne corrected him. "Dr. Tanner."

Major Brannan who was rapidly losing his temper with the colonel and said, "During the autopsy it was discovered that the alien had no reproductive organs. Whether all the aliens are the same or not is still a matter of question. How they reproduce is something we have been unable to discover, but nobody is going to be having sex with our alien."

"It would certainly be interesting to see what they would have reproduced," the colonel said. "Or even how aliens have sex. I'd buy a front row seat for that one."

"Yeah, I just bet you would," Daphne scoffed. "Maybe it's a female. We don't know for a fact that Ari is male. If so, would you be willing to volunteer your sexual services? You know, like you said, do a service for your country?"

Colonel or not, to her you had to earn respect before she gave it and this guy was a total jerk.

The colonel looked intently at Daphne like he was trying to figure out if she was serious.

Major Brannan had to fight back a smile. He knew the colonel could make things hard for them. He had a reputation of one who liked throwing his weight around. Major Brannan could see that reputation was well deserved.

"After hypnotizing Dr. Carmichael we discovered there are more than one type of alien as you heard today," Major Brannan said. "That is something other abductees have also reported. This is something other..."

"Yeah, her story sounded like something she had seen in a sci-fi movie to me, mantis type beings, reptilians, shape shifters, and seven foot tall stick figures...," the arrogant colonel laughed.

Daphne could no longer keep her composure and interrupted. "What was your initial thought when you learned about aliens crashing to earth? Did you believe they were real, or maybe you thought someone had smoked some wacky tobaccy and was hallucinating."

Major Brannan stepped in. "I know it sounds unrealistic, but you've seen our resident alien so you know they're real. Not everyone and everything is a carbon copy of what we are or have become accustomed to."

"I'll have to get a hold of the reports of the claims of these women who said they were abducted and had sex with aliens and then had their babies," the colonel said returning to that topic. "What do you think? They made it up for attention or any chance of it being real?"

"While some abductees claim they have been impregnated by one of these other type of aliens we have no way to validate their statements. Kylie isn't the only one who has described these other beings," Major Brannan said. "Whether or not any tests have been run on the infants that supposedly resulted from this encounter is unknown."

"Interesting," the colonel said. "Well, my plane is waiting."

Major Brannan and Daphne waited before he was gone before saying anything.

"I'm worried about Kylie," Major Brannan said. "If it's discovered she does indeed have alien DNA, they'll definitely want to run experiments on her."

"My friend will not be treated like some guinea pig or test animal," Daphne said.

"I just hope and pray that choice isn't out of my hands. They could hold her against her will in the name of national security. I'll protect her anyway I can."

"You damn well better!"

62

Bidaiari, or Ari as they now referred to him, true to his word had been answering questions that Kylie presented to him. The sessions where they questioned him appeared to wear him out.

He was responsive to the questions she asked and did try to educate her in their ways and thoughts. There were still some topics he would absolutely refuse to answer.

At most they were getting two or three questions answered a day, but one bit of information Ari did give them which terrified them all was that he was not being held captive. He could walk out anytime he wanted, and there was nothing they could do to stop him.

Kylie had seen other aliens walk through walls and doors defying physics, so when he made this statement she wasn't entirely surprised.

Did he stay behind because the others of his kind had no way of rescuing him, she wondered? What would be his purpose in staying if he could leave? Was he here at Area 51 to study and observe as he had said his role was previously? Here he had access to the military and the ability to read their thoughts. When they were alone she intended to ask him just why he did stay if he had the ability to leave.

Kylie had a few days off and she and T.C. had originally planned to go stay at the Archer's cabin, but now she was wanting to change those plans.

"What's wrong with going to the cabin?" T.C. asked. "I thought you'd been looking forward to checking the place out and spending time there."

"I was. I mean I am," Kylie said. "I just want to save that for another time."

"O.K., fine by me," T.C. said. He pulled up his laptop and

looked for somewhere close enough to go for just a few days. "As long as we're together it's all the same to me where we go."

"How about Lake Tahoe? Here look at this place," T.C. turned the laptop around so she could see the photos of the place he found online.

"That looks beautiful. What amazing views! Can we get it on such short notice?"

T.C. made a phone call and said, "Start packing."

It was an eight hour drive, so they decided to fly instead of driving and rent a car when they got there. That would give them more time to enjoy themselves.

When they arrived they were impressed by the views. It was absolute paradise for those who appreciated the great outdoors.

Kylie gazed around in wonder taking in the view of Lake Tahoe itself, a large freshwater lake nestled in the Sierra Nevadas. The water of the lake was clear with snow capped peaks of the mountain range in clear view of the cabin they were staying in.

Kylie stared out the window deep in thought watching the snow coming down. Even through the double-paned windows you could hear the wind whistling outside. It was a good time to be indoors in front of a fire curled up with the one you loved.

She turned around and watched T.C. adding logs to the fire. When he saw her he patted the spot next to him for her to join him.

Kylie knew she had to use this opportunity to tell him everything. Like he had said, 'No more secrets.' She planned to live by that creed.

The fire was crackling and the snow was falling outside the window, none of which Kylie could enjoy until she had unburdened her heart. T.C. had to know everything there was to know, and then she would give him a chance to back out of the marriage.

That evening by the fireplace Kylie told T.C. everything.

63

He never for a second considered changing his mind about the marriage. He knew how difficult it had been for her to tell him everything that she had experienced, and he loved her the more for sharing it with him.

"How could you even think for a minute I would change my mind?" he asked her. "I committed myself to you the moment I asked you to marry me."

"I thought the DNA part may be what would send you running," she said.

"As far as I'm concerned all women are aliens," he said with a big grin on his face.

At that point she knew, they were in this together whatever happened.

That night the aliens came for her.

She had been so happy now that there were no more secrets between them. After being reassured he wasn't going anywhere they had found their way to the bedroom.

T.C. had taken the condoms he had brought with them and walked into the bathroom pulling her by the hand with him. He held the condoms over the toilet.

"I want you to have my baby," he said. "O.K.?"

"Now?" she asked.

"I don't want to wait any longer. I want us to get married right away. As soon as we get back to Vegas. I want you to have my children. The sooner the better. It happens when it happens, but when it does I will be the happiest man alive. A wife I adore and our child together is all a man could ask for. I plan to grow old with you," he said as she watched him holding the condoms over the toilet. "O.K.?" he asked.

She nodded in agreement tears of happiness in her eyes. He

dropped the condoms one by one into the toilet and said, "No changing our minds now, agreed?"

She reached over and flushed the toilet. "Agreed."

She and T.C. had just finished making love. They had gone to bed when the sun went down and talked about their future and made love until midnight.

They planned to contact their friends and have their wedding the weekend after they returned to Vegas. They wanted to start their family right away. T.C. had said they might as well start practicing, and they had spent the last few hours doing just that.

She had slipped on a nightgown because it was chilly in the room, but T.C. was still lying on the bed in the nude.

T.C. said. "When I can walk again I'm going to take a cold shower and get some sleep. You wear me out woman."

"Me?" she laughed. "I rolled over to go to sleep hours ago, but someone kept me up."

"You kept me up too," he said, meaning something entirely different from what she meant.

Kylie laughed. Her laughter ended abruptly as she watched two aliens step right through the cabin's closed closet doors.

64

The aliens motioned for her to follow them. She looked over at T.C. lying right beside her but he appeared to be frozen, unaware of what was going on right in front of him.

He had been talking to her just a second ago. She knew he wasn't asleep, yet he couldn't move. He seemed totally oblivious to the alien's presence not more than three feet away from him.

She tried to fight it but seemingly against her will she rose and one of the aliens took her by the hand. He stepped through the wall pulling her along with him. How was that even possible?

She was in bare feet with no jacket only in her nightgown, yet she didn't feel the cold of the snow under her feet or the cold air blowing around her.

She was led to the light where she then entered the spacecraft. She mindlessly followed the aliens down a long hall. They passed several closed doors. She thought she heard crying behind one of the doors, but the sound stopped as abruptly as it had begun.

She entered a room that was in darkness with only a muted light. When her eyes adjusted to the dim lighting she noticed the room was vacant other than a metal table in the center of the room. She had been on that table before, she was sure of it.

She had a feeling of déjà vu, as though she had been here before and experienced this same experience. Perhaps that was why she felt terrified.

She was unsure why she felt this way, as they had never harmed her in any way that she could recall, though she knew her past memories with the aliens were vague at best. Nevertheless, she felt an unease she couldn't explain.

She was told to lie down. She saw no way out and did what she was told.

The two aliens who had brought her aboard stepped back as a tall, slender type alien came forward. This is the type alien she referred to as the mantis type alien for lack of any other way to describe him.

Kylie herself was close to six feet tall and this alien would have easily towered over her. He emanated kindness, and she felt he meant her no harm. He pushed her nightgown up to her thighs and inserted something into one of her legs. He withdrew a sample from her leg which as a geneticist she assumed was meant to be a DNA sample, as there would have been no other explanation for the procedure.

Once he departed with the sample he had removed from her she pulled her nightgown back down and began to sit up thinking they were done with her.

Another alien entered the room and gently told her to lie back down. Perhaps he had been standing behind her all along, but it was only now she was aware of his presence.

This alien too was taller than Ari and the aliens who came to bring her to the spacecraft. She watched him as he came and stood by her side.

He seemed familiar for some reason she couldn't comprehend. There was a gentleness about him and he had a calming effect. She began to relax in his presence.

His appearance was different from the other aliens. His appearance was more human than that of the others. His head was smaller as were his eyes. They did appear to have an Oriental look as though he came from Asian ancestry. His eyes were not over-sized as the other aliens' eyes.

He was able to portray his thoughts to her. He 'told' her he would always be there when she visited and had been with her in the past at her other visits. He seemed kind and she felt comforted with him by her side. In his presence her fear subsided almost as though she had been given a tranquilizer.

No sooner had she begun to relax when she felt the presence of another being enter the room. Darkness seemed to surround him. Her fear returned, and she was even more fearful than before. She shivered uncontrollably.

This alien emanated the feeling of power and of one totally lacking in compassion or kindness. One without a heart or soul.

She watched in fear as he turned so she could see him. He was taller than some and a bit shorter than others. He would have been considered little more than average height for a human. He had the appearance of a human in looks, but human he was not.

He stared down at her with a lack of emotion of any kind. His eyes were like black, empty pools. He showed no kindness as the others had done.

The aliens who had brought her aboard watched him for a sign as though he were in charge and they were there to do his bidding.

She saw he had the appearance of a good-looking man, one that would have turned heads in another setting. Just to look at him you could see and feel he was cold and devoid of feeling. He was wrapped in some type of long, shimmering cape that seemed to cling to his body with a train that trailed in his wake.

Even though human in form she knew he was an alien. He must have felt her thoughts. He changed his looks in front of her. A shape-shifter.

Yet again he had the appearance of an extremely attractive man and she thought he did this to become attractive to her, to appeal to her. He didn't. She felt repulsion.

He walked over and ran his hand through her long hair and caressed her cheek with the back of his hand. His hand was as cold as ice. He turned her head forcing her to look at him.

He looked into her eyes with black, soulless eyes. She turned her head away from him which seemed to anger him.

He stormed to the end of the table and pushed her nightgown up to her hips. He took her legs and roughly spread them apart leaving her exposed. She was unable to fight him or stop him.

He dropped his cloak to the floor and she could see he wore nothing beneath the cloak. When the cloak was removed it was clear to see he was obviously aroused. Without a doubt she now knew his intentions toward her. She tried to scream, to beg for him to leave her alone, but no sound came out.

At this point he climbed on top of her mounting her. She was unable to move or to fight him off. It was as though she was restrained. She felt pain as he roughly entered her and thrust himself inside her.

The other alien who had told her he had always been with her walked over to her head and placed his hands on the sides of her head. At his touch the pain ceased but the terror did not.

As he pulled out of her she could feel his semen run down her thigh. He climbed off her and looked down at her. He ripped her nightgown and it fell open exposing her breasts.

As she watched in fear wondering what he would do next he shape-shifted yet again. He changed into a Reptilian with lizard eyes and skin with wart like bumps that resembled that of a frog.

He bent over her touching her breast running his claw like hand down the length of her from her breast to between her legs. He bent over and flicked his lizard-like tongue licking her breast.

After he finished with her he left the room. The other alien who had held her head helped her up off the table.

She dropped to the floor and sobbed. She had just this evening made love with her fiance, a true act of love; and then this alien creature came and defiled her.

When T.C. came to he looked through the cabin for Kylie and spotted her outside through the window. She was standing in the snow with nothing on her feet, her nightgown torn hanging loosely from her body. She appeared to be in shock.

He noticed that her nightgown was ripped and lying open exposing her to the elements. One breast was exposed with long claw marks running from her breast to her stomach.

He ran outside and picked her up and carried her in. He wrapped her tightly in a blanket and briskly ran his hands up and down her arms trying to warm her. He led her over to the couch and as quickly as he could with shaking hands stoked the fire. He led her over close to the fire holding her in his arms to warm her up.

She didn't need to say anything. He knew she had been taken.

It was obvious from the evidence of the ripped nightgown, the claw marks, and her catatonic appearance what had happened to her while she was in their custody.

He had actually seen the aliens before they had frozen him in place and he had been helpless to stop them from taking her.

He ran a warm bath and led her to the bathroom. He gently removed her nightgown and noticed the claw like marks on the inside of her thighs and on her breasts. He spotted blood and something else on the inside of her leg, a thick bluish fluid.

He hung his head in despair that he had been unable to stop this violence that had taken place against the one he loved, a woman he cherished.

65

It was over a week before she would let T.C. touch her intimately again. It was their love that finally won out. She couldn't blame him for the alien's actions.

He made tender love to her showing her that theirs was an act of love.

He had called in to work and told them that she had come down with the flu on their trip. It gave her some time to heal before having to face Bidaiari again. He knew that would be difficult, especially since she had explained he could read her thoughts. She couldn't hide anything from him.

He offered for them to both quit their jobs and move away. It was a generous offer. She knew that it wouldn't matter where they were. She knew wherever they were the aliens would find them if they wanted to. She declined his offer but loved him even more for offering.

T.C. had wanted to have their wedding when they returned home, but now he thought it best to give her some time to heal both mentally and physically.

When she returned to work she asked for a private meeting with only Daphne, Alan, and Major Brannan present. She didn't hold back. She told them everything that had been done to her. She said she didn't know if she could work with Bidaiari any longer after what had happened.

Major Brannan had come to think of her as another daughter. Their relationship may have been rough from the beginning but that relationship had changed the night she had been there for Daphne when she was mourning her baby daughter and dead husband. Now he would do anything to protect her as if she were his own.

For a time the major was able to tell the higher-ups that the alien had closed up and had refused to answer any other questions. They agreed to give it a little time, but only a little. The information he held they deemed too important not to pursue.

The stress was too much for Kylie. She had become sick to her stomach and feeling poorly since they returned. Major Brannan agreed to giving her some time off, but warned her that when she returned the higher-ups insisted she begin the questioning again more vigorously to make up for lost time.

66

Every morning and evening Kylie was sick to her stomach and could hardly eat. She woke most nights experiencing terrifying nightmares. She was losing weight she could ill afford to lose. T.C. knew he had to do something to get her mind off what had happened. The stress was making her extremely ill.

He thought about taking her to the Archer's cabin but wanted it to be good memories for her when she went. They planned to go often and he didn't want any of these memories to be connected to the cabin.

He found a bed and breakfast in Utah and made plans for the two of them to spend a week there. She perked up at this idea and agreed to his plan.

The time at the bed and breakfast was just what she needed. She was eating better, getting sick less, and spending time in the fresh air. The views alone made her forget about the stress and relax.

They had gone snow skiing and ice skating and even roasted marshmallows and made s'mores over the fire.

On the last day she admitted she dreaded going back to work, but she knew the work was important and needed to be done.

They decided to go ice skating one more time before they packed up to leave. They skated for about an hour and the color had returned to Kylie's cheeks.

"I'm going to skate over and get our blanket and the thermos of hot chocolate. Want to join me?" T.C. asked.

"You go ahead. I'm going to take a few more laps around the lake before we have to go," Kylie said giving him a kiss before she skated off. He stood and watched her graceful moves for a few minutes with a big smile on his face.

"How did I get so lucky?" he asked himself.

He turned to go to the SUV to get the blanket and hot chocolate when he heard the ice cracking and heard her scream. He turned just as she fell through the ice. He skated to her as fast as he could.

He didn't fear for himself, the only concern he had was for Kylie. He didn't see her head come up or see her try to climb out of the lake. His legs shook as he skated. He was terrified.

He worked his way carefully to the spot where she had gone in knowing if he fell in himself he would be no help to her. Lying on his stomach on the ice he fished around for her looking into the water. He couldn't see her. All he saw was blackness.

Frantically he plunged his arm into the icy water as far as it would reach. Nothing. Had she been swept farther down the lake and was under the ice frantically trying to get out?

Finally reaching around underneath the ice he felt some strands of her hair and reached down and grabbed a handful. He refused to release her hair for fear of her falling deeper or being swept under the ice out of his reach losing her entirely. With his other arm he reached in and after several attempts was able to grab her under her arm.

He knew he had to work quickly. His hands were going numb, and he feared she would go into hypothermic shock if she hadn't already.

He struggled to pull her up while lying on his stomach almost falling into the lake himself. He reached down as far as he could to drag her lifeless body out of the ice. Between the dead weight and the additional weight of the water and her ice skates it was rough going bringing her to the surface.

He was going on pure adrenaline at this point. He reached down for every bit of strength he had and finally pulled her on top of the ice.

He quickly checked to see if she was breathing. She was but her heartbeat was faint. He quickly took his own jacket off and wrapped her in it and with her in his arms skated to the edge of the lake.

He pulled her ice skates off and then his own dropping them in the snow. He ran for the SUV. He gently placed her on the front seat lying the seat back and turned the heater on full blast.

He ran to the back of the SUV for the blanket. He wrapped her tightly in the blanket like a cocoon. The frigid water was running off her pooling by her feet and soaking the seat she was on.

He hadn't even noticed his own teeth were chattering and he was shaking from head to toe. His feet in socks only were numb to any feeling.

He jumped behind the wheel heading for the nearest hospital which was quite a distance away. He called 911 and told them to send an ambulance and to meet him along the way.

His tires lost grip a few times and he almost lost control. He had a close call with a tree, backed up, and regained traction while constantly searching the road for the ambulance.

A police car with flashing lights came up behind him and then pulled up beside his vehicle and motioned for him to follow. The police car turned on it's sirens and traveled as fast as he could considering the road conditions with T.C. right behind him. He was giving him a police escort to the hospital or until the ambulance reached them, whichever came first.

He reached over and rubbed Kylie's arms briskly with one hand while steering with the other. He checked to be sure the heater vents were aimed at her to warm her. She was so cold. She was turning blue before his eyes.

Not normally a praying man he begged God to spare her life.

Would she make it to the hospital? Would she survive this?

67

The ambulance caught up to them after a few miles. He jumped out of the SUV and climbed into the back of the ambulance with her in his arms.

One of the policemen in the car who had escorted them to this point stepped into the ambulance and draped a blanket around T.C.'s shoulders before leaving him and Kylie in the care of the EMTs.

The other policeman told him he would be sure his SUV was driven to the hospital. He would leave the keys and a note of where it was parked with the nurse in the emergency room. It was a thoughtful gesture,, but all T.C. had on his mind was if Kylie would survive.

The paramedic had rapidly cut off Kylie's drenched clothing and had already begun treating her. One EMT wrapped her in heat packs and heated blankets while the other began running an IV with warm fluids to warm her from the inside. One of the EMTs checked her heart for cardiac arrest and began monitoring her vitals.

She still hadn't regained consciousness. Once they had her stabilized with sirens running they raced for the hospital.

One of the EMTs then turned to T.C. to warm him up. He had been completely unaware of how cold he was. The EMT removed the blanket the policeman had been kind enough to leave with him long enough for T.C. to strip out of his soaked clothes.

The EMT gave him a dry, warmed blanket and thick socks. His hands shook with cold and fear. He needed help putting the socks on.

The EMT placed heat packs in strategic areas of his body as he had done to Kylie to warm him up so he didn't suffer the same fate.

He then turned his attention back to Kylie to keep an eye on her vitals.

T.C. never for a moment took his eyes off her. He watched the care the paramedic was giving her and knew until they arrived at the hospital there was nothing more that could be done for her.

After arriving at the emergency room Kylie was whisked away on a gurney, and T.C. was led to another room. A doctor checked him out. All the while his mind was on Kylie and praying she had recovered consciousness and would survive this.

A compassionate nurse handed him some scrubs and a pair of crocs to wear and told him while he dressed she would see if she could find out how his wife was doing. He didn't correct her.

T.C. paced the halls while the doctors examined and treated her. Code Blue had been called and there was an entire team working on her.

Whenever a nurse went by he attempted to get some answers. One sympathetic nurse finally brought him a cup of coffee. He held it more for warmth than to drink.

It all finally caught up with him and he got the shakes. He set the coffee cup down before he spilled it.

He was led to a chair in the hall where he could keep a watchful eye on the door to Kylie's room. He refused to leave the area where they were treating her.

Every time a doctor or nurse walked in or out he got a glimpse inside the room and could see them working on her. Several IV bags hung by dripping their miracle drugs into her. Would they be enough to save her life? How long had it been? What was taking so long?

He started to call Taylor to tell him what had happened when a doctor came out of the room looking exhausted. He pulled his mask down from his face to speak to T.C.

T.C. turned his phone off and stood looking at the doctor expectantly asking, "How is she?"

The doctor said, "She's going to be alright. You got her out of the water and emergency aid quickly and saved her life by doing so. She's not completely out of the woods yet, but she's stable. We'll know more within the next 24 hours. We're going to admit her to ICU, but she's holding her own."

T.C.'s tears flowed. "I don't know how to thank you."

"She hasn't lost the baby, but we're going to keep a watch on that. There's still a good chance she could lose it."

T.C.'s head jerked up. "Baby?"

68

Did he just hear that right? Did the doctor say baby?

The doctor looked up, "You didn't know?"

"No," T.C. said.

"It's early in the pregnancy yet, but no promises on if the baby will survive. Your wife however should have a full recovery. It's a good thing she was healthy and has a strong heart."

T.C. thought about what he said about having a strong heart and the information Kylie had shared with him about the aliens fixing her heart when she was a child.

"Does she know? About the baby, I mean?" T.C. asked the doctor.

The doctor answered, "She's under sedation now and she was unconscious when she was brought in, so if she didn't know before no one has told her."

"Can I ask you not to say anything until she has time to recover?" T.C. asked.

The doctor answered, "I'm sorry but she'll need to know when she comes to. She'll need to be examined again soon to see how the baby's doing. There's a good chance she'll lose the baby. You'll need to tell her as soon as possible."

The doctor started to walk away. T.C. called out, "Doctor, how far along is she?"

T.C.'s fists were clenched. He knew the answer to this question could destroy Kylie. If there was even the slightest chance the baby was a result of her encounter with the alien he didn't know what she'd do.

"I would estimate no more than four or five weeks, but you would get a more definitive answer from the OB/GYN."

T.C. quickly calculated and realized that time frame was right about the time when they had been at the cabin when she had been violated by the shape-shifter. If she was indeed five weeks along it was before, but at four weeks it was at the time when they were at the cabin. In that case, it could be his or the aliens.

How was Kylie going to take this news? He knew she would immediately start calculating the time just as he had.

His mind raced with thoughts of what they would do if they discovered the baby was the aliens. How could they know for sure? Would she want to abort it? How did he feel about that?

Would it be alien or human? How would he handle it if indeed it turned out the baby wasn't his? He honestly didn't know.

"Please Lord," T.C. prayed. "Please let this child be a product of our love and not a result of her being forced upon by the alien. She deserves this happiness."

When Kylie woke up T.C. was sleeping in a chair by her side holding her hand. Before he even had an opportunity to tell her she was pregnant, the OB/GYN doctor briskly walked in and began talking about the baby.

To say Kylie freaked over the news would be an understatement. The nurses rushed in and had to sedate her.

69

Kylie and T.C. exchanged their vows once they returned to Vegas not wanting to delay it any longer. She had still been recovering from the accident so they had a small outdoor ceremony at Black Canyon where they had gone kayaking on their first date. It was the perfect wedding for them.

What was important to them was that they were husband and wife, not the ceremony itself.

Daphne had proved herself as an invaluable friend and had arranged everything for the wedding while Kylie was recuperating.

They had family and a few close friends in attendance. The Archers had come, Gordon her young next door neighbor from Phoenix had served as the ring bearer, Olivia, Major Brannan, Alan, and Daphne, while T.C. had his brother, a few friends, and his co-pilot in attendance.

Her first day back to work her first priority as far as Kylie was concerned was a meeting with Bidaiari to get some much needed answers.

Major Brannan and Daphne stood with Kylie at the door to the adjoining room where Bidaiari was living. They would be watching from the one-way mirror.

"We're right here. If you need us or would prefer for us to be in there with you just give us a signal and we'll be in there in a moment," Major Brannan said.

"Bidaiari's never made any moves to hurt me. I'll be fine," Kylie said.

She took a deep breath before she entered the room where he was being held.

Bidaiari appeared to be pleased to see her. He seemed concerned about her. Between the time spent at the cabin and the bed and breakfast, her stint in the hospital, and her recovery at home she had been gone for about nine weeks.

Bidaiari stood as though to greet her. Immediately he looked at her stomach area and stared. He bowed to her confusing her. He had never done this in the past and it confused her now.

It equally confused Daphne and the major in the other room watching.

"What the hell's he doing?" Daphne asked.

"I'm not sure. It looks like he's bowing. I have no idea why he did that. I wish she would have asked him," the major said.

After what seemed like several minutes Bidaiari spoke to her through his thoughts, 'A new life is within you.'

Kylie said, "Just what kind of life is what I need to know."

She sensed confusion from Bidaiari. Then he seemed to understand.

'It is a human child. The child comes from you and your man.'

"You're quite sure of this?" Kylie asked. She felt relief at what he had told her. One thing Bidaiari never did was lie to her. He either told her the truth or refused to answer.

'It is a beautiful child. A child perfect in every way. Do you want to know the sex of the child?'

"No, I do not. I want," she hesitated for a moment. Kylie needed a little more reassurance. "I need to know," she said. "This is hard to talk about..."

'You wish to know if the child came from the seed of the alien,' Bidaiari said through his thoughts to her. 'You wish to know if it is he who planted his seed in you during the breeding act that made this child.'

"Yes," Kylie said. "One way or the other I have to know. Until I do know, I can't..."

Bidaiari read her conflicted thoughts and seemed puzzled and alarmed by what he was reading from her, 'You would destroy this child? Remove it's existence? Stop it's life force?'

"I don't know," Kylie said truthfully. She could sense Bidaiari's anger, something she had never sensed from him before."My husband and I want children. I don't want a child that comes from an alien, especially one who forced himself on me the way he did. If that were the case I honestly don't know what I would do, but I'm running out of time to make that choice. I have to know. Please Bidaiari, can you tell me without a doubt that this child is from me and my husband?"

'The child belongs to you and your husband. It is yours and his,' Bidaiari said.

Kylie rose to leave and said, "Thank you. I had to know."

After she left when she could no longer read his thoughts Bidaiari opened his mind and thought, 'She doesn't understand. She has been chosen. She is the chosen one. Our future may very well depend on this child. It is the long awaited for child of hope. Under no circumstance can it be destroyed. Everything must be done to assure it's safe passage into this world.'

Daphne had gone out in the hall to meet Kylie. The major stayed behind watching Bidaiari not really trusting him. He noted the countenance of his face had changed after Kylie left.

"What are you up to?" the major thought to himself. "Were you honest with Kylie?"

The major had no idea that Bidaiari could read his thoughts from the other room.

Bidaiari projected his thoughts to the other aliens, 'She is the chosen one! The child must be saved and protected at all costs. It is the child of hope for which we have been waiting for. The child's existence is vital to our survival.'

70

Major Brannan sat in his office that afternoon with the door locked and the lights out. He was deep in thought and troubled.

The alien had known from the moment Kylie had walked in the room that she was pregnant. At just over two months along she wasn't showing any visible signs of the pregnancy. How did he know? And what in the hell was the bowing all about?

When Kylie had asked about whether the child was the aliens or her husbands she didn't catch that Ari evaded answering her question directly. He simply told her the child belonged to her and her husband.

The major had insisted that Kylie tell him word for word how the alien had answered. It was the way he answered that concerned him greatly.

Was he reading more into this? Perhaps. Did he trust the alien? *No! Hell, no!*

Did the alien even know for certain the answer to the question. That was something that truly baffled and concerned him. He was locked up, how would he know? But yet he seemed to know everything that happened to Kylie.

Since he himself couldn't communicate with him he only had Kylie's word to go on. She had clearly believed him as she showed obvious relief when he answered her.

What did the alien mean by his answer? That the child belonged to her and her husband. Did he mean it was theirs to raise or that it was indeed conceived by T.C.? Was it a play on words?

The major went over and over this in his mind contemplating every answer Bidaiari had given.

He didn't know why, but he was even more uneasy now that Kylie was convinced it wasn't the alien's offspring. Perhaps it was because she was so desperate to believe him that the child was that of her and her husband.

Major Brannan wasn't reassured by the way he had answered

her. The answer had seemed evasive, or was that just the way the alien knew how to express himself? He would have preferred a definitive yes or no answer.

Major Brannan stood up, let out a deep sigh and walked over and turned the lights on. He opened his door and told his secretary to call Daphne, Kylie, and Alan in for a meeting.

When they all arrived and settled in Major Brannan said, "We have a dilemma here. The higher-ups are hounding me about the results of your DNA tests."

Alan started to speak but Major Brannan said, "Hold that thought, Alan. Am I correct in the fact that you were unable to determine *beyond the shadow of a doubt* the source or the anomaly of the DNA you tested from Kylie? And please just answer yes or no. I really don't want to hear any details I'll be forced to report to my superiors."

"The source is undetermined," Alan said catching on to where Major Brannan was going with this. "No, it is not *definitive*."

"O.K.," Major Brannan said. "I'm going to go with that. So, I can tell my superiors honestly that there has been no verification of any alien DNA found in Kylie's DNA test, correct?"

"Correct," Alan answered with only a slight hesitation.

"Then that's all they need to know," Major Brannan said. "No further tests need to be done, understood? Perhaps any DNA samples or revealing notes you may have written on the matter should disappear permanently."

Daphne walked over and hugged her father. "You're the best."

"Wait, I'm not through," Major Brannan said. "I think it's best if we don't spread the news of the pregnancy until we absolutely have to."

"I understand," Kylie said.

"I'm not sure you do," Major Brannan said. "I don't want the higher-ups to think due to your DNA issue that the child is something they can have any claim to."

"Claim to?" Kylie said with fear in her voice.

"What I mean by that is, I don't want them to have any reason to request any testing on the child. You've been through enough. You deserve to have a happy, normal pregnancy and love your child and give it a normal life," the major said. "And congratulations by the way."

"Thank you," Kylie said. "For everything."

The major looked at Alan and asked, "Do you understand?"

Alan understood perfectly. What he had discovered was to be kept to himself. Even Kylie would be left in the dark. What he had discovered while she was on leave would be between him and the major only. All evidence and any DNA samples and notes he would need to destroy immediately.

The new samples of her DNA tested since she became pregnant were alarming in the fact that the original anomaly discovered that they believed to be alien in origin had replicated itself.

Did that mean the alien DNA was taking over, reproducing or that it had something to do with the child she was carrying? Could she be carrying the child of an alien and that was causing this new anomaly?

Alan could certainly understand why the major was fearful of others discovering this fact. What it meant nobody could possibly know, but this information Alan was assured would not go beyond him or the major.

These samples taken since her pregnancy also must be destroyed. Kylie must never be allowed to study them for herself.

Kylie deserved some normalcy after all she had gone through. Knowing what he had discovered would serve no purpose to share with others. That knowledge leaking would be harmful to Kylie. He was determined that the knowledge remain contained.

After the others had left the room the major said to an empty room, "God help me and her both if the top brass discover she could possibly be carrying the child of an alien."

71

Kylie had finally begun to relax and stop worrying about who the baby's father was once she had spoken to Bidaiari. She bought a *'What To Expect When You're Expecting'* book, a baby name book, and a pregnancy journal. She was now enjoying the pregnancy as any first time expectant mother should.

T.C. was accompanying Kylie to her first doctor visit. He had been secretly reading up on the subject of pregnancy. If the baby was indeed his, which he still had his doubts about which he kept to himself, then they should be able to hear the heartbeat at this doctor visit.

If the baby wasn't his, then the heartbeat wouldn't be heard for another week or two. Of course even then it could be his, but at that point it could also be from the time with the alien.

T.C. thought to himself, "Please let us hear a heartbeat today and remove this doubt that is burdening me."

Regardless of the answer of who fathered the child he would love and protect Kylie and the baby with every fiber of his being. She deserved nothing less.

Kylie had filled out all the paperwork on her medical history, been weighed in, and had her vitals checked. She sat on the end of the examination table wearing a paper cover swinging her feet back and forth nervous with anticipation.

Today at her first OB visit the doctor would examine her to determine how far along she was and then they would check to see if they could hear a heartbeat.

T.C. tried to reassure himself that even if a heartbeat wasn't detected today it didn't necessarily mean the baby wasn't his. He had after all had numerous occasions to father the child both before and after the time she had been with the alien.

Whatever it was or whoever fathered the child it would be

their child. He would raise it and love it as his own. In moments of weakness however, he couldn't help but to wonder what he would do if the child resembled the reptilian alien. He did his best to believe that it was indeed a human child, a child from him and Kylie as Bidaiari had reassured Kylie it was.

The doctor was giving Kylie a pelvic exam and asked her when her last period was. Kylie gave the date of approximately three weeks before their visit to the cabin. The doctor asked her how sure she was of the date. After the pelvic exam she measured Kylie's abdomen and made notes for her medical records.

"If your calculations are correct we should be able to get a heartbeat today," the doctor said to Kylie and T.C. "Would you like to hear your baby's heartbeat?"

Kylie and T.C. held hands as the doctor ran the fetal Doppler across her abdomen searching for a heartbeat.

T.C. found he was holding his breath while listening to what sounded like a swooshing sound.

"Is that the heartbeat?" T.C. asked.

"No, no heartbeat yet. Perhaps it's too soon," the doctor said unable to find anything.

T.C. looked crestfallen.

"That doesn't mean there's a problem, just that it's too soon. Perhaps you aren't as far along as you thought," the doctor said.

T.C. knew very well what that could mean and so did Kylie. She looked ready to burst into tears as the doctor sat back and started putting the fetal monitor away.

72

"Please," Kylie said barely over a whisper. "Would you try one more time, please. It's important."

The doctor saw the look on Kylie's face. She assumed it was due to her fall into the icy lake and a concern for the baby. The doctor said, "Let's try again just to be sure."

The doctor was about to give up again after finding nothing thinking Kylie wasn't far enough along. Just before the doctor pulled the monitor off her belly the room filled with the sounds of a rapid heartbeat.

Kylie broke out in a big grin and looked at T.C. with a look of sheer joy.

"Sometimes babies like to hide and cause us undue worry," the doctor said.

T.C. felt himself go weak with relief. If they were picking up a heartbeat by this date he was pretty sure the child was his.

"I would estimate at this point that you're nine weeks along," the doctor said. "If you're experiencing morning sickness that shouldn't last much longer. You're almost through the first trimester of your pregnancy."

"That's our baby," Kylie said listening to a strong heartbeat. A tear ran down the side of her face. She reached out for T.C.'s hand and gave it a squeeze.

T.C. felt himself having to fight back tears. This was a day he had looked forward to from the time he knew that Kylie was the woman he wanted to spend his life with.

"Congratulations," the doctor said. "Your baby is about the size of a grape and about an inch long right now. He's constantly moving, but you won't be able to feel him for awhile. You're in good health so I don't foresee any problems."

T.C. picked up on something the doctor said. "He? It's a boy?"

"Just out of habit I say he, but at this date we don't know the sex of the child. If you want to know you can find out when we do an ultrasound when Kylie's about 20 weeks into the pregnancy."

Where in the past weeks Kylie had been torn about how she felt about having the baby she was now all smiles.

She had been reassured by Bidaiari's announcement that the baby came from her and T.C. Now with the heartbeat confirming she was already pregnant at the time she had been with the alien, she could enjoy the pregnancy knowing it was indeed her husband's baby. She had a new outlook and looked forward to the baby's arrival.

Kylie and T.C. went out for lunch after they left the doctor's office. "I'm sorry about how I acted initially," Kylie said over lunch. "I was just so afraid that..."

"I know," T.C. said reaching for her hand. "But the doctor told us today that you're nine weeks along so that should reassure you. That's my baby you're carrying."

73

"I'm so jealous," Daphne said. "Taylor and I are trying for a baby, too."

"Really?" Kylie said grinning. "Oh, Daphne. That would be wonderful."

"Taylor told me if we had a little girl we could name her Emma in honor of the baby I lost. It was a nice gesture on his part, but I think we need a new beginning and a new name for our own child. I hope it happens soon, if not it certainly won't be for lack of trying," Daphne laughed.

"Too much information," Kylie laughed with her friend.

"So how big is the little rascal now?" Daphne asked rubbing Kylie's stomach.

"I'm about three months along now," Kylie answered. "The book says it's about the size of a lime."

"Taylor and I are so proud that you and T.C. asked us to be the godparents," Daphne said. "We'll spoil him or her and protect it with our lives."

"I know you will," Kylie said. "You're a dear friend. Thanks for always being there for me."

"My dad was so touched when you asked him to be the honorary grandfather. Did I tell you when I came over he was looking online at baby stuff?"

"No," Kylie laughed.

That was certainly a different man that the "Winston" she had first met Kylie thought. She knew she could rely on him to protect her. It could have been very different without his help with the higher-ups wanting to run tests due to the claim from Bidaiari of her carrying alien DNA.

She was well aware it was only a matter of time before they discovered she was pregnant. She knew that may just reawaken their interest in her.

74

The major's superiors had sent a new list of questions for Kylie to ask Bidaiari. The questions were on the subject of military installations and of past actions the aliens had carried out which was news to Kylie.

The major walked into the lab where Kylie was deep into her work and looked around to be sure no one else was around to overhear the conversation.

"I've just been informed a few people will be sitting in watching and listening to when you speak to Bidaiari later today. It may be a good idea to go in and give him a heads up and ask him not to discuss anything about the baby and your pregnancy."

"Good idea," Kylie said.

"I know they won't be able to hear or understand what he's portraying to you, but some of them are pretty observant and may pick up on something.

"Any reason they're coming in?" she asked.

"The list of questions are concerning the aliens' intent as far as their visits and about weaponry and I assume this is too important just to get a written report on his response. They may have additional questions they may want to ask depending on how he answers at the time, too," Major Brannan said. "But that's just my assumption."

Kylie went in ahead of time to ask Bidaiari to keep any discussions on the baby and the pregnancy out of this meeting. When she entered the room he stood and bowed. He had begun to bow every time she came in the room, something he never did with anyone else.

She repeated to Bidaiari that she wished to keep the fact that she was expecting a secret from those who came in with their questions.

He seemed puzzled by her request. She explained she preferred the superiors were kept unaware of her pregnancy as long as possible.

She didn't want them to even consider what it may mean for the child to have been passed on the alien DNA.

He reminded her that at any time she wanted a topic kept secret to merely think her thoughts and he would know them. She didn't like to be reminded of that but realized it may prove to be an asset one day.

75

Kylie was all business when she walked into the room where Bidaiari was sitting and waiting. As she entered he stood and bowed. She winced hoping the others hadn't noticed the gesture and wouldn't question her about it.

She projected her thoughts to him to please stop doing this. People would wonder why he had begun bowing to her when he hadn't done so before.

She thought perhaps the aliens honored women who were bringing new life into the world, but this was only a guess on her part.

"Bidaiari, there's some people here today observing and they gave me a list of a few questions they would like me to ask you. They have concerns as to why you and..." she hesitated not knowing what to call them, "your kind, as a lack of what to call you..."

He communicated with her the thought 'Bidairai. They are Bidaiari.'

"Are you saying your people are called Bidairai, not you specifically, but as a group?" Kylie seemed confused by what he was trying to tell her.

'The ones who come to visit are Bidairai, travelers.'

"So Bidairai means travelers? It's not your name or the name of your planet?

'Correct.'

Kylie began to ask the next question but he stopped her wishing to explain further.

'Bidairai is a word we learned in a mountainous region from an old sect of people. It is from one of the oldest languages on this planet. They protected us at one time and promised to always do so. It is in honor of them and fitting to what we are, travelers. It is the name appropriate for what we are, though the word is not from my planet.'

When Kylie translated this Daphne began searching on Google to see if she could discover the language or the people he was referring to.

Kylie glanced down at the list and decided she wouldn't necessarily ask the questions in order. Since this topic came up she would stay on the topic. "Can you tell me the name of your planet or it's location?"

'The name would mean nothing to your people. Just because you have a name for something doesn't mean that is how we identify it.'

"I understand," Kylie said. "Please bear with me. I need to repeat your answers so those observing will have the answers to the questions as I ask them." After she translated Bidaiari's answers she paused.

'You may continue with your questions,' Bidairai said.

"What should we call you if Bidairai is more a term for what you do. Is there a name we can call you?"

'Ari is fine. That appears to be easier for your people to pronounce and to remember.'

"O.K., Ari," Kylie smiled remembering how she had first came up with the name Ari.

'I now understand when you people make that movement with your face that it means you are happy.'

"Face?" Kylie asked confused.

Ari reached over and pulled the sides of her mouth upwards. 'Forgive me, but this is not something I am capable of doing. This movement confuses us. We don't understand this feeling that we don't experience. We are curious about it.'

Kylie explained to the people in the other room observing that he was referring to people smiling. He had mentioned this in the past so it must have been something that left an impression on him.

Major Brannan stepped in and whispered in Kylie's ear, "The colonel is requesting that you get back to the questions."

Kylie said looking towards the mirror, "Colonel, I understand you're anxious to get to the questions, but Ari has agreed to answer questions but in return he may have questions of his own. He is interested in learning about us and our ways as we are about him and his people. We are learning together. It helps us in communicating with one another."

The colonel was sputtering mad that a civilian, regardless of her doctor status, had dared speak to him in such a manner. And in front of other officers no less.

"Ari, can you tell me where your planet is located?"

'Our planet was in a different solar system from that of yours. Light years away. Our planet no longer exists.'

Kylie translated his answer to the others listening in.

"Can you tell me why you and others like you are visiting our planet?"

'Your planet is similar to what our planet had been like. We find it compatible.'

Kylie knew this answer was going to raise some new concerns and questions. "What is the purpose of visiting here? There must be a reason for your visits?"

'Me and others like me, the other Bidairai, do as we are told. We come to observe and learn.'

Major Brannan came in and handed her another note with a question they would like answered immediately.

"Ari, as I'm sure you can understand there are some who are concerned about the reasons for your visits. Are there plans for those of your kind to make your home on this planet?"

'I can't answer that. I do not have that knowledge.'

Kylie seemed frustrated by his answer. "You've told me in the past that you all know what the others know, so I find it hard to believe you don't know the reason for the visits or what they have planned. Can you please..."

'I know what the others of my kind know. There are other kinds who give us the orders. We follow their orders.'

"What have your orders been as far as coming here?"

'To observe and learn.'

Kylie decided to slip in a few questions of her own. "You not only observe, but there are times people here on earth are abducted, taken aboard your spacecraft. What is the purpose for this?"

'To observe and learn....in cases like yours when there are medical problems we sometimes fix them. Our knowledge is far advanced from the knowledge of humans. We do this as a courtesy for helping us. In return some of our alien DNA is implanted into the person treated. It benefits us both.'

She left the part out about fixing her and implanting DNA but translated the rest of his thoughts.

The major came in and handed her a phone. "The colonel would like to be able to speak to you personally."

"Just a moment, Ari." She held the phone to her ear and listened.

The colonel wasn't convinced she had just translated everything Ari had conveyed to her. The colonel said she listened to his response for a much longer time than it took for her to convey his message. He wanted to know if she was telling them everything.

Kylie assured him that Ari just took a little longer to think about the answer and translate.

The colonel then told her he wanted to come in and see if he could communicate with the alien himself. He had some questions he wanted addressed immediately and directly.

"Would it be alright if someone else joined us, Ari?"

'No more questions.'

When the colonel heard the response he came in anyway.

Ari looked directly at Kylie and said, 'If they want more answers in the future, they will ask them through you only.'

Kylie translated his response, furious that the colonel had barged in like he had.

The colonel knew he had to back down if he wanted any information in the future. He wasn't used to others telling him what to do or deciding how things would be done, but in this case he knew he didn't want to blow it. "Can you ask him when we can return with more questions?"

Ari was finished. He chose not to respond to the colonel or to Kylie.

"He isn't responding. I guess we're done here Colonel Hazard, that is unless you'd like to try waterboarding our 'guest' to try to get more answers *directly* out of him."

She stormed out of the room.

211

76

The higher-ups had been coming twice a week for the question answer sessions with Ari.

Kylie was over four and a half months along when after one of the sessions she saw Colonel Hazard and Lieutenant Colonel Ward confront Major Brannon outside the adjoining room to where Ari was held.

She wasn't sure what that was about but she went back to the lab to continue her work.

There was something about the way the colonel had looked at her that gave Kylie some concern. Was it that he wasn't happy the questions weren't going fast enough? She was doing all she could do.

Bidaiari was only willing to be pushed so far in a day. The questions seemed draining to him. She had to wonder if he felt he was betraying his own kind by even answering the questions.

After Colonel Hazard and Lieutenant Colonel Ward left, Major Brannan called Daphne into his office for a private meeting.

"The only reason I'm not including Kylie in this meeting is because of her pregnancy. I don't want to upset her. Well, actually that's what the meeting was about."

Daphne said, "What was the meeting about? Kylie?"

"Colonel Hazard wanted to know if she was pregnant. I evaded his question playing dumb. I don't know if he bought it or not, but I know when he left he wasn't satisfied with my answer," Major Brannan said.

"How did you answer him?" Daphne asked.

"I said I'm sure she would tell me if she was if she thought it was any of my business," he said. "I was trying to make a point."

"Why would he care if she was pregnant or not? She's still doing her job," Daphne said.

"I know," the major said. "I'm deeply concerned about this situation. My biggest fear is that it's due to the fact of her having alien DNA."

"That was never proven," Daphne said.

Her father looked at her.

"Oh," Daphne said in a subdued manner. "Does Kylie know?"

"No," her father answered. "And let's keep it that way. The only other one who knows is Alan, and I trust him to keep it to himself. And you damn well better do the same if you want to protect your friend and sister-in-law."

"You can certainly trust me," Daphne said. "She's my best friend. I only want what's best for her and her baby."

"I do trust you," he said. "Who I don't trust is that Lieutenant Colonel Ward. He's liable to keep pushing the colonel about this, especially when they learn she is indeed pregnant. It's only a matter of time. It isn't something she'll be able to hide for long."

Daphne looked sincerely worried just thinking about what this could mean. She knew it was impossible to fight the government, and in this case they could claim the security of the country as their reasoning behind it.

"We have to warn her," Daphne said. "We have to do something."

"If you recall they wanted to find all the women who have been abducted and claimed to have gotten pregnant by an alien and have the children tested. If he knew Kylie was pregnant, who they already suspect of carrying the alien DNA, they may be even more adamant about testing the baby and Kylie," the major said pacing back and forth.

"She doesn't really show yet. Well, not too much," Daphne said. "She's showing, but she's been able to hide it so far. She won't be able to for much longer though. What are we going to do?"

"I don't want to worry Kylie, but this is a very serious matter. I'm afraid if I let her know she'll act differently around them," the major said.

"Do you really think she's at risk?" Daphne asked. "What should we do?"

"I've been giving it a lot of thought. This is what we need to do..." Major Brannan shared his plan for Kylie's safety with his daughter.

"That's really extreme," Daphne said after he laid out his plan.

"This is an extreme matter," the major said. "It's not something we dare take lightly. The minute we do, her safety and that of the baby is at risk. If you had sat in the meeting and heard them you would know exactly what I'm talking about."

77

Taylor called his brother and insisted they get together, just the two of them for dinner.

Kylie was working late so T.C. was quick to agree. He was tired of eating alone. Taylor said he would do the honors and make dinner himself at his and Daphne's place.

T.C. showed up with Taylor answering the door with an apron wrapped around his waist and tongs in his hand.

T.C. laughed, "She has certainly domesticated you. Actually it suits you well, and I'm happy for the two of you."

Taylor said, "Let's eat, and then I have something to discuss with you. Daphne will be joining us later."

"It'll be good to see Daphne. I don't get to see the two of you enough as it is. Is that steaks cooking on the grill I smell?" T.C. asked as he followed Taylor out to the patio.

After dinner when Daphne explained to T.C. what she and her father feared the lieutenant colonel and colonel's plans may be for Kylie and the baby he turned white as a sheet.

"What do I do?" T.C. said. "Should I just take her and disappear?"

"I think that's exactly what you're eventually going to have to do," a solemn Taylor said.

"Seriously?" T.C. asked in shock. "This is America. How can they just take her and keep her and ..."

"Our biggest fear is they'll kidnap the baby or just demand it taking possession of it claiming national security. If they come prepared for that they'll have the black government standing behind them giving them the right to do so," Daphne said. "If they take Kylie they could make her disappear."

T.C. sat back at the table trying to take it all in.

"I think it's best you don't tell Kylie about it for now or she

215

may give herself away when she sees them. She wears her emotions on her sleeve, and they would catch on that she was on to them. That just may force their hand and push their agenda forward. She'll need to know soon though," Taylor said.

Taylor let that sink in for a minute then continued. "We need to plan this out so when that time comes you're ready to run and go into hiding at a moment's notice. But it's important that you're prepared. We have to plan this so they won't be able to find the two of you."

"I think the only thing delaying them at this point is to be sure Kylie definitely is pregnant before they make their move. Plus, one thing that may hold them up is the fact that she's the only one Bidaiari's communicating with. They need the information he has," Daphne said. "But I don't think we have a lot of time."

"How long do you think we have?" T.C. asked.

"My guess would be a few weeks to a month or two. You probably need to leave in a few weeks before it gets to the point where they'll make a move."

T.C. looked worried sick. Not the evening he had expected to spend with his brother but he was thankful they were looking out for him and Kylie.

"Maybe they'll wait till the baby's born, but that's doubtful. They stand a better chance of getting away with this quietly if they take action before the birth," Daphne said.

"Here's what me and the major have come up with so far..." Taylor said leaning forward and pulling out some papers to go over with T.C.

T.C. was still in shock over this whole revelation, but he knew if he wasn't prepared he stood a good chance of losing both his wife and child.

"O.K.," T.C. said. "These plans need to be infallible. It's not going to be easy to hide from the government. You do realize that."

78

"Tell the Archers hi for me," Kylie said. "I think that's great that you're having Philip take care of your financial planning. Don't forget to take the paperwork with you that I signed, too." Kylie said as she was dressing for work.

"I wish you were going with me," T.C. said. "I don't like leaving you behind."

"I wish I was going, too," Kylie said. "If you wait till next week I could go with you one day."

"I need to get this taken care of. Philip was kind enough to set up time for me at a moment's notice. I wouldn't want to let him down," T.C. said.

"You're right," Kylie said. "Give them my love and tell them I hope to be able to visit soon."

"Stay with Taylor and Daphne tonight, and I'll be back late tomorrow morning," T.C. said.

"I don't know why you think I need to stay with them. I used to live on my own you know," Kylie said smiling at her over-protective husband.

"Humor me," he said. "You weren't pregnant then."

He looked at what she was wearing and said, "You're not wearing that to work are you? Aren't you having the question session with the colonel and Bidaiari today? That dress is a bit too revealing. You should wear something looser to hide your baby bump."

Kylie looked in the mirror and pressed her dress up against her belly and stood sideways smiling at her bulging belly. "I've really popped out the last few weeks, haven't I? I won't be able to hide my pregnancy much longer. I'm definitely showing."

Kylie took the dress off without questioning him about it and he walked over to her closet and pulled out a dress that would hide the pregnancy a little better. "Here, this is better. I don't want that dirty old man ogling you."

Kylie laughed, "I doubt he would be turned on by a pregnant woman."

"I think in this case you'd be surprised," T.C. said.

He watched her step into the dress and back up for him to zip her up. He noticed it wasn't as loose as it had been and so did she.

"I'm proud of my baby bump," Kylie said gently rubbing her belly. "I'm looking forward to the day I can share the news and not worry about hiding it."

She was definitely at the point where her pregnancy was obvious. Normally he would have been proud of that fact, but now it only made him realize they needed to step up their plans.

She turned around and he ran his hands over her pregnant belly. "I love the fact that you're carrying my child." He stepped back admiring her.

She was even more beautiful than ever. Who ever said pregnant women weren't sexy was just plain crazy.

"I'd better get going if I'm going to make it to the Archers by the time I told them I'd be there," he said.

Kylie wrapped her arms around him holding him tight. "This will be our first night away from each other since we've been married. Just don't be late tomorrow. Remember, we have an appointment for our ultrasound."

"How could I forget," T.C. said. "Kylie, I hope you know how much I love you. I'd do anything for you."

"I know," she said. She patted him on the rear and said, "You better get going."

79

The meeting with the colonel had been canceled and rescheduled for two weeks later.

Major Brannan came to Kylie and said, "I think it's best if we go ahead and continue with the question session with Bidaiari. We still have questions from the list they gave us we haven't asked him yet. They can always catch up by watching the videos of the meeting between you and Bidaiari."

"That's fine with me," Kylie said. "I'm running out of time if they have a lot of questions left. I'll be giving birth in four months, so we need to get these questions asked while we can."

Major Brannan thought to himself, You're absolutely right. You are definitely running out of time.

He made a mental note to himself to go over the map and plans with Daphne before the end of the day.

The discussion that day with Ari was about the timing of when the aliens first began visiting and why then, how they discovered planet earth was compatible to them, and what that meant exactly as far as their future plans.

Kylie felt he was much more open to answering these difficult questions with no outsiders observing from the other room, but today he seemed nervous and upset. She asked him if there was something bothering him.

'You are in danger,' Bidaiari said. 'The others who bring the questions have plans for you, bad plans.'

Kylie was clearly upset by this declaration and asked him, "What kind of plans, Ari? How do you know this?"

'I will tell you when I have the answers. Soon you must leave this place.'

Kylie didn't wait to see the major and Daphne when she was finished with the questions. She went and sat in one of the lounges where she could be quiet and alone with her thoughts. What did Bidaiari mean by his warning to her?

Kylie got up and went to the major's office to relay the information Bidaiari had given her but he wasn't in his office.

Major Brannan and Daphne were sitting in a video viewing room going back over the video of the meeting discussing it's importance.

"Oh no," Daphne said. "Have you noticed what Kylie's doing? Go back a bit."

"See there." They watched another two minutes of video, "and there she did it again," Daphne said pointing.

"Did what?" her father asked. "All I see her doing is, oh..."

"That's what pregnant women do. They rub or cradle their belly. It's a protective, loving gesture, but anyone who's been around a pregnant woman may pick up on that," Daphne said. "Plus it makes it very evident that she's pregnant."

"I remember you doing the same thing when you were pregnant with Emma. Not only that, but see here," the major stopped the video at a certain point, "she seems visibly upset by something Ari has said to her. We need to find out what it was," the major said.

"We can't chance that the colonel or lieutenant colonel won't notice. We're out of time, aren't we?" Daphne asked.

"You better call her in. We need to prepare her," the major said.

"Not while T.C. is gone. She's going to need him for comfort hearing something like this," Daphne said.

"Only until T.C. gets back tomorrow then. Make plans to get together with the two of them tomorrow and go over everything. We don't dare wait any longer," the major said. He only hoped they hadn't waited too long already.

Kylie was going over the answers Bidaiari had given her at their question answer session that day.

"I think today was one of our most informative sessions, don't you," Kylie asked.

"Yes, it was," the major said watching Kylie gently rub her belly. "The general will be anxious to see the video."

Before the major asked Kylie about what Ari had said that had upset her she told him.

The major listened and tried to reassure her that he would keep an eye and an ear open and let her know if there was something to be concerned about."

Kylie stood to go and the major could clearly see her lab coat was tight and exposed her pregnant belly.

"I'm glad the colonel won't be coming for another two weeks. I know he already suspects you're pregnant, but I think you're past the point of being able to cover it up."

"Does it really matter if he knows?" Kylie asked innocently.

She would soon find out that it mattered very much.

80

Disclosure agreement or not and the threat of jail was nothing compared to the threat of losing his wife and child, so he told the Archers everything. They were already aware of Kylie's alien abductions but were shocked to hear about an alien being held at Area 51.

They hadn't even known where Kylie worked for sure, but they had suspected it considering the location and the secrecy involved. Working with an alien, now that was something they had never considered.

When T.C. got to the part of the alien sexual encounter Pilar burst into tears. "She's such a loving, kind person. Why did that have to happen to her?" She wiped her tears and asked, "I don't mean to be insensitive, but could the baby be the aliens?"

T.C. said, "I've asked myself the same thing for the last few months. I don't think so because of the timing, but when the doctor asked her if she was sure about the timing of her last period it made me wonder if perhaps the time wasn't as accurate as we thought. The timing is very close. I don't think so, but it's entirely possible."

"Would you be able to tell?" Philip asked.

"You mean by looking at it?" T.C. asked.

"Yeah, or take any kind of lab work," he answered.

"Kylie has taken extensive lab work on herself in hopes of ruling out her having alien DNA and was unable to find anything conclusive. But like she said, what did she have to compare it to. It's not like she's ever studied alien DNA before. I'm sure she'll do the same on the baby once it arrives."

"What about after the birth? Would the baby look like an alien?" Philip asked. "If it isn't yours, I mean."

"For crying out loud, Philip. They have enough to worry about. Please don't add to his concerns."

"You're right, I apologize for my insensitivity," Philip said.

"This is just a bit out of the norm."

"You're only saying what all of us have wondered ourselves," T.C. said. "Kylie said some of the aliens resembled humans. Other than the Oriental look to the eyes she said she may not have even known they were alien. Others she said looked to be of a Nordic ancestry. She said they appeared human to the point that if someone encountered them on the street they would never suspect anything."

"But you said the alien who had intercourse with her..." Pilar couldn't finish her thought.

"Yeah, he was a shape-shifter. In his true form he was Reptilian," T.C. said. "If the baby was born and resembled that, honestly I don't know what..."

Pilar took him in her arms and said, "Let's enjoy the pregnancy as much as possible and not borrow trouble. Speaking as a doctor, our bodies have a way of rejecting something foreign. Perhaps if it had come from the alien that's what would have happened, so that could be a good sign."

81

The three of them sat up all night making plans for the couple's new life. While T.C. was with the Archers Kylie was enjoying the evening with Daphne and Taylor. She was blissfully unaware of the imminent change in her life.

After a time Philip excused himself and made a phone call. T.C. could hear him raise his voice a few times but seemed calm when he returned.

"The good thing about the cabin is there is absolutely no way to trace it to us even if they came looking for her through us. The fact that it's on the Hualapi Indian Reservation ownership must remain in the native American's hands, so while it has been turned over to us for our exclusive use the ownership remains in the original owner's name on paper. No one other than our son knows about it."

"And the shaman and midwife," Philip interrupted.

"True, but you can be assured the Hualapi people won't speak to any government agent," Pilar said.

"It sounds like we'll be safe there at least until after the baby's born," T.C. said. "That had been a big concern, where we would go until after the baby was born and what to do about the birth. I'll have to tell Kylie as soon as I get back. So far she's been kept in the dark. I think at this point she needs to be aware."

"It won't be what she had originally planned. She'll have to have a home birth, but I don't foresee any problems," Pilar said.

"I don't know how Kylie's going to take the news of having to deliver the baby in the cabin. The major already warned me that we would be discovered immediately if we turned up at a hospital," T.C. said. "I have to admit I'm uneasy about it myself. I'm just thankful you'll be there to deliver the baby."

"I'll be there for the birth, but I think it would be unsafe for us to visit before then just in case we're being watched. The midwife will take good care of her up till the birth and report to me how she's doing," Pilar said.

"The cabin is on such a large piece of land you won't have to worry about running into anybody," Philip said.

"I'll arrange for the midwife to bring groceries every week. She can check on Kylie while she's there and in case of emergency she's close by," Pilar said.

For hours they made plans from Philip transferring their money to offshore accounts. He planned to move the money around until it was untraceable. Eventually it would be changed over to their new names and moved yet again.

The Archer's son Paul who was a computer genius had agreed to make them a few false identifications and supply them with passports and a past history in their new names.

They would at least initially move a few times and change names and identities to make their trail harder to find.

T.C. gave the Archers unopened, prepaid phones he had purchased just for emergency contact.

"Don't delay in calling us when the time comes for the birth. We're about an hours drive away and just in case we're being followed we would have to lose them before we came," Philip said.

"It isn't ideal for a first pregnancy, but Kylie's in excellent shape. I don't foresee her having any problems in childbirth," Pilar said. "She's been under a doctor's care for the first half of her pregnancy, so that's a plus. The midwife has delivered dozens of babies on the reservation. She'll give her good care. She's a little unorthodox, but she's very good at what she does."

They left nothing to chance and made extensive plans. They knew it wasn't amateurs that would be searching for them, so there was no room for error.

They were outside on the porch saying good-bye to T.C. All three of them had heavy hearts and a lot on their minds.

"I can't believe something like this could happen in the United States," Pilar said as she hugged T.C. as he was preparing to leave. "This should be a time of joy for the two of you."

Philip said, "Don't think you're doing Kylie any favors by

leaving her in the dark too long. She needs to know so she can have time to prepare mentally."

"She's strong. She'll handle it," Pilar said. "I feel bad you having to leave your twin brother and everyone behind. There's no telling how long you'll need to go in hiding."

"You may never be able to come back, at least as Kylie and T.C. Tanner. Have you considered what that means as far as family is concerned?" Philip asked.

"Yeah, I know it won't be easy. It's tearing me up. I think once we change our identities that's who we'll have to be for the rest of our lives if we wish to remain safe and out of their reach. Taylor and Daphne are talking about joining us in a few years once we're at the point where we can settle in one place," T.C. said.

"Don't ever let down your guards. And don't think for a minute that wherever you are that they'll lose interest in the child. I would suggest you leave the country as soon after the baby is born as possible for your own safety," Philip said.

"You should be able to travel safely by the time the baby is about six weeks to two months," Pilar said.

"Getting out of the country you need to be very careful. We'll work on that. For now we just need to assure you're safe until the baby comes," Philip said.

Pilar had also given him directions and keys to use her great-aunt's home in the south of France when they were on the run. She had passed away and left the home to Pilar. She hadn't changed it into her name yet either, so it was another place they could go for a time that would be untraceable.

"The midwife will get word to us once you arrive," Pilar said. "I'll make sure the place is stocked with food and cleaned up before you arrive."

"One more thing," T.C. said pulling a folded piece of paper out of his pocket. "Kylie had these items on a list to order on Amazon for the baby. Could you order the things you think we'll need from the money from one of our accounts? I know it's a lot to ask but I want her to have the things she wants for the baby. I don't want this situation to be any harder for her than it already is."

"I'll do that. I'll find a way so it doesn't come in my name where they can trace it back later when they're looking for you," Pilar said. "Don't worry. By the time you arrive at the cabin everything should be in place."

"Thank you seems inadequate," T.C. said.

"Vaya con Dios. God be with you," Pilar said.

They stood on the porch and watched as he drove away.

82

Kylie stood with her hand at the door to the medical center. Before pulling the door open she looked at T.C. and said, "Sex or no sex?"

He reached down and nuzzled in her neck and said, "I'll never say no to sex with you, my love."

Kylie laughed and said, "You know what I mean. Do we want to find out the sex of the baby? They should be able to tell us today."

T.C. said, "I'll go with whatever you decide. I'm a little old-fashioned. I think I'd like to find out at the birth. If you really want to find out today though; that's fine with me."

Kylie opened the door and walked in. Looking back at T.C. she said, "Let's wait. It doesn't matter to me whether it's a boy or girl. I just want a healthy baby."

"And a human one," T.C. said quietly as she walked up to the registration desk to sign in.

A woman sitting in a chair looking at a magazine must have overheard him and looked at him giving him a strange look.

Kylie came back and had just sat down next to him when a nurse opened the door that led to the examination rooms and called out, "Kylie Tanner."

The nurse told her to lay back on the table and the diagnostic radiologist would be right with her.

Kylie sat at the end of the table and gently laid down. "I've been so excited about having this done. We'll be able to see the image of our baby. It makes it seem so much more real."

T.C. looked at her protruding belly and said, "Yeah, it's real alright. Looks like a cantaloupe in there."

"It'll resemble a watermelon by the time I'm ready to give birth," Kylie said gently rubbing her belly.

A young woman walked in and introduced herself as Jenny the radiologist who would be performing the ultrasound.

"Is this your first baby?" Jenny asked as she pulled Kylie's top up exposing her protruding belly.

"Yes, this is our first," Kylie said.

The radiologist rubbed a gel across Kylie's abdomen. "I know that's cold, sorry about that."

She moved a wand type instrument across Kylie's belly. "How far along are you?"

"Twenty-two weeks," Kylie answered. She was watching the monitor where the image of their baby appeared.

T.C. walked closer to the monitor. He hadn't known what to expect. He was amazed that you could clearly see the outline of the baby.

"There's the head," the radiologist said. "And there's his arm."

"It's a boy?" T.C. asked.

She answered, "Oh, sorry; I automatically call it a boy out of habit. Would you like to know the sex of your baby?" she looked for an answer from Kylie.

Kylie looked at T.C. He said, "Whatever you decide."

Kylie said, "No, it's our first. We'll wait. We want to be surprised."

Watching the ultrasound they watched the baby draw it's legs up and put his hand up near it's face. They were amazed at how clearly you could see the baby and all his movements.

"There's just one baby in there, right?" T.C. asked.

Kylie looked surprised by his question and said, "I never even thought about that."

"Why do you ask?" the radiologist asked. "Are you trying to have your entire family all at once or do multiple births run in your family?"

"My husband is a twin," Kylie said. "I never even considered that I might have twins."

"Let's check just to be sure one isn't hiding behind the other one then," she said running the wand all over Kylie's belly. After a few minutes she said, "Nope, just one baby."

"What's that?" T.C. pointed.

"That's the heartbeat," she answered. "Your baby appears to have a strong heartbeat. Looks healthy to me. I don't see any problems."

"You're sure everything looks normal?" T.C. asked.

"Yes, everything's fine," the radiologist said. "Nothing I see to worry about."

She took some measurements and made some notes in the medical records. "I'm going to print out a picture for you all to keep. Your baby's first picture."

They had the rest of the day off and went home. Kylie propped her feet up and rested while T.C. made them lunch.

After lunch they decided to go for a leisurely walk. Kylie knew it was important to exercise and stay in good shape to prepare for the birth. With the hours she was working she was having less opportunity to do so.

"I was wondering up to what point I should keep working," Kylie was saying as they walked. "I can probably work right up till the end, but I was thinking it might be nice for the two of us to have a little time off together before the baby comes. What do you think?"

T.C. knowing she wouldn't be working up till her due date said, "Let's play it by ear and see what happens. The part of the two of us having time together sounds wonderful to me."

He stopped and took her in his arms. As he held her close kissing her he felt a thump in his stomach area.
Kylie drew back putting her hand on her belly and said, "I just felt the baby. The baby just kicked."

"Is that what that was?" T.C. asked with a surprised look on his face. "I felt that, too."

He ran his hand tenderly across her belly. He was more determined than ever to protect them.

83

That afternoon while Kylie was taking a nap Taylor had called T.C. on the prepaid phone and told him they couldn't wait any longer to tell Kylie.

Daphne sensed the colonel and lieutenant colonel had something up their sleeves. They had come in that morning unannounced looking specifically for Kylie. They wouldn't even tell the major what they wanted her for, only that they would be back in two days when Kylie returned to work.

They also informed him they wanted to bring in a few people of their own to try to communicate with the alien.

Daphne thought if they found someone else who could communicate with Ari there would no longer be a need to delay whatever their plans were for Kylie.

What exactly those plans were, she and the major had not been able to uncover. The fact they were being so secretive about it, they knew it wasn't something good.

After Kylie woke up T.C. told her what they feared for her and the baby. Kylie was still in shock trying to take in what T.C. had told her when Daphne and Taylor arrived. The major had thought it was best if he kept his distance from these meetings to give him deniability if needed in the future. As long as the top brass still trusted him they would confide in him so he could continue to help Kylie.

Together they went over all the plans.

"The only problems I foresee is if when the time gets close if they start having you followed. If that happens it may be harder getting you out of town without a tail," Taylor said. "We have you covered, but if they do catch on you may still be followed. You'll have to lose the tail before you start heading in the right direction.

"If that happens we'll need to change vehicles once we lose

them," T.C. said.

Taylor scribbled a note to himself and said, "I'll take care of that. I'll have an extra vehicle left in two or three different areas. You would need to head in one of the areas where one of the cars is stashed until you can lose the tail then quickly switch cars. We have plenty of cars at the garage we can use so no problem there, but if they do follow you you'll definitely want to lead them away from the direction where you're ultimately headed."

Daphne said, "The biggest threat and it's a big one, is if they decide to come and take her from work. In my father's opinion that's what they would do. They wouldn't have to deal with you T.C., and they could quickly whisk her aboard a flight and disappear with her."

Kylie shook her head and said, "I can't believe this is happening. If we lived in Russia or China, yeah; but this is insane."

"Welcome to the new America," Taylor said. "A secret government working behind the scenes oblivious to most Americans. I'll tell you, when I was a Navy Seal I saw some pretty underhanded things our government did all in the name of so-called freedom. That's the excuse they give anyway. In actuality they appear to have their own dark agenda."

"Your training as a Seal is coming in handy in helping us," T.C. said.

"Yeah, well; we shouldn't have to be worried about hiding from our own government, but it is what it is. They can be pretty dangerous so we really need to get this right and be sure the two of you are out of their reach," Taylor said.

"We need to have these plans memorized and ready to implement at a moment's notice. If they attempt to take her at work that's the most dangerous plan and one that is most likely to fail," Daphne said.

"It can't fail. That's why we have to work out all the details now and make sure everyone knows what to do and doesn't falter," Taylor said.

T.C. said, "Since the plans if she's taken from work are the most at risk can we go over those plans again? I want to be sure Kylie knows exactly what to do."

Daphne cleared her throat and said, "T.C. if your plane is on the ground at the time we'll whisk her aboard and then just take off immediately without waiting for clearance. My father has done some research and found that you can safely land at this location." Daphne pulled a map out of her handbag for T.C. to study. "You'll have to fly below radar."

"Steal a jet from the government?" Kylie asked. "Nothing so far is a criminal act, but that would definitely be something they could put us in jail for."

"Jail would be the least of your problems," Taylor piped up. "We need to get you out of their reach. The important thing would be to get you to safety," Taylor said.

T.C. looked at the map and layout of the airport thoroughly to be sure the landing strip was long enough to safely land the Janet Boeing 737-600 he would be flying.

"That should work," T.C. said. "I can do this."

"If that's the route you have to take a car will be left there for you," Daphne said. "From there you'd have to drive to pick up the next car Taylor's going to arrange to leave for you in case the first one is identified by someone who's seen it parked there."

The thought of T.C. having to steal a jet, a government owned jet no less, went against everything she believed in. But then so did being kidnapped and having her baby taken from her by that same government.

"And what if I'm not flying that day or if I'm in the air or..." T.C. said.

Daphne said, "As a last resort we'll arrange to get her through the tunnels under Area 51 and out that way."

"What!" T.C. stood up. "That's way too dangerous."

"Like I said, that would be our last resort," Daphne said. "And that option would have the most risks."

"What are the risks, Daphne?" Kylie asked.

"Actually there are several with this scenario," Daphne answered. "The first would be if they come to take you with no warning and they take you into their possession. At that point we haven't figured out a way out of yet. We have to be sure it doesn't get to that point."

"And the other risks?" Kylie asked quietly.

"They could have the building locked down. The other risks are getting lost in the tunnels. My father has secured a map for us in the tunnel for us as he thought..."

"Us?" Kylie asked.

"Us, if it comes to getting you out through the tunnels we have two guards who will be helping us, and of course I'll be going out with you myself," Daphne said.

"That's too risky," Kylie said. "I can't risk them jailing you or the guards for aiding me. I won't have that on my conscience."

"No problems with that. They won't even know I assisted you. Nor will they learn about the guards, but they'll only be able to assist us up to a certain area," Daphne said.

"If there's a map for you to follow to get out that sounds fairly safe. As far as safe goes with this whole scenario," T.C. said.

"Not really," Daphne said. "Those tunnels have been closed off for years. Some areas are radioactive..."

"I won't risk my baby's health," Kylie said.

"You won't be. The radioactive areas are clearly marked and along with the map my dad left an EMF detector. If we venture in an area that's radioactive it will set off an alarm immediately," Daphne said.

"I don't like the sound of that, and if the tunnels have been closed up for years who's to say that they aren't sealed up or that you can even get through," T.C. said.

"That could be an issue in certain areas," Daphne admitted. "Some of the tunnels go nearly a mile underground. There are elaborate underground chambers that fork off in different directions going as far as almost 20 miles from Area 51. One way or another we'll find our way out."

"And then once you find your way out," T.C. said. "You know as well as I do that the ground surrounding Area 51 is littered with motion and thermal detectors. That area is better secured than the White House or Fort Knox."

"That's true," Daphne said.

"There's no way of someone approaching anywhere near the land without being detected. It won't be any different trying to get off the land, especially if they put out an alert to look for her. Those guards aren't your typical rent-a-cops. They're paid to kill if it comes to that. How do you expect to get off the land if you find your way out of the tunnel?" T.C. was clearly worried about this alternative.

"I have a contact who's in charge of a group who visit Area 51 on a regular basis. He'll contact the others. They'll spread out and once we get out of the tunnels and past the fence line they'll get us out quickly," Daphne said.

"No one said it would be easy," Taylor said.

"No, nearly impossible. You still have to get past the monitors and the guards monitoring the area," T.C. said.

"I'm sure at that point they'll be on high alert too with them searching for Kylie. Let's face it, if it gets to that point that's where the danger will be the largest threat," Taylor said.

Daphne said, "The best plan is for you both to leave before it gets to that point."

T.C. said, "What if we just go now. Wouldn't that be best? They don't know at this point that we even suspect them and they wouldn't be expecting us to leave."

"The longer you have to hide in the nearby vicinity the more chance of them finding you before you can get out of the country," Taylor said. "I think we still have a few weeks, but it would be best if you left before that point."

"And how are we going to get out of the country? Surely our passports will be flagged," Kylie said.

"Paul Archer is going to get us new identities and arrange passage out of the country," T.C. told Kylie.

"Paul? Are you sure about that?" Kylie asked.

"I know what you're thinking, he hasn't been able to face you since he was responsible for the death of your parents. Maybe he thinks this is a way to pay you back," T.C. said. "He's agreed to do this."

Daphne said, "My dad should have a better idea of what the colonel has planned when they come next when Kylie's there. They're not going to give up this opportunity to get the answers they desperately need from Bidaiari. That alone will buy you some time."

"Didn't you say they were bringing in others to try to communicate with him?" Taylor asked.

"So far in the past he hasn't communicated with anyone else. So that's probably not a worry," Kylie said. "Besides, he reminded me if I had something to communicate with him that I didn't want others to know I could just come to him and think it and he would know. I'll ask him to refuse to work with the others."

They spoke for hours on the topic. There was no room for error. They knew who they were dealing with.

"Please know, all of you, that I realize how much trouble you've gone to to protect us, me and the baby. You're putting yourselves at risk. And T.C. you're giving up so much. Your family, your livelihood, everything. I can't expect that..." At this point Kylie broke down crying and left the room.

"It's a lot for her to take in at once, and then being pregnant on top of that. It's a damn shame she can't just be happy and enjoy her pregnancy," Daphne said.

"Doesn't make you think too much of our government, that's for damn sure," Taylor said. "When it gets to the point that they think of human life as collateral damage..."

Daphne said, "Enough said. We all need to stay on our toes and be prepared at a moment's notice and be ready to act. Go comfort your wife. We'll let ourselves out," she hugged T.C. as they got up to leave.

The two brothers hugged each other. They had always been so close that it was going to be hard to say good-bye when that time came.

With Kylie not yet being six months along they had thought they still had a few months, but now it appeared things were being moved up.

84

Colonel Hazard arrived at Area 51 along with Lieutenant Colonel Ward and half a dozen other people. The colonel explained to Major Brannan that he would like for each of the people he brought to try to communicate with Ari.

As the major took them down the elevator to the area below where Ari was being kept the colonel explained, "I would also like a few additional questions asked. Perhaps they can go in one at a time asking their questions and see how he'll respond."

"We can certainly try," the major opened the door to the observation room with the one-way mirror and told them all to have a seat.

For most of them it was the first time they had ever laid eyes on an alien, and while they had been briefed for the task at hand it was still shocking to see a living, breathing alien.

Kylie and Daphne were already in the room with him. They had gone ahead to prepare him for the colonel's arrival and to let him know what the colonel had planned as far as trying to find someone else to communicate with Ari.

Ari sent a warning to Kylie that the others had arrived. She let Daphne quietly know so she wouldn't be overheard, "It appears we have company. Ari says the others have arrived."

'Thank you, Ari.' Kylie sent her silent thoughts to Ari.

Kylie was asking Ari questions as though she was continuing her line of questioning without letting on that she knew the others were in the other room.

The colonel barged into the room saying, "I think we can forego that line of questioning for now. Would you and Daphne step out into the hall for a moment, please."

As Kylie was rising from her seat the colonel watched her very carefully. He was trying to determine if he could see if she was indeed pregnant, but in preparation for his arrival she had worn an X-Large lab coat hiding her stomach.

Ari sent his thoughts to Kylie, 'This one is a threat to you.'

Ari was clearly agitated by the colonel's intrusion into the room. He began pacing and looking over his shoulder at the colonel.

The colonel walked over closer and said, "Ari, I would like to speak to you myself. I have a few questions for you."

Ari made a threatening move towards the colonel who quickly backed away. He didn't turn his back on him until he had the door open and left the room.

85

The colonel was furious at Ari's response to him. "That alien is a danger!"

Kylie said, "Colonel, perhaps he feels threatened by your presence. He's never made an aggressive move in the past. You barge in to his space and want him to answer your questions, yet you treat him in a very hostile manner."

As the colonel was speaking to Kylie, Daphne quietly went and joined the others in the adjoining room. She felt it was more important to keep her eyes and ears open when the colonel and lieutenant colonel were around. She sat in the back of the room where she would be unnoticed sitting in the shadows but was still able to hear their conversation.

"Why won't he speak to me or the others? What is it about you that he'll only speak to you? This is totally unacceptable. This is a military matter and we have questions." He directed his question at Kylie.

"It isn't up to me who he chooses to speak with," Kylie answered. "Perhaps he feels your intentions towards him are less than honorable."

The colonel opened the door to the adjoining room and asked one of the young women who had come with him to step out into the hall.

As she did so the colonel said, "You are to take her in the room with him and demand that he speak to her. We can't have him just communicating with you. If something were to happen to you we would be back to square one."

"I'll be glad to take her in there with me," Kylie said. "But as far as who he's willing to speak to, that isn't up to me...or you, for that matter."

The woman held a paper with a few questions the colonel had asked her to try to get answers to. Kylie could see the paper shaking in her hands.

"You needn't be nervous. He's not dangerous," Kylie said.

"The hell he's not," the colonel said clearly disturbed by Ari's reaction to him. "We don't know if he's a threat or not. He could be playing all of us, stringing us along while others of his kind make their plans to annihilate all of us and take over our planet."

Kylie stepped forward and said quietly, "Colonel, he can feel your thoughts even from here. You might want to be careful and try to hide the animosity towards him if you want him to cooperate and answer your questions."

"Get in there. I have several people I plan to send in there today," the colonel angrily stepped back into the room to observe. "We're wasting time."

The woman followed Kylie into the room standing behind her for protection.

"Ari, this is..." She turned around and told the woman, "Sorry, I didn't catch your name. Introduce yourself."

The woman made a tentative step forward and gave him her name. She asked him, "May I ask you a question?"

Ari made a move towards her leaning into her face which terrified the woman making her stumble backwards.

Ari was clearly playing his part well. The woman read off the first question and stared at Ari waiting to see if he would answer.

"Is he saying anything? How can you tell? I don't think he's going to answer me," the woman clearly terrified said.

"No, he's not responding. Why don't you try another question?" Kylie kindly suggested.

She portrayed the message to Ari, 'Good work.'

When the woman got no response from him she was only too happy to leave the room.

Next the colonel sent in a Navy officer who also had no luck with him. After four more attempts the colonel asked for Kylie to step outside.

When she was out in the hall he said, "I believe our alien just doesn't want to work with us today."

"Why don't you give me the questions and let me see if he will answer for me," Kylie said.

Kylie went back inside and sent her thoughts to Ari, 'I believe it's working, but I really need you to give me some good information so he'll realize I'm his only hope to work with you. As long as he believes that I believe I'll be safe.'

'You are not safe,' Ari warned, 'but I will answer what I can.'

As Kylie was reading over the list of questions to ask Ari the lieutenant colonel said to the woman who had first gone in to try to communicate with Ari, "When we have her take the pregnancy test I want you to accompany her to the bathroom."

"Yes, sir," she said.

The lieutenant colonel reached into his bag and pulled out a home pregnancy kit and handed it to the woman.

86

Kylie asked Ari, "What is it that made your kind aware of us on planet earth? Had you visited other planets first, and why the interest in our planet?"

Ari answered, 'We searched through several solar systems in search of other life forms or for a place to make a new home. It was when your people set off atomic bombs when we first became aware of your existence.'

Ari continued with his thoughts, 'At first we thought your planet was disintegrating much as ours had, until we learned it was by your choice that you were destroying your planet.'

Ari appeared sad. Kylie could sense his emotions as well as his thoughts.

'This act was beyond our comprehension. To destroy each other and the place that fed you and that you called home, we do not understand this.'

Kylie felt inclined to tell him neither did she, but knew the military men listening in wouldn't be happy to hear her condemning their acts and siding with the alien so she simply portrayed this thought to Ari.

As Kylie was telling the others in the adjoining room his answer Daphne quietly exited the room while their attention was elsewhere. She stepped into the room as though she had just arrived from upstairs. "Oh, sorry. I thought you all were through in here."

Daphne quickly whispered in Kylie's ear that she would wait for her in the bathroom on the south end of the hall and to come alone. She then said, "Sorry again for interrupting."

Kylie wondering what it was about picked up with the line of questioning where she had left off. "So it was the atomic bombs that brought our existence to your attention?" Kylie asked.

'Before that we were under the impression there was no other life in your solar system.'

"Am I understanding correctly that you could see the explosion of the atomic bombs from where you were?" Kylie asked.

'The atomic bombs broke open the ozone layer causing serious damage. That act affected the world as you know it,' Ari said to her. 'We have been watching your people since then.'

Kylie repeated his answer so the others in the adjoining room would clearly understand.

When Kylie finished speaking Ari said to her, 'We are saddened by the people of your planet destroying your planet from within. One day, you too, will suffer the fate we did in losing our planet if these actions continue. Then perhaps it will be your species who are in danger of survival.'

After that answer the colonel sent in a note telling Kylie to forego the other questions and to ask about their capabilities as far as affecting our weapons.

Kylie read the extensively, detailed note and told Ari she had just a few more questions for the day. She could see he was tiring.

Kylie told him there had been a few incidents back in the 1950's that had occurred at military installations, one in Great Falls, Montana at the Air Force Base and the other only a few miles away that they would like to ask about specifically.

Kylie read directly from the colonel's notes, "'*Several UFO's were observed by both military bases at the same time missile silos were shut down. The procedures required to make the missiles inoperable hadn't been carried out. This occurred once the spacecraft had been sighted. Did your kind have anything to do with shutting down the missile silos?'*"

Ari answered. He leaned close to Kylie and told her, 'We have the capability to stop any aggressive action from your military, from not only killing each other but from destroying the planet. If you don't appreciate and protect your planet, there are others who will.'

At that Ari let her know he was done with their questions.

87

The colonel stood to leave at the end of the question session. He said to the lieutenant colonel, "I need to leave immediately to report this to my superiors."

The others would be flying out separately with the lieutenant colonel. He now stepped forward and said, "Before we leave Dr. Carmichael..."

Kylie spoke up, "It's Dr. Tanner, in case you forgot I was married."

"Yes, it's very confusing with both you and the major's daughters being Dr. Tanner. Anyway, I would like you to take this pregnancy test." The lieutenant colonel looked around and motioned for the woman holding the test kit in her hand to step forward. "Lieutenant Kraft here will accompany you to the ladies rest room."

"Lieutenant Colonel, I think you're out of line. I'm an employee here at Area 51. You're not my boss. I have my right to privacy," Kylie said.

"Actually, you don't," the lieutenant colonel spoke up. "The papers you signed when you began work here..."

Kylie said, "Forget it." She grabbed the pregnancy kit out of the woman's hand and began heading towards the bathroom. Angrily she turned around and said, "All I've done to aid you people and this is how you're going to treat me? Seriously?"

"There's a bathroom right here," the lieutenant colonel yelled at her. "Follow her," he said to Lieutenant Kraft when Kylie continued walking down the hall.

Kylie without turning around said, "That bathroom is out of order. I'll use the one down the hall."

As she opened the door and stepped inside she looked around for Daphne but didn't see her. The door opened behind her and Lieutenant Kraft stepped inside.

"Get out!" Kylie yelled at her pointing at the door. "You can wait outside. It's bad enough what you people are forcing me to do without standing there and watching me."

"I'll just wait right outside the door," Lieutenant Kraft said backing out of the bathroom. "I'm just following orders."

After the lieutenant stepped back into the hall one of the bathroom doors opened and Daphne was standing on top of one of the toilets hunkered down so her feet wouldn't show from below the door. She put her finger to her lips for Kylie to be quiet and motioned for her to hand the pregnancy kit to her.

Daphne took the pregnancy kit and used her urine sample and handed the kit back to Kylie to give to the woman standing outside the door.

After the woman left Kylie paced the hall angrily. Once everyone had entered the elevator and the elevator doors closed she opened the bathroom door and said, "The coast is clear. They're gone."

Daphne came out and said, "I overheard what they planned to do. At least with my urine sample the test will come back negative. It'll buy you a little time before you have to deal with that issue again."

Kylie said, "Thanks." As they walked down the hall she gently put her hand on her stomach as though to protect her child. "I think it's probably time for me and T.C. to leave."

Daphne knew the time they bought with the negative pregnancy test would only buy them a short amount of time. Very soon, there would no longer be any way to deny what would be evident for all to see.

Yes, it was probably best they leave now.

88

Kylie was packing a few items of clothing for both her and T.C. for when they left Vegas. She looked around at their home knowing everything would have to be left behind.

The worse part was T.C. having to leave behind his twin brother. They were so close she knew it wouldn't be easy for him. Material goods she knew could be replaced, but having to leave loved ones behind was tearing them up.

T.C. was in the living room with Taylor who was going over the places where they were leaving cars for them. If they were followed they would have to lose their tail and would need to change cars.

Taylor had arranged for someone to pick up the car they drove so none of the cars would give any indication of the direction they had traveled.

It was Wednesday and they were planning to leave after work Friday evening. They thought that would at least give them the week-end as a head start and there were no plans before then for another session with Ari.

"We'll get those cars in place tomorrow," Taylor said.

"Thanks," T.C. said standing and hugging his brother. "Thank you for everything."

The two brothers cried at the thought of the loss of each other's company. They had always been very close and weren't sure when they would be able to be together again.

89

Kylie went into work for a few hours Thursday morning but was leaving early as she had a doctor's appointment. She knew she would be without a doctor's care for the rest of her pregnancy and wanted one last assurance everything was O.K. with her and the baby.

T.C. had arranged time off to go with her and also had the following day off which would be Kylie's last day. They weren't aware of it at work, but T.C. wouldn't be returning to work at Area 51. He would bring their car into the garage and have it packed and ready to go. They would be leaving this week-end.

The closer the time came to their leaving the more frightened T.C. was every time Kylie had to go in to work or was out of his sight.

Another session with Ari wasn't scheduled until the following Tuesday. By that time they should safely be at the cabin with no trail left behind of where they had gone.

The major would tell them only that Kylie had called in sick and perhaps they could postpone the meeting with Ari buying them even more time before it was discovered they were gone.

After her medical appointment T.C. tried to convince her to call in and take the rest of the day off considering she would only be working a couple hours anyway. Kylie thought since she only had another day she needed to go back to wrap up a few projects and to tell Ari good-bye. She felt she owed him that.

When she arrived back at her lab the major had left a message for her to come to his office immediately. He had been frantically trying to call her to tell her not to come back in but had been unable to reach her. Both Kylie and T.C. had turned their phones off when they went in for the doctor's visit and had forgotten to turn their phones back on.

When she arrived he told her to come in and close the door. Daphne had just arrived and was walking in the door behind her.

The major said, "I heard that the major and lieutenant colonel are coming in this afternoon. It appears your pregnancy test came back positive."

90

"What?" Daphne said. "That can't be right. I took the test for her myself. Maybe they're trying to trick her into telling them something."

The major opened a drawer and said, "Just to be sure..." he pulled out a pregnancy kit and handed it to Daphne. "Go take another test."

Five minutes later Daphne came out beaming from ear to ear. "You're going to be a grandpa. Taylor and I are going to have a baby. Oh my God, I can't believe it. I didn't even suspect...Oh Kylie, I'm so sorry. I thought I was helping you and..."

"It's O.K.," Kylie said. "I think I'm beyond hiding it at this point anyway. Congratulations, I'm so happy for you and Taylor both."

The major smiled and got up and congratulated her hugging her. He quickly broke away and said, "I don't want to put a damper on your good news. I can't tell you how thrilled I am for you, but right now we have to figure out why they're coming now and not just waiting until Tuesday."

"Obviously they now think the test results confirm what they were already thinking," Kylie said. "But after bringing in several people to try to communicate with Bidaiari and being unsuccessful they'll have to realize I'm their only hope in getting the answers they seem to so desperately want."

The major's secretary stuck her head in the doorway and said, "You said to let you know when I heard anything new. The major's plane has just landed."

"You two head out of here until I see him and see what I can find out," the major said. "And leave your phone's on!"

As they walked down the hall Kylie squeezed Daphne's hand and said, "I'm so happy for you both."

"Don't tell T.C. yet," Daphne said. "I'll tell Taylor tonight. I don't want to tell him over the phone, but I think you better call

T.C. and let him know the major is here and knows you're pregnant."

"O.K., I'm going to go downstairs and see if Bidaiari has picked up on anything," Kylie said. "That'll give me a chance to tell him good-bye."

Daphne said, "I'll meet you down there in about ten or fifteen minutes. We can wait there for Dad's call to give us a heads up."

Kylie texted T.C. as she was about to step into the elevator and go downstairs. She knew she wouldn't have a signal long enough to call him.

When she arrived she found Bidaiari greatly agitated and relieved to see her. 'They're here. You need to leave.' Bidaiari said. 'Go. Now.'

"You mean the colonel?" Kylie asked.

'Yes, and the other one.'

"I need to leave right now?" Kylie asked, believing Bidaiari knew things she and the others had no way of knowing.

'You need to leave through the tunnels. If you need me concentrate hard. I will project my thoughts to you but you will be at a distance. Know you are capable of this. You must do this.'

Kylie looked scared. The time had come. They were so close to leaving, just days away and now they had discovered she was carrying a child and were coming for her.

If only she would have listened to T.C. and stayed home. Now it was too late. She knew Bidaiari was right. She didn't dare chance it. She had to run.

Bidaiari reached out and gently placed his hands over her belly. She felt a quickening, a surge of life within her. It felt as though the child was responding to his touch.

With his hands still on her belly he dropped to one knee bowing his head and sent his thoughts to her, 'The child within you is the child of hope. Hope for humans and for our kind. One we have waited for with great anticipation. You, Kylie, are the chosen one. You are special in a way you...' He jerked his head up and quickly rose.

Kylie was immediately overwhelmed by his intense sense of fear.

'Run! Run!'

Kylie turned to leave as quickly as possible. 'Thank you, Bidaiari. For everything.'

'Run!' he was agitated unlike she had ever seen.

91

Kylie's phone was ringing but she didn't dare stop to answer it. She was in too much of a hurry. She was taking Bidaiari's advice.

She was about to get on the elevator when she found the lieutenant colonel and a woman dressed in a lab coat blocking her way.

"You needed a pregnancy test to tell you what's so obvious?" the woman said looking at Kylie's swollen belly. She was obviously not only pregnant, but far along in the pregnancy.

He stared at her stomach with a leer on his face. The lieutenant colonel said, "Dr. Tanner, come with us."

"Sorry, but I have somewhere I need to be." The lieutenant colonel reached out grabbing her wrist and pulled her onto the elevator. "That's an order." He pressed the elevator button to shut the door.

"You forget," she said. "I'm not in the military. And you're hurting me." She attempted to jerk free of his grasp, but he had a tight hold on her.

They took her to a room on the floor above, the lieutenant colonel never for a moment loosening his grip on her. The room had a metal table in the middle of it with stirrups much like in an OB doctor's examination room. There was a table set up with a tray holding two syringes.

"What's going on?" Kylie asked frightened at what she was seeing, wondering what it was they had planned for her.

"This is Dr. Sanford. She'll be performing an amniocentesis on you," the lieutenant colonel said.

"Like hell she will," Kylie said. "That's an intrusive medical procedure that could possibly cause me to miscarry. If I wanted those tests run I would have had my own doctor perform the procedure. You're certainly not going to do this against my will."

"This isn't a matter of choice. We believe you to be carrying alien DNA and now you're pregnant. From what the alien told us

252

that could be a threat to our nation. If we discover your baby to carry..."

The doctor put her hand on his arm to get him to stop talking. "One step at at time. Let's get the procedure done and go from there. Lieutenant Colonel, you can leave now. I'll continue from here."

"I'll be with the colonel and the major. Come find me when you're finished here," the lieutenant colonel left.

Kylie could hear him enter the elevator outside in the hall. The doctor put a firm grip on Kylie's arm as she tried to leave. The doctor said, "Take your clothes off and lie down on the table. Put your feet in the stirrups."

Kylie stood there looking around for a way out.

"Let's make this as simple as possible," the doctor firmly said. "Remove your clothing and lie down on the table. Don't force me to do it for you. You're not leaving this room until this procedure is completed."

92

Kylie was searching for a way out. She was desperate. They didn't care about her or her child, only in promoting their own agenda. And in this case it was her child that was their agenda. She had to do something and quick.

Kylie sat on the side of the table to make the doctor think she was going to comply with her orders. She was ready to run as soon as she had the opportunity to do so. Right now the doctor was between her and the door.

The doctor turned and was filling one of the syringes with some fluid. "This will help you relax during the procedure. I'm going to put you out for a time. You're going to sleep through the entire procedure. When you wake up, it will all be over. This will relax you and the baby both, so the baby doesn't move as I insert the needle."

The doctor thinking Kylie sitting on the table was a sign that she was going to not give her any trouble relaxed her guard.

The doctor turned to Kylie and explained, "As you may or may not know an amniocentesis is performed by inserting a needle into your stomach and removing a small amount of the amniotic fluid the baby is in. You'll be asleep. You won't feel a thing."

Kylie could feel the baby thrashing about inside her as though he had a sixth sense of what was about to happen.

Kylie thought to herself, I'm a geneticist, of course I know what an amniocentesis is and about the tests run. But she thought it was best to let the doctor talk and give her more of an opportunity to make her move.

However, she also knew it was unusual to put the mother and the baby out. They could do anything they wanted while she was out and she would be helpless to stop them. Not that she planned to give them an opportunity to so much as touch her or her baby.

Where was Daphne? She should have been looking for her by now. She could certainly use her help.

The doctor continued explaining, "Some of the amniotic fluid will be removed by a needle to determine a prenatal diagnosis of chromosomal abnormalities, and we're hoping it will show us if the child you carry is a carrier of alien DNA."

Kylie edged herself to the edge of the table where she could jump off when she had a chance to escape.

"We'll examine the fetal DNA for genetic abnormalities, which will help us determine whether your baby is a threat to society. If so, we'll simply abort it and study the dead fetus."

"Like hell you will," Kylie came off the table grabbing the doctor's wrist holding the syringe she was about to inject into Kylie to put her and the baby to sleep.

The doctor lost her balance falling to the floor knocking over the tray with the instruments with a loud clatter. The syringe rolled away and both of them dove for it. The doctor quickly flipped onto her hands and knees and was closer to the syringe than Kylie.

It was just out of reach when the doctor pushed herself forward with her hand just about to grasp it. Kylie took her elbow and slammed it into the doctor's nose.

"Ow!" the doctor shrieked falling over and grabbing her nose. "You broke my nose." Blood poured out of her nose running between her fingers, but she wasn't giving up.

She rolled over and reached for the syringe yet again, but before she could grab it Kylie grabbed her ankle to pull her out of reach. The doctor was able to grab the syringe just as Kylie had yanked her by the ankle.

Kylie quickly sat on the doctor straddling her and knocking the wind out of her. Kylie grabbed the wrist holding the syringe and squeezed until the doctor lost her grip dropping the syringe with the knock-out drug.

She and the doctor both tried to grab it, but Kylie was one determined woman. She put her knee in the doctor's back to keep her down.

The doctor tried to push her off of her. Kylie had too much at risk to give up. This was a fight she was determined to win.

Kylie reached for the syringe, but it had rolled just out of reach. If she reached for it the doctor would be able to get out from under her.

Daphne stuck her head in the door and said, "Thank God I found you. What..."

She looked shocked when she saw the woman being held underneath Kylie.

"Grab that syringe, Daphne. Hurry!"

Daphne spotted the syringe and ran and picked it up, and handed it to Kylie who without hesitation removed the cover off the end of the needle and plunged it into the doctor's neck pressing the plunger quickly to release the drug and knock her out.

Before the entire contents emptied the doctor had already gone still and was out like a light.

"Did you kill her?" Daphne asked in shock watching the entire thing.

"I'd like to. Come on, we've got to get out of here." Kylie said pushing herself up off of the doctor.

"We need to leave now," Daphne said as she followed Kylie down the hall at a brisk run. "They plan to take you with them today, by force if necessary."

"Lead us to the tunnels."

As they stood by the elevator they could hear it running. They looked to see what floor it was on and could see whoever was on the elevator was coming to the floor where they were waiting. "Come on." Daphne said grabbing Kylie by the hand and heading for the stairwell.

As the door closed behind them they heard the elevator ding and the doors open. They ran down a floor which was the floor Ari was on. The guards used to seeing the two of them didn't try to stop them as they ran to Ari's room. Kylie asked if there was anything he could do to give them some time to get away.

He said, 'Go. I will do what I can to keep them away long enough for you to get in the tunnels.'

Daphne's jaw dropped, "OMG, I just read your thoughts. I read an alien's thoughts. I heard him."

Kylie grabbed her and said, "We've got to go. As they stepped into the hall the colonel and lieutenant colonel stepped off the elevator coming in their direction.

"Bidaiari, help us," Kylie yelled.

Daphne said, "Look, they're frozen in place." She ran her hand in front of their face. Nothing. No response.

Bidaiari projected his thoughts to them, 'Go!!'

93

"I don't know how long they'll stay frozen, but we need to get moving," Kylie said. The armed guards too were frozen at the exit to the floor where Ari was housed.

Daphne ran back and grabbed one of the guard's key cards, just in case they needed help getting out of this building and into another. It was better to have a back-up plan in case the guards that were going to help them were held up along the way or didn't show up.

As they ran towards the tunnels Daphne called the two guards who would help them escape. Thankfully they were both working today. They were going to meet them at the entrance to the next building where Daphne and Kylie's passes wouldn't work to open the doors.

Kylie quickly grabbed her phone out of her purse and put in the code that would let Taylor and T.C. know they were on the run and which mode of exit they would be using.

When they got to the next building the guards were nowhere in sight. "There's no time to wait," Daphne said. She took the stolen key card and swiped it. Nothing. The light remained red.

Daphne tried swiping the key card again and the light turned to green allowing them to enter the next building. "Yes, let's go!"

"We still have a ways to go before we get to the tunnel, are you O.K.?" Daphne asked looking back at Kylie. She was worried about a pregnant woman in her last trimester running and what the stress could do to her and the baby.

"Just keep going," Kylie said. "I'll rest a bit once we get deep in the tunnels."

One of the guards texted Daphne and said they would meet them at the tunnel entrance.

Daphne and Kylie had to slow down and appear as though they belonged in these halls when two men stepped out of one of the rooms. They glanced at the women but kept walking.

"How much further?" Kylie asked after going through another building and going down two floors of stairs.

"We're really close now, but this part may be dicey," Daphne said. "We're entering Hangar 18 where they keep the alien spacecraft. It's guarded similar to the floor where Ari's kept."

"Heavily guarded in other words," Kylie said. "With guns."

As they turned the corner Kylie pointed ahead and said, "The stairs to the tunnels are at the end of the next hallway. We have to go down several flights of stairs and then we'll be at the entrance to the tunnel where we're going in."

They turned the corner and Kylie jumped back when she saw two armed guards walking the hallway. "Now what? Is there another way to get there?"

Daphne peeked around the corner and said, "That's our help. Come on."

The guards motioned for them to hurry and opened the door to the stairwell for them. Once they were at the bottom one of the guards said, "Stay back out of sight until I check to be sure the coast is clear."

They could hear the guard outside talking to someone. The man had been about to take the stairs when the guard stopped him telling him the floor was being washed and it was slick. It would be best to take the elevator.

Once the man was out of sight the guard opened the door and motioned for them to come. That's when they heard the alarm going off. Red flashing lights went off in every hall.

"Hurry! Open the door!" one of the guards yelled. "This whole building is about to be locked down."

94

T.C. jumped in his SUV and tore over to Taylor's auto repair shop. Taylor had already received the text too and was hoping the women had at least been able to make it to the tunnels.

There would be no cell service that far below ground surrounded by tons of concrete, so it was unlikely they would hear from their wives again anytime soon.

The guards that were helping them would contact them once they made it out of the tunnels themselves. They could only go so far to get the women to safety and then they would be on their own.

Taylor sent his employees home with the exception of one of his mechanics he trusted. The mechanic's wife was part of their plan to escape.

She came in through the back door locking up behind her. If needed, she would be wearing a wig similar to Kylie's hair and drive out of the garage with Taylor. He was in hopes that if they were being watched they would think it was T.C. and Kylie and chase them. That would give the real T.C. and Kylie a chance to leave in a different vehicle in the opposite direction.

T.C. nervously paced in Taylor's office. "I wish we'd hear something from them. I never should have let her go back to work. We should have just left as soon as we knew she could be in danger."

"We thought we had more time," Taylor tried to reassure his brother, while at the same time was worried sick about his own wife.

Taylor got his brother a drink of water from the water fountain and said, "Getting through the tunnels is going to take time. At the earliest it will be tonight before they get out. It could be as long as tomorrow. They'll have to travel through miles of tunnel."

Before the mechanics had left for the day Taylor had given them instructions to bring a car from the back into the garage and back it in.

When T.C. had arrived Skip, the mechanic, had backed in T.C.'s SUV next to the other car. He then put T.C.'s bags in the backseat of the other car. If they had to change cars the bag would be easy enough to grab quickly. These would be the vehicles used in their escape. It was too risky for T.C. to use his own vehicle.

Everything was ready on their end, now if only the girls could make it out safely they'd be prepared and ready to go.

"It should be us picking them up when they get out of the tunnel. We should be there for them," T.C. said dropping his head into his hand pushing his hair back away from his face.

"They would pick up on us being there and hold us for questioning. The conspiracy theorists they're used to seeing hanging out around there and won't think anything of it other than to try and chase them off."

"I just feel so helpless," T.C. said.

"I know. I had the same argument myself," Taylor said. "These guys have a network and are already in place. They're all set to pick up our wives the moment they step foot outside the fence and get them to safety."

"This stress can't be good for Kylie or the baby," T.C. said.

"Or for you either," Taylor said. "We just have to wait at this point and be ready."

As Kylie, Daphne, and the guards exited the stairwell the alarm and flashing lights went off. They knew they only had thirty seconds until the building went into lock down.

One of the guards rapidly opened the door to the tunnel with his key card just as the light to the door turned red. He barely had the door open when the entire Area 51 shut down locked tight. Nobody would be going anywhere as long as the code remained in place.

The door slammed behind them. "At least no one else will be able to get in the tunnels for a time. That should help," the guard who had unlocked the door said.

"Won't the doors to the tunnels be locked down, too?" Kylie asked.

"No, only the entrance and exit doors to and from the tunnel. The doors in the tunnels themselves were built decades ago, and since they aren't used anymore they never changed it over to the new system," he answered.

Daphne said, "We have to get in a little further and then you can stop and rest a bit, Kylie."

"I can keep going as long as I have to," Kylie said. "I know what's at risk here."

They traveled about half a mile further into the tunnel before they came to two backpacks left and concealed for them by Major Hazard. The backpacks contained a map of the tunnels with different routes highlighted for them to choose from. There were bottles of water, some protein bars, and both Daphne and Kylie had given him a pair of their running shoes to include in the backpacks, as they knew they would have to be doing a lot of walking. He also included flashlights, an emergency flare, two pairs of night vision goggles, bolt cutters in case they needed to cut the fence to get out, a portable radiation detector, and a warm camouflaged blanket for them both in case they were there overnight, either in the tunnels or the desert.

The guards studied the map and chose the route they thought would bring them out in an area which would be the safest exit for them.

One of the guards pointed out what they considered to be the best route explaining to Kylie and Daphne, "You'll be underground a little longer, but it's better to do most of your traveling below ground out of sight than above ground where they'll be searching for you by ground and by air."

"It's a lot of walking," the other guard said. He looked at Kylie who was obviously very pregnant. "Can you do this? It will be about a 16 mile walk. That's an awful lot of walking for a woman in your condition."

Kylie reassured them she could walk the distance as long as she rested occasionally. When the guards looked at each other doubtfully Daphne spoke up and said, "She's in better shape than I am. She'll make it."

"O.K., then." the guard rolled the map up and led the way.

They walked a few miles and at that point insisted Kylie sit and rest a bit before moving any further. She drank one of the bottles of water and ate a protein bar then put her head back and shut her eyes.

She thought about what they had planned to do to her and to the lengths they were willing to go. That thought alone terrified her. But what they didn't know is she was even more determined than they were.

95

The guards carried the backpacks for them as they made their way through the tunnels. The tunnels had been closed up, no longer used for close to half a century. They smelled of dampness and decay. Standing water stood in some areas of the tunnels.

As they walked through the tunnels each intersecting passageway was identified with a number which corresponded to markings on their map. The tunnels ran as far as the eye could see. Thankfully they were well lit up.

As they passed some of the doors Kylie noted that they had signs with the symbol for radioactive and other signs with the wording Warning Radiation Hazard.

"Hold up a minute," one of the guards said as he set one of the backpacks down and pulled out a portable radiation detector. "I'll keep my eye on this. Some of these areas can be dangerous to go through."

The tunnels had a musty smell to them, and it was clear no one had been back here in the area they were then walking through for some time. There were discarded metal cables along the ground much like those used in mines.

After traveling a short distance by the tracks they came to several carts which the guard pointed out had once been used to transport bombs and was called a bomb trailer. It was those carts that had run on the tracks years ago carrying the bombs.

As they walked the guard told them of how the area surrounding Area 51 had been used for testing dirty bombs in the late '50's. "The area we're going through now is close to where the bombs were stored and transported."

He was interrupted by his radiation detector making a clicking sound. They kept walking a few steps and the clicking increased in frequency.

"We need to double back and take a different route. With the radiation level increasing we can't risk it," he said as he guided them back the way they had come. When they had walked back a good ways they stopped and looked over the map choosing a new route.

Some of the doors they came to were sealed off and they would have to change their route yet again. At times it seemed as though they were making no headway. Everything looked the same, miles and miles of long, straight concrete tunnels with huge air ducts running above their heads the length of the tunnel.

"Not exactly the scenic route, is it," Daphne said to lighten the mood.

They sat after walking for several hours to give Kylie time to rest a bit. One of the guards whose wife had recently had a baby told her she could prop her legs up on his lap and he would massage her legs. He said he remembered well that when his wife was pregnant anytime she was on her feet her legs would swell and ache.

Kylie's legs were indeed swollen and her back ached something fierce. Thankfully she was used to walking as she had hiked for years and had always been physically active.

She took one of the back packs and used it for a pillow and spread the blanket out to lay on. She could still feel the hard, concrete floor beneath her.

She took the guard up on his offer to massage her legs. She knew they still had quite a distance to walk and that was just while they were in the tunnels. Then they had to make it through the desert until they were picked up.

The air was stuffy and had an unhealthy feel to it in this area of the tunnels. Kylie had to wonder what toxins her lungs were breathing in from the humid, stale air and how it would affect the baby.

As she was lying there the guard rubbing her legs looked at her swollen belly. He could see the baby was active as her dress was tight across her belly due to the baby. You could see movement beneath her dress as the baby kicked.

He was mesmerized watching it. He felt he had a stake in getting this unborn child to safety and was determined to do just that.

Daphne, too was sitting by Kylie's head watching the baby kick and thinking that she too would be feeling that in months to come with her own child. Taylor would be so happy to learn he was going to be a daddy.

Daphne was brought out of her daydreaming when she saw a movement out of the corner of her eye and screamed jumping up. The others looked up, the guards reaching for their weapons.

96

The colonel, lieutenant colonel, and the doctor were in the major's office having a heated discussion.

The doctor had a bandage on her nose and blood on her lab coat. Her eyes were swollen. She was still groggy from the knock-out drug and had a hard time holding her head up. She slid down into her chair and fought to stay awake.

"How could you let her get away?" the colonel bellowed at the lieutenant colonel. "You were to stay with them and guard her, bringing her to the plane after the procedure was completed."

"You have..." the major began.

The colonel turned and glared at him. "And where's your daughter? What part does she have in all this?"

"I don't believe she was scheduled to work today, so just leave her out of this," the major said furious. "You have no right to come in here and take one of my employees hostage. To even think of what you had planned to do to her."

He took a breath feeling his heart pounding rapidly in his chest. He reached in his drawer and put one of his heart pills under his tongue.

The lieutenant colonel said, "So, where is she? Is she hiding somewhere in the building? We have to find her."

Colonel Hazard turned to the major, "Where would you suggest we look for Dr. Tanner?"

"I would suggest you get on that plane of yours and leave before you find yourself slapped with a lawsuit."

"Lawsuit? For what?" the colonel bellowed.

"For taking an American citizen hostage, planning to do a medical procedure on her without her consent..." the major said.

"Which has yet to be performed due to the ineptness on the part of these two," the colonel said pointing to the lieutenant colonel and the doctor who was still fighting the effects from the sedative Kylie had stuck in her neck.

"Not for lack of trying on your part," the major said. "You took her hostage and planned to kidnap her. Where in this nation do you think that's acceptable?"

"For reasons of national security," the colonel said planting his hands on the major's desk and leaning towards the major screaming in his face.

The colonel stood at the end of the major's desk pointing his finger at him. "Do you not recall when President George W. Bush signed into law the Patriot Act? That law has a lot of wiggle room and leaves a lot to interpretation. And that is how I am taking possession of her and the unborn child, whether you like it or not. That child she's carrying could be a threat to our nation."

"You threatened to abort her child," the major stood up and screamed right back at him.

"You're out of line, major," the colonel said. "I'm your superior and I can have you..."

"Maybe superior in rank, but not as a human being. What kind of man would even consider doing such a thing?" the major paced the floor. "I'll be reporting you. In the meantime, get out!" He pointed to his door.

"We need a search party to locate her," the colonel said.

"You'll do no such thing. If I found her, let's be clear. I would not turn her over to you. We'll do this the right way. We can have the baby tested after it's born for any abnormalities and any indication of alien DNA, but so far with Kylie that's been a bust. What makes you think you'll find any different results with the child?"

"Fine! We'll do it your way then," the colonel said. "Come on." He motioned for the lieutenant colonel and the doctor to follow him out.

"You better hope and pray she doesn't have any complications in her pregnancy due to the stress you've caused," the major yelled loud enough for them to hear as they walked down the hall.

As they left his office he sank to his chair grabbing his heart hoping the medication would kick in soon.

He knew the colonel gave up too easy. He knew there was no way he would just let this go until the birth of the baby.

"You're just going to let her go?" the lieutenant colonel asked sputtering mad. He had to hold the doctor up so she could walk.

"As far as he knows, we are," the colonel said. "As long as he's not willing to help us, he doesn't need to be kept in the loop. We'll have her house watched. She'll have to go home sometime, and we'll pick her up then. By the time the major finds out she'll be out of reach where he won't have any say in the matter."

97

Daphne screamed and jumped up. The guards reached for their weapons thinking someone must have found them in the tunnel.

"Sorry, sorry," Daphne said pointing at the ground. "It's just a big, hairy spider. I'm terrified of those things."

"We should probably get moving," the guard Justin said.

The guard who had rubbed Kylie's legs for her gently laid her legs on the ground and stood holding out his hands to give her a hand up. "It's a shame you have to go through this, especially while pregnant. What do they want with you anyway?"

"Sorry, classified information," Daphne spoke up.

"No problem," he said.. "Understood." And he did. When you became an employee at Area 51 you were used to the government's secrets and being kept in the dark.

He bent over to pick the blanket up. He folded it and stuffed it back in the backpack and threw the backpack over his shoulder.

As they walked along Kylie asked him how old his baby was. "She's three months now. She's just starting to roll over and smile. It seems like everyday she's doing new things."

He pulled her picture out of his wallet to show Kylie. "Her name's Faith. She looks just like her mother."

"She's a little doll," Kylie said. "And thank you. You were right. My legs were swollen. It's much easier going on now. I'm sorry, you're helping us putting your own jobs on the line and I don't even know your name."

"It's Chris. I didn't mean to cross any boundaries or anything. It's just I remembered how much my wife's legs bothered her, and I know you still have a good ways to go yet."

"How much farther?" Daphne asked.

"It looks like about eight more miles," Chris answered.

"What do you think is going on up above?" Justin asked.

"I imagine there's a huge search party going on," Daphne said. "People looking for the two of us."

"Actually, I imagine that search is pretty contained," Justin said. "If the reason for your escape has to do with top secret information they wouldn't want too many people to know about it."

"That's true," Daphne said. "I didn't think about that. That would definitely make it easier."

"The guards will be on alert to watch for you though, both inside and out," Chris said. "It's once you exit the tunnels that you're going to have a problem. I don't think you have to worry about them finding you as long as we're down here."

"I'm worried about the sensors once we make it outside," Daphne admitted. "I don't know how we're going to get around that. Getting to the fence line is going to be problematic."

"Even once you get to the fence line, if you make it to that point they won't stop there. They have no one to be accountable to out here. They can make you disappear and no one would know," Chris said. "Not meaning to scare you, just something you need to know."

"We'll have help waiting," Daphne said, "once, *not if*, but once we get to the fence."

"We'll do what we can to aid you in that," Chris said. "We, meaning us guards..."

Kylie bent over holding her stomach and leaned against the wall. Chris rushed to her side. "Are you alright?"

"A pain, nothing serious. It's just a little uncomfortable. Probably all this walking hasn't helped," Kylie said.

"You're under a lot of stress. That's not good in your condition," Chris said.

They stopped to let Kylie rest awhile. She fell asleep while the others kept watch.

As Kylie slept Chris kept watching her stomach and could see it tighten up at times. He knew that wasn't a good sign.

When her stomach tightened Kylie would whimper in her sleep. Being a man of faith he prayed she didn't go into premature labor, and she would be safe and have a healthy baby.

"We've gone twelve miles already," Justin spoke quietly so as not to wake Kylie. "I know that's a long ways for you to walk, but this exit will be the least risky. You'll be about sixteen miles west of Area 51 when you come out. They probably won't expect you to come out that far, if they've even come to the realization that you went in the tunnels."

Chris was looking at the map over his shoulder and said, "It looks like less than four miles now till we reach the exit. Once you get out, the quicker you make it to the fence line the better your chances. I would suggest you rest until dark and go then."

Daphne pulled out her phone to text the person who was in charge of picking them up once they reached the outside.

"You won't be able to get a signal in here with all this concrete and being so far below ground," Justin said.

"Yeah, I'm pretty sure she will," Chris said pointing at some cables above their heads. "I believe those are radiating cables."

"You're right," Daphne said. "Smart guy."

"What's that?" Justin asked.

As Daphne texted her message for pickup and another to her husband Chris explained how a leaky coax or leaky feeder worked.

"It's a communications system used in underground mining and tunnels. The coaxial cable runs along the tunnel sending and receiving radio waves. Basically it works like an antenna. The cable is leaky from the slots in it's outer conductor allowing the radio signal to reach the length of the cable."

"That's way over my head," Justin said, "As long as it works."

"It's odd though. Granted they're often used below ground like this, but if these tunnels haven't been used in decades why are they here? That technology wasn't available when these tunnels were in use," Chris said.

"They were put in when...," Daphne caught herself about to reveal the information about the alien spacecraft. "Sorry, they did open some of the tunnels again for a time for something they were working on they wanted kept under the radar. I'm not sure if they're still in use or not, but if so we shouldn't stay in this area any longer than necessary."

Kylie woke up and sat up trying to orient herself. Chris told her they were less than four miles from the exit. She didn't know whether to be excited or worried by that news.

She knew they were going to have to rely on the guards that

worked with Chris and Justin to help them out or they would be caught. It terrified her to think of what it would mean if they took her into custody.

They walked on for over another hour. The air seemed to change as they got close to the exit.

"This I'm afraid is where we'll have to leave you," Justin said as they reached the door that led to the outdoors.

The guards left them at the door wishing them the best of luck. They were headed back and would enter the building down a little ways and call for a ride so they would have time to convince the other guards to turn their heads when the sensors went off, or to somehow shut them down for a time and claim a malfunction with the equipment.

They had to get back to their post to take care of that before the two women left to go outside. That would also give the women time to rest and leave under the cover of darkness.

It was already the day after they had first entered the tunnels. Daphne and Kylie both knew their husbands were most likely nervous wrecks not being able to be kept up to date on where they were at this point.

"I don't know if I can do this, Daphne," Kylie said. "I'm terrified."

"You can do it, Kylie. You have to. Look how far we've come already. We've made it this far, we'll make it the rest of the way," Daphne tried to reassure her friend.

Kylie tried texting T.C., but they were in an area of the building where they no longer had the radiating cables and she wasn't able to reach him.

Daphne checked her watch and said, "It's time, Kylie. We have to move and we have to move quickly."

Kylie stood preparing herself to leave the tunnels. She felt Ari's presence. It was so strong she turned around expecting to see him standing there. Then she heard his thoughts in her head.

'You can do this, Kylie. Your baby's life depends on you making it. The child brings hope to many of both worlds. You, Kylie, have been chosen to bring this child into the world. Do not fail. Go with confidence. You will be safe.'

The girls unloaded the backpacks eliminating and leaving behind anything they felt they could do without. They kept the few bottles of water that were left, one flashlight, the flare, night vision goggles which they wore on top of their heads so they could quickly put them on as needed, kept one blanket and emergency flare. The rest they left behind in the other backpack choosing to just carry one.

"We'll need the flare to signal our ride where we are," Daphne said throwing the backpack across her back.

She stepped forward and pulled Kylie in her arms hugging her and said, "We can do this. Ready?"

Kylie said, "Daphne, thank you. You're so special. I can't believe you've put yourself in danger for me."

"Remember what we said about friends. They're there in good times and bad. They're there for each other. Besides, I have to protect my godchild and my baby's cousin."

Kylie took a deep breath and said, "Let's go."

Taylor peered out the window and said, "The car's still there. They're watching the place. I would bet there's someone watching your house and mine, too."

Skip, his mechanic and his wife Holly, were sitting waiting in case they were needed.

T.C. jumped when he heard his phone chime with a text. Taylor's phone did the same.

"They're out of the tunnels. They're still on the grounds, but they're on the way," T.C. said.

"Who was the text from?" Holly asked perking up after a long night of waiting.

"The guy who's waiting to pick them up," T.C. answered. "They texted him earlier and let him know their approximate location of where they would be exiting the tunnels. He's got them in sight watching with his night vision binoculars."

"So far he says there's no sign of the camo guys in the white trucks. That's a good sign." Taylor looked up from his phone and said, "Maybe under the cover of darkness..."

"Don't think for a minute those sensors don't work at night," T.C. said. "You know as well as I do that's the most guarded government installation in the United States. They aren't safe yet."

"Maybe the fact that they came out so far from Area 51 is in their favor," Taylor said.

100

Once Daphne and Kylie stepped out into the outside and the door shut behind them there was no turning back. It was pitch black out. Away from the city and out with nothing around you but a sky full of stars, there was a blackness so thick you couldn't see your hand in front of your face.

"Put your night vision goggles on," Daphne said. "But if you see car lights or any kind of light quickly look down and remove them or they'll blind you."

"How do we know where the sensors are?" Kylie said as she stepped forward.

"We won't be able to see them. We'll just have to hurry and hope we can beat them to our pick-up site before they spot us and come for us."

As they trudged along they could hear the crickets and night sounds. An occasional coyote howled in the background giving Kylie goosebumps. She would hate to have to spend the night out here.

As hot as Vegas was during the day, the night time temperature in the desert was cold. Kylie thought about wrapping the blanket around her but was afraid it would just delay her.

"Here they come," Daphne groaned pointing at a stream of headlights heading their way. "Take off your night vision glasses, but keep going. Don't give up."

The fence was in sight by the time they were surrounded by at least half a dozen white trucks. The guards just sat in their trucks with their engines running.

"What are they waiting for?" Daphne said. "What do they think we're going to do, walk up and give ourselves up?"

The truck's headlights shone lighting their way. When the guards didn't make a move Daphne quickly dropped the backpack to the ground and pulled out the wire cutters.

"Come on, let's go," Daphne said. "They're just sitting there.

And here comes another truck. Maybe that's who they're waiting for."

"They're frozen. The guards are frozen," Kylie said and began laughing hysterically. "Thank you, Ari."

They ran for the fence. Daphne bent over and cut the fence from the ground up, a hole large enough for them to crawl through. Before they had a chance to get through, the other truck came flying up.

Daphne held the fence open as wide as she could and told Kylie to hurry and get through. She told her once she got on the other side not to wait for her but once she was through to run.

The truck doors opened that had just pulled up. Kylie was struggling to get through the fence when she heard the voice of Chris one of the guards who had helped them.

"I'm so sorry. We just got back," he looked over at the other trucks and said to Justin. "What are they doing? Why are they just sitting in the trucks?"

"It doesn't matter," Daphne called out. "Help me get this open so we can get out to safety." She wasn't about to go into explanations of how the other guards had been frozen by an alien who was several floors below ground at Area 51.

Kylie struggled with her added girth as Chris held the fence open as wide as he could for her to crawl through on her hands and knees. The fence caught on her dress and ripped it but she made it through to the other side. Daphne was right behind her.

As she was going under the fence she told Chris and Justin to get back in their trucks and get out of the area and play dumb to what just happened. She assured them the other guards would never know they played a part in their escape.

Daphne made it under the fence and caught up with Kylie. She grabbed her hand and ran as fast as she could for the road.

Their legs were torn up from the desert foliage they had to run through, but they had made it off the property safe and sound.

Daphne stopped only for a moment and shot off the flare. In about 45 seconds an RV came flying up beside them. The door to the back flew open and an older man helped them in. Once they were inside he signaled for the driver to take off.

"You girls alright?" he asked as they sped off.

"We are now," Kylie said. "Thank you, thank you so much!" She broke down sobbing, finally able to let out her emotions. She hadn't believed they would make it out without being caught, but they had.

"I can't imagine how you girls got onto the property and off again there at Area 51, but we were given orders not to ask any questions," the man who had helped them into the vehicle said.

The girls didn't say a word.

"Sure would like to know," the man repeated himself under his breath. "If it'd been me, I would've been shot for sure."

The dust from the road left a large rooster tail behind them as they flew down the dirt road but no one followed. They had made it.

101

T.C. and Taylor both became increasingly worried as time passed. It seemed improbable that their wives had any chance of making it past the sensors once they were outside the tunnels.

"I don't know how we agreed to letting them go through the tunnels," Taylor said. "What chance do they possibly have of making it off the land without being caught?"

"I don't even want to think about it. Why didn't we leave earlier when we had the chance? They must be exhausted. They already had to walk the distance of half a marathon through the tunnels," T.C. said. "And pregnant on top of that."

"Holly, maybe you better get dressed in case we have to run for it," Taylor said. "The clothes and wig are in the women's bathroom."

"Sure," Holly said getting up and heading for the women's room.

Before she left the room she turned to the two men who were worried about their wives and said, "You need to have faith. Kylie's as tenacious as a pit bull when it comes to protecting her baby, and Daphne; well, I've never seen her give up on anything."

T.C. paced, his hands shook. "If anything happens to her I'll never forgive myself. I swear if anything happens to them whoever is responsible I'll hunt them down..."

T.C.'s phone pinged. "They're out!" He shouted. "They made it out. They're on the way here." He wrapped Taylor in a bear hug.

T.C. stared at the screen on his phone and said, "I just got word they've been picked up and they're safe. Exhausted, but safe. Thank you, Lord!"

Taylor said, "With us being watched it might be better to arrange to pick them up somewhere. We can both leave in the cars and double back. I can wait till I know you and Kylie are safe on the road and have Daphne dropped off somewhere else."

"You're probably right," T.C. said. He rapidly texted the

message and named a safe spot close to where one of the cars was left so they could switch cars if need be.

Holly stepped out of the bathroom dressed in her disguise as Kylie with a small pillow under her top and a wig resembling Kylie's hair. Even though she was fairly tall herself, she wore heels since Kylie was tall. They would be a distance from the men watching them, but they didn't want some little thing to make them suspect anything was amiss.

T.C. looked Holly over and said, "Yeah, that should work. Especially in the dark. I think they'll go for it."

They had placed a pillow on the passenger seat so she would sit up high due to Kylie's height.

T.C. and Taylor hugged each other and wept, promising to get back together as soon as it was safe to do so. It was hard to let go. Even harder to say good-bye. There was no way to know how long it would be before they would see each other again.

Skip opened only one side of the garage doors and made sure the men sitting in the car watching had time to get a glimpse of "Kylie" before she got in T.C.'s SUV. As Taylor pulled out of the garage he hesitated just long enough in the car's headlights so the men in the car watching them could get a good look at his face and see that "Kylie" was also in the car.

Chances were the men watching weren't even aware T.C. had an identical twin. They were just hired muscle. Taylor sped off down the road with the other car quickly following.

Once they were out of sight Skip opened the other door of the garage and motioned for T.C. to go. He left in the opposite direction leaving his headlights off until he made a turn onto another road.

He raced to pick up his wife and unborn child. He swore he'd never let either one of them out of his sight again.

102

T.C. could barely take his eyes off his wife. He didn't dare let his guard down for a minute as they drove for the cabin where they would make their home for the next few months.

He didn't want to even contemplate what was in store for them after that. He knew they would be on the run for quite sometime to keep their child out of the hands of the shadow government, a government within a government.

Kylie exhausted from the stress and the long arduous journey out of Area 51 slept soundly as T.C. drove. Her face was filthy, her dress torn, and she had blood on her dress which she assured him wasn't hers but that of a doctor whose nose she had bloodied. She had never looked more beautiful.

He continuously checked his mirrors for any sign of a tail, but he began to relax after they had been on the road for awhile and had seen no evidence of being followed.

Taylor leaving the garage with Holly dressed as Kylie in T.C.'s Land Rover seemed to have worked. When he sped out of the garage the car that had been watching the garage immediately began following him.

They hadn't been very good at their job as Taylor only allowed them to follow him long enough to be assured of T.C.'s escape before he lost them by making some quick thinking maneuvers.

Taylor had texted T.C. when he had picked up Daphne safely. That would be the last they would be able to communicate for some time. It just wasn't safe to do so. He had advised T.C. to take the battery out of the phone and toss the phone in the next body of water they passed just as a precaution, and he would do the same.

Kylie woke and reached for T.C.'s hand squeezing it. "I was so afraid we wouldn't make it out of there. I don't know where they were planning to take me. Can you believe they actually talked about aborting our child as though we had no say in the matter. Our government has gone too far when they get to the point..."

"Ssh! Calm down, honey. You don't want the baby to feel your stress. You're alright now," T.C. said reaching over and rubbing her belly.

She had experienced some pains during the walk through the tunnels and during their escape off the land, but the baby seemed to have settled down now.

"How much further?" Kylie asked. "I'm so tired. I just want to fall into bed and sleep for the next 24 hours."

"We should be there in about 20 or 30 minutes," T.C. said.

"I wonder what Ari meant when he said our baby was hope for the world's survival. He said I had been chosen to bring this child into the world," Kylie stared off into space pondering his words.

Kylie looked down at her stomach and said, "Someone just woke up. It just felt like he or she was kicking me from one side to the other. It must be a boy. This is one strong little fella."

"Maybe we should have found out the sex," T.C. said trying to not think too much about what Ari had said. It just stirred up his doubts again about who or what had fathered the baby.

T.C. however was unable to put Ari's message out of his mind. From the sounds of it they weren't finished with Kylie or the baby. And if she was chosen, did that mean she did carry an alien child?

103

They arrived at the cabin which was situated on the Hualapai Indian reservation. Kylie was touched when she saw that Pilar had some of the baby items she had wanted to purchase all set up just waiting for the arrival of their child.

T.C. looked around. The cabin was small and rustic. It was homey. It would be peaceful out here. It was only for a few months but he was thankful they had a safe place to stay.

T.C. looked through the cupboards and fridge and saw they were well stocked. The Archers were truly good friends. Their son would aid them on the next part of their journey by setting them up with new identities and helping them to get out of the country after the baby came.

"Oh, honey, come look," Kylie called from the other room.

T.C. walked into the bedroom and felt a great wave of contentment as he saw his wife smiling admiring all the baby items.

"Look at this little portable bed. It's perfect. We'll be able to take this with us when we leave too. And look at these precious little outfits. We have receiving blankets and diapers and..."

"It looks like we have everything we'll need for the baby," T.C. said smiling down at her.

"As long as we have each other that's all we need," Kylie said. "Just the three of us."

"You've had a really tough day, honey," T.C. said stroking her hair. "Why don't you take a shower and get some sleep."

Kylie slept the next day until almost noon. When she woke up she found T.C. outside sitting on the porch drinking a cup of coffee.

It had been dark when they arrived last night so they hadn't been able to see much around the cabin. She was quite surprised at the breathtaking view. They were in the midst of a luscious forest but peeking through the trees stood massive cliffs. The panorama really was spectacular.

"It's beautiful, isn't it?" T.C. said. "I've been enjoying the view and the peacefulness of it all."

"This will make it much easier to be cooped up here for the next few months," Kylie said coming over and kissing him on the top of his head. "The air smells so fresh. I'm going to enjoy being here with you."

They heard someone walking through the forest near the cabin and T.C. whispered to Kylie, "Go inside."

Before she had a chance to get up someone called out, "It's Makawee. I'm your midwife, a friend to Dr. Archer."

The native American woman then stepped from the forest revealing herself. "Do not fear. The good doctor has told me to care for you as if you were one of our own. You will have your peace and be left alone other than me coming to check on you from time to time."

104

T.C. and Kylie stood to greet the Indian woman who stepped from the forest. She introduced herself as Makawee, Kylie's midwife.

She asked if they had everything they needed and told them she would do their shopping for them and to just let her know of their needs. She would get messages to Dr. Archer as needed she reassured them. She wished to examine Kylie and they stepped inside the cabin.

T.C. stood in the doorway to their bedroom and watched as the midwife lifted Kylie's top and felt all around her belly. "The child is restless in your womb. I will bring you a tea that will help the child to settle."

The midwife felt from one end of her belly to the other and said, "The child will see the light of day in about ten weeks. You must rest and let your mind be at peace. Only then can your child be calm."

She left as quickly as she came.

"What did you think of the midwife?" T.C. asked.

"She came highly recommended to me by Pilar, but I'm still glad Pilar will be here for the birth, too," Kylie said. "I never thought I'd be giving birth at home or in a little cabin in the woods."

"Does that worry you?" T.C. asked as he came and sat at the side of the bed.

"A little," Kylie said. "I just worry in case something goes wrong. In other ways it feels right, natural."

"Remember your midwife said for you not to worry and be at peace so the baby will calm down," T.C. said. She felt the baby stirring within her even as he spoke.

T.C. laid his hand on her belly and immediately felt a hard kick. Kylie and T.C. laughed.

She sat up and asked, "Can we take a walk and look around a

bit? It's beautiful here. I want to see where I'm going to be living for the next few months."

"Don't you think you should rest?" T.C. asked.

"I slept until almost noon. I think I got plenty of rest. I'll rest and put my feet up when we get back," Kylie said.

They walked hand in hand to the outskirts of the forest and could see some of the Indians in the land below. One was riding a horse and there was a woman with a child in a sling on her back. Most wore your typical western style clothing. There were an occasional few in native clothing, one was a pregnant woman with another child by her side.

There were several children dressed in typical American style clothing. They ran and kicked a ball stirring up the dirt where they played. It was a picturesque scene.

When they returned to the cabin Kylie heated them up some soup she had found and after eating laid down to rest.

105

T.C. had fallen asleep himself while Kylie was napping. He woke to the sounds of her moaning and tossing and turning about on the bed. He looked at her and she was clutching her belly. Tears ran down the side of her face.

"I'm having pains," Kylie cried. "Really sharp, intense pains."

He immediately woke up fully alert and said, "When did they start?"

"They woke me up about ten minutes ago," she clutched her belly and squeezed her eyes shut as another pain came. She clutched the sheet from the bed in her hand while the pain lasted.

"The pains are hard and close together," Kylie cried. "You need to call Pilar or the midwife."

As he stood to pull on his pants he could see her belly tighten up hard as a rock. "T.C., please...get help. Tell them to hurry."

The midwife came quickly and examined Kylie. "The baby is coming too early. It can not survive if it comes now." She had Kylie rise her feet above her head by putting them up against the wall as she laid in the bed.

The midwife went to the kitchen to make her an old Indian traditional tea from tea leaves and herbs gathered from the forest in hopes it would stop the pains.

T.C. whispered to her, "Can you stop the pains?"

"I don't think so. Perhaps, as long as the waters don't break." She shook her head and said, "The pains came upon her too fast and hard."

A Native American man in native dress and moccasins walked into the cabin soundlessly and walked into the bedroom where Kylie was lying.

T.C. started to head towards the bedroom to ask the man to leave.

The midwife held his arm and explained, "That is the shaman. He has come to see the future of the child."

The shaman ran his hand in the air over Kylie's belly speaking in the Pai language the dialect of the Hualapai people. He then held both hands over her belly and made a gesture as though he were drawing something out of her and walked outside shaking his hands.

The midwife explained, "He is removing any bad or playful spirits that may be calling the child into this world too early. I think he's too late though. The child is too anxious to enter this world."

The shaman walked back in and said, "This child will arrive when the time for her to arrive comes, not before. There is something special about this child. She is a holy one. She will bring hope to many of all kinds. She will be a great leader. She will be called Hope."

The midwife seemed taken aback at his words. "It's too late. You're wrong. The child is coming." She called out after him.

The shaman merely shook his head in disagreement with what she said and walked back into the forest and disappeared among the trees.

106

The pains continued as night fell. The pains didn't increase but they didn't lessen either. They were coming almost every five minutes.

Kylie was inconsolable fearing her child was not going to survive. The next time the midwife checked her she checked to see if Kylie was dilating. Not only had she begun to dilate, but she had begun bleeding.

T.C. said, "We need to get her to a hospital. Maybe it's not too late for them to save the baby."

Both T.C. and the midwife looked up startled as the forest lit up with bright lights. T.C. feared they had been found.

They had been found, but not by the government as he first assumed. The aliens had come to take Kylie.

T.C. and the midwife were frozen into a trance like state and were unaware when the aliens entered the cabin.

The alien who had told Kylie in the past that he had been with her always came and put her in a dreamlike state. He then scooped her up into his arms and gently carried her aboard the spacecraft.

Kylie came to on what appeared to be an operating table with several aliens around her. She began to panic thinking they were taking her child from her. She gasped and cried out as a strong labor pain ripped through her.

'Quiet now! We have come to save the child,' the alien explained to her. 'The child is not yet ready for this world. We are fixing the problem.' He placed his hands on the side of Kylie's head, and she immediately felt comforted and the pains stopped completely.

After a time he leaned over Kylie and said, "The baby is safe and resting within you."

She saw another alien step between her legs with some type of long, slender instrument which he inserted into her. She began to panic not knowing what he was doing.

The other alien again touched her head and said, "He is only inserting a part of us into the child. It is necessary for the child to continue to live, to survive."

When the alien completed his work and withdrew the instrument he stepped back and bowed and left the room. The alien by her head stood back and told her she could get up, it was time for her to go.

"All is well now with the child. You can return and wait for the baby's safe arrival," the alien said as he helped steady her when she stood.

Kylie walked into the living room and watched as the midwife and T.C. seemed to come out of a trance.

"What are you doing up?" T.C. said coming to her side in a panic.

"You must not get up. It will bring the child on..." the midwife began.

"The pains have stopped. Everything's O.K., I think everything will be alright now," Kylie said.

Once the midwife examined her again she shook her head and said, "That must have been a strong batch of tea. I just knew the child would come with no breath of life before the dawn. I was wrong. The child survives."

107

Pilar had taken a chance and come to visit. She explained she felt it was worth taking the risk after what the midwife had told her. She wanted to examine Kylie for herself to be reassured.

Kylie told her how the aliens had performed some type of operation on her which saved the baby and stopped the pains.

"I'm certainly glad they have the know-how to do that," Pilar said. "I feared the worst. I'm so thankful everything's alright with you and the baby. I would advise you to still take it easy though. You need to make it at least another month and preferably two for the baby's chances to survive to increase. You still have over two months to go before the child is full term."

"I never thought I'd be happy the aliens came to visit," T.C. admitted. "She hasn't had another pain since then."

"The baby seems fine," Pilar said. "A strong heartbeat and active."

T.C. told Pilar and Kylie what the shaman had said when both he and the midwife thought they were going to lose the baby.

"That's almost word for word what Ari said," Kylie said in amazement.

"He's a holy man who seems to see the future," Pilar said. "I've seen him in other instances that simply astounded me."

Pilar stood and said, "I'm so thankful both you and the baby are doing better. I don't think I should chance coming again though, unless you have any other issues or until the baby comes."

After Pilar left they sat down and began making a list of baby names. They narrowed it down to a few names but still hadn't decided for sure.

"I guess we could narrow it down to two or three names for both a boy or a girl and then wait till the baby is born and see what name seems to suit him," Kylie said.

"The shaman said she," T.C. said.

"Everyone else has said he," Kylie reminded him.

"I guess it will be one or the other," T.C. said smiling.

108

The next weeks passed with Kylie getting bigger as her time to give birth was just a few weeks away. She was slower getting around and not as active. The extra weight was making her uncomfortable. She was counting down the weeks.

They had been safe so far. T.C. realized the ones looking for them would realize it would soon be time for the arrival of the baby. Would they begin their search again in earnest at that time? He hoped he and Kylie would be long gone by the time that happened.

There were no more visits from the aliens. Things had been quiet.

They took daily walks through the land the cabin was on but only watched the activity from the reservation from a distance. It was best they remained unseen by others.

On one of their walks they had come across a creek. It was in an isolated area of the reservation. T.C. came to fish and Kylie would watch or nap in the shade being soothed by the sounds of the running water.

Kylie was sitting on the front porch of the cabin when a doe and two fawn stepped into the clearing. The deer looked over at Kylie but seemed unconcerned by her presence.

Kylie watched them and was disappointed as the mother stepped back into the forest with the fawn following.

Kylie got up and quietly walked over and stepped a little ways into the forest to see if she could see them. She went farther than she realized when she could see though a space between the trees a small grassy area.

A pregnant native American woman stepped into the clearing below. She laid a blanket that she had been carrying in an area underneath a tree. She stepped out of her native dress and leaned back against the tree.

Within a few moments of watching her Kylie realized the

294

woman was in labor and about to give birth there on her own. She never uttered a sound. Kylie sat in the grass and quietly watched her.

When it became time for her to push the woman leaned against the tree squatting over the blanket. When her next contraction came she held onto the branch above her head and silently bore down to push the child from her womb.

Two pushes later Kylie could see the child's head emerge between her legs. The woman reached between her legs while leaning against the tree and eased the child out. She laid the child on the blanket below with it's cord still attached. She wrapped the baby in a blanket vigorously rubbing the child until it began to cry.

The Native American woman buried the afterbirth below the tree where she had given birth. She then sat and held the child to her breast feeding him. A short time later she put her dress on over her head, gathered up her newborn child, rolled up the blanket, and walked back towards the living area of the reservation.

Kylie sat back going over in her mind what she had just witnessed. The woman had never made a sound. She stood or squatted through the entire birth. She was all alone and had given birth in the most natural way. It had been an amazing sight to see. Rather than feeling she had intruded on a private scene she thought perhaps there was a reason she had witnessed this birth.

109

T.C. watched Kylie try to get comfortable but the additional weight of the baby was making that difficult. Her back was aching when she woke up and the position of the baby was making it hard for her to get around. The baby had dropped and was low causing her discomfort.

Kylie stood by the edge of the creek in one of her few dresses that still fit her. She pulled her dress over her head and dropped it at her feet. Naked she walked into the creek as T.C. stood watching as he fished. Even at almost nine months pregnant he was stricken by her beauty. He admired the swell of her belly and her swollen breasts.

She splashed around in the creek for a few minutes and started splashing him where he was standing at the edge of the creek. "Come in and join me."

"Since you've scared all my fish away I might as well." He set his pole down and stepped out of his shorts and joined her.

"I feel weightless in the water. I should have thought of this before," Kylie said.

T.C. swam over to her and treaded water beside her. They swam for awhile and then went to shallow water where they could reach the bottom.

He held her in his arms while she floated for a time with her huge belly protruding from the water. She turned over and swam into his arms and kissed him. He gently made love to his wife there in the shallow part of the creek.

They swam over to the edge of the creek where they were still submerged in the water but could rest against the edge. They sat and talked about the days ahead and discussed where they would go when the time came for them to leave.

They got out of the water and spread a blanket and dozed in the sun for awhile wrapped in each other's arms. When they woke up they went for one more swim before heading back to the cabin.

Rather than put her clothes back on Kylie did her best to wrap a towel around her belly but it wouldn't reach around her girth. She just shrugged and remained as naked as the day she had been born. She loved not feeling constrained by tight clothing.

As T.C. watched her he could see her belly grow taut. He wondered if the contractions were beginning. He had felt her belly growing rock hard when they were in the water but hadn't said anything.

He knew her time would come soon. She wasn't due for about another two and a half weeks, but when the midwife had last examined her she said it could be any time.

That evening after dinner Kylie said, "I think we better get serious and get our list of baby names narrowed down. Have you picked any favorites?"

He said, "I like Noah if it's a boy."

Kylie said, "I like that, but how about Timothy Noah?"

"No juniors. He deserves his own name," T.C. said.

"He wouldn't be called Jr. Your middle names would be different and besides everyone calls you T.C. They could call him Timothy," Kylie argued her case.

"They won't be calling me T.C. for long. We'll have to change our names when we leave here. If we called him Timothy that might be something that would give him away one day as far as his true identity and put him at risk."

"I see what you mean," Kylie said.

T.C. asked, "Did you have a name picked out for a boy?"

"I liked Timothy," she said. T.C. gave her a look. "OK, I also like Forrest. The name Forrest would remind me of our time together here."

"That's a nice thought. We'll keep Forrest and Noah as our choices for a boy," T.C. said.

"How about a girl's name?" T.C. asked.

"I like Brook," Kylie said.

"Brook, I like that," T.C. said. "Forrest, Brook...very earthy names."

"Did you have a girl's name picked out? Not that I think we'll need one. Everyone has called the baby he and him since I've been pregnant," Kylie said.

"Except for the shaman, don't forget," T.C. said.

"Except for the shaman," Kylie admitted.

"I thought about what both Ari and the shaman said about the baby. I think if it's a girl Hope would be a perfect name for her," he said. "The shaman as much as said her name is Hope."

"Hope," Kylie said thinking about it. "I like it. Not that I think we'll be using it. I know this is a boy. This baby is far too active and troublesome to be a girl."

"That's the very definition of a girl – troublesome," T.C. said smiling at his beautiful wife.

110

In the morning they went for a walk but made it a short one as Kylie was uncomfortable. Her back was hurting and the baby low in her womb was causing her discomfort when she walked.

As they headed back to the cabin Kylie said, "How about I make us lunch and we eat down by the creek? I'd like to swim for a little while. It eases the pain in my back and takes the pressure off my stomach."

T.C. said, "That's fine, only I'll make lunch while you sit and put your feet up. Then we'll go have a picnic and a swim. I'll even give you a back massage down by the creek."

T.C. watched her as she sat with her feet up as he made lunch. She eased down in the chair placing a pillow behind her back. She was gently rubbing her belly and taking long, deep breaths letting them out slowly.

Her clothes had all become stretched tight the last few weeks and fit tight across her belly. Even from the kitchen he could see her belly grow hard beneath her hands. As her belly hardened she began the breathing exercise they had seen in the Lamaze vlog they had watched on YouTube.

"Are you sure you want to go to the creek today?" He asked her concerned that the walk had been too much. "We could just eat here and then you could take a nap."

"No, I really need to go to the creek. Being in the water relieves me of this weight. It really feels good to feel weightless again after carrying this added bulk around."

He packed their lunch in a basket and grabbed some towels and a blanket for them to sit on while they ate and so she could lie down afterwards and rest.

Sitting by the creek they enjoyed the soothing sound of the running water and the beauty of the open sky. They both loved the outdoors and had spent more time outdoors than indoors since they came to the cabin. With this spectacular setting they didn't want to go indoors anymore than they had to.

T.C. noticed Kylie just picked at her food and ate very little. Two or three bites and she pushed her plate away. She leaned back enjoying the scenery. She followed the flight of a hawk for a time and then rolled over and took a short nap. When she woke up she was ready for a swim.

T.C. had draped his arm loosely over her belly as they rested and had begun timing when her stomach grew hard. It was about every five minutes, sometimes only two minutes between contractions. She was still weeks away from her due date, but from the signs of things this baby was restless and ready to be born.

She pulled her clothing over her head dropping them at her feet by the edge of the blanket. She headed for the water. She told him being free of the tight fitting clothes and in the water seemed to give her more comfort than anything. She stood by the creek's edge slowly rubbing her enormous belly.

She felt quite comfortable in their private swimming area being in the nude. No one ever came to this area and they had their privacy.

He joined her in the water and instead of a brisk swim they leisurely treaded water. He was watching her carefully and he could see in her face that she wasn't as relaxed as she had been yesterday in the water.

"Let's go closer to shore," she said.

When he swam up to her side she was clutching her stomach.

"Kylie, are you in labor?" T.C. asked.

111

T.C. watched her breathe through the contraction. When he asked if she was in labor it was a minute or two before she could respond.

"Yes," she said. "The pains woke me this morning, but they weren't too bad. When we walked they began getting a bit more uncomfortable. They're pretty consistent now. They're getting harder and closer together."

"We should get back to the cabin," T.C. said.

"No, please," Kylie said. "Let's just stay here a bit longer. It helps being in the water. It really does."

"We need to call Pilar," T.C. insisted, "and let the midwife know. He had been carrying their satellite phone with him whenever they left the cabin for the last month just in case she went into labor while they were out or in case of an emergency.

"Please wait just a bit longer," Kylie pleaded. "I want to do this just with you for as long as I can."

"I can at least call them and let them know so they'll be prepared. I can tell them you aren't ready for them to come yet," T.C. pleaded.

"No, they'll want to come check me. I just want it to be the two of us," Kylie begged. "Please."

That thought made T.C. nervous and it was against his better judgment, but he agreed as long as she gave them plenty of time to make it to the cabin for the birth.

"Don't worry. This is our first. It will probably take hours," Kylie said.

He held her as she floated in the water as he had the other day. It seemed to soothe her, but the pains soon became harder and more frequent to the point where she found it hard to relax.

She asked him to hold her up but let her stomach below the water. She leaned back against him and he wrapped his arms around her holding her just below her breasts. Being in the water did seem to bring her relief. When a contraction came on he took one hand and gently rubbed her belly through the contraction.

The pains increased in intensity more quickly than either of them expected and began coming closer together.

She crawled up the bank on her hands and knees. She barely made it up the bank before a hard contraction came on. Still on her hands and knees she breathed through it and relaxed laying on her side after it was over.

He was a nervous wreck watching her thinking they had waited too long to make the call. She looked like she was about to give birth any minute with the contractions as strong as they were.

"You better make those calls," Kylie said as another contraction began almost as soon as the one before it ended.

Before he had a chance to get up to make the call, she grabbed his hand squeezing hard through the contraction.

The minute the contraction ended he ran for the phone and dialed Pilar first since she had the furthest to go. He then called the midwife who told them to stay by the creek, and she would come check Kylie there. She could then help him get her to the cabin.

Kylie was on her hands and knees breathing through another contraction as the midwife made her appearance.

The midwife watched her through the next contraction and could clearly see the contractions were close together and pretty intense. She told Kylie to lie on her back or squat, whichever position was most comfortable for her and she would check to see if she was dilating when the next contraction came.

T.C. helped Kylie onto her back and she immediately could feel the beginning of the next contraction starting. The midwife told her to put her legs on her shoulders as she examined her.

When the contraction began the midwife checked her to see if she was dilating. The midwife finding her to be almost fully dilated went ahead and broke her water. She gently laid Kylie's legs down and stood saying, "You're going to be a mother today. She looked at the sky. Before the sun goes down the child will arrive."

"We better get her to the cabin now," T.C. said.

Kylie said, "I want to have the baby here. This is such a beautiful, peaceful place."

T.C. thought she was delirious from the pain, but the midwife agreed that it was the perfect place to bring a child into the world.

She gave T.C. a list of things she needed brought from the cabin for the birth.

112

T.C. hesitated not wanting to leave Kylie's side. It was only then he realized he was still naked from their swim. He covered himself and looked sheepishly at the midwife.

"I've seen it before," the midwife said. Seeing that he was hesitant about leaving Kylie she said, "I know where the things are I need. I'll go get them. You stay with your wife."

T.C. asked Kylie, "Are you sure this is where you want to give birth?"

"Can you think of a more beautiful place? It's who we are," Kylie said. She told him about the birth she had witnessed of the young native American woman. "It was natural as birth should be. That's what I'd like for us and our child."

He helped her through the next pains holding her up against him. She was becoming restless, unable to get comfortable.

He slipped into his shorts before the midwife returned embarrassed at having quite literally being caught with his pants down.

By the time the midwife returned Kylie's pains were coming every two minutes consistently. She could no longer talk through them.

"Where's Pilar?" she cried between contractions. "I wanted her to be here."

"She's on her way. Don't worry, we're prepared to bring the little one into the world with her or without her," the midwife said.

She told Kylie to get in whatever position was most comfortable for her to complete the birthing process.

Ten more minutes of contractions and Kylie leaned against T.C. with her head on his shoulder. The pains were intense, much harder than she had ever thought they would be.

"I can't do this," Kylie cried. "It hurts so bad. Please, I can't do this anymore."

"No one can do this for you," the midwife said. "You'll be

fine. You're a strong woman."

T.C. felt helpless as she cried as another contraction overwhelmed her. The midwife examined her to see if there were any changes since her water broke.

Kylie lowered herself onto the blanket exhausted. T.C. rubbed her head and encouraged her through each contraction.

"You're fully dilated," the midwife said. "Your baby will be in your arms soon and the pains forgotten."

113

T.C. noticed the shaman sitting on some rocks on the other side of the creek. His hands were raised in the air and he appeared to be praying to whatever god he prayed to. T.C. didn't mind his being there to witness the birth. For some reason he felt comforted by his presence.

Kylie wanted to get into another position. She squatted on her knees with her arms around T.C. using him as support when the contractions came on.

Pilar stepped into view and saw that Kylie was in hard labor.

"This is certainly unconventional," she said in reference to Kylie giving birth by the creek.

Did the labor pains come on suddenly or did you choose to have the birth here?" Pilar asked.

"Kylie's choice," T.C. said. "She wanted to have it here. I didn't know about that until her labor was pretty far advanced."

The midwife directed T.C. to be prepared to help his child in the birth process. "Catch your child as he first sees the light of day. Help bring him into this world. He is about to make his presence."

Kylie not needing to be told listened to her body and began pushing through the next contraction. When the contraction was over she was exhausted and sweaty from the hard work. When the next contraction came on she automatically knew to push. She gave it everything she had in her.

"The head is right there," Pilar said. "Push, Kylie. Push hard. Push that baby out."

Her face turned red from her efforts. The baby's head didn't appear to have moved at all through all her attempts to bring him into the world.

On the next contraction Kylie pushed with every bit of strength she had and the baby's head made it's way through the birth canal, it's little face exposed.

Pilar said to T.C., "Be ready and don't drop him. He'll be

slippery."

One more push and the rest of the baby slid out with ease into T.C.'s waiting hands.

Kylie was totally exhausted from the efforts of giving birth and the midwife helped ease her onto the blanket. T.C. held the baby in his arms crying with relief and joy. "You did it, Kylie."

Pilar showed T.C. where to cut the cord when it was time. The midwife took the baby as it began squalling and walked a few steps away.

T.C. and Kylie looked at each other grinning at the first cries of their baby.

"What is it?" Kylie asked. "Boy or girl?

T.C. looked amazed. "I forgot to look."

114

Pilar looked the baby over and attended to it while the midwife returned to finish taking care of Kylie.

"Is everything alright?" T.C. called to Pilar. He had been concentrating so hard on delivering the baby and not dropping it, then cutting the cord, that he didn't even think to look to see whether it was a boy or girl.

Pilar brought the baby over and laid her skin to skin atop her mother. When she placed the infant on her mother she said, "It's a girl. A beautiful little girl."

"A girl," T.C. said smiling from ear to ear. He looked over in the direction of the shaman, the only one to have proclaimed they would have a girl. The shaman was gone.

Kylie and T.C. admired their baby looking her over.

T.C. silently looked her over and thought to himself that she seemed human. He saw no signs of her resembling an alien. She looked perfect to him.

Kylie held the baby to her breast to let her suckle. The baby immediately latched onto her breast and knew what to do. Kylie and T.C. smiled at each other in awe of this little child they had made and delivered together.

He reached down and kissed Kylie's forehead and said, "You did it. You brought our little girl into the world. You did an amazing job."

Where he came from T.C. didn't know, as one minute the shaman was gone but now he stood looking down at the baby nursing at her mother's breast.

The shaman gazed into the child's eyes who seemed alert and looked back at him. "The baby is of this world, but not of this world. She belongs to two worlds. Many will look to her for answers. She is the hope of two worlds. She will be called Hope."

T.C., Kylie, and Pilar all contemplated what he meant by his words.

They all had their own thoughts on the matter considering the story of the child's conception. That's a story which would forever remain a mystery - *or would it?*

Did his words mean she did indeed come from the alien, or that she also carried alien DNA but was the child of T.C. and Kylie?

Perhaps one day they would have the answer, but for now they just wanted to enjoy and love their baby. T.C. decided he needed to let the question of her paternity go and just be the father he desired to be.

Pilar asked, "What are you going to name her?"

"Hope," both Kylie and T.C. answered without hesitation.

115

T.C. and Kylie were finally alone with their baby. Before she left Pilar had helped them to the cabin and had bathed both Kylie and the baby and prepared them a light meal. She dressed Hope in a white nightgown with pink rosebuds and wrapped her in a receiving blanket handing her to her mother to nurse.

It was hours after the birth. The baby was lying on the bed between them. They gazed adoringly at their baby daughter. She seemed unusually alert for a newborn and appeared to watch them as they watched her every move.

T.C. looked at her and knew in his heart that regardless of her origins he would love her and protect her with everything he had in him. As far as he was concerned he was determined to put the question of where she came from behind him. He would think of her as his own, which he suspected she probably was.

"She looks just like you," T.C. said to Kylie.

"And here I thought she looked like you," Kylie said. "She has your cute little nose and your chin. I hope she'll have your smile."

They were amazed at every little sound or movement she made. They couldn't seem to keep their hands off her. All the pain of the labor forgotten as they were completely mesmerized by this little beauty.

"We better get some sleep," Kylie said after a few minutes. She handed Hope to T.C. to put in her bed by the end of their own bed where she would be near by. "She'll be wanting to be fed again in a few hours. We'll have to learn to sleep when we can."

T.C. was woken from a deep sleep. He thought he was dreaming at first when he looked towards the baby's bed and saw three aliens staring down at her. He watched helplessly as one reached out and gently touched the baby. They then bowed, turned and left, one looking at him intently as he turned to leave. He nodded acknowledging T.C.

He had fallen back asleep when the baby began crying. Kylie said, "Honey, can you bring me the baby so I can feed her?"

Half asleep he walked over and changed her diaper and then reached to pick her up to take to her mother to be fed.

If he would have been holding her he would have dropped her. When he had looked into her eyes it was as though he was watching their future unfold through her eyes.

Looking intently into her eyes he could see two men grabbing Kylie. They were dragging her away screaming while a tall, blonde couple stood by with what he somehow knew was Hope when she was still a child. He was nowhere to be seen in the picture.

He blinked and looked again only to see the baby, a perfect little girl whose looks favored her mother.

He promised himself he would quit drinking the midwives herbal tea thinking he had been hallucinating. Between that and very little sleep he convinced himself he had imagined the whole thing.

He had let his fears get the best of him. Had he been seeing things because he was half asleep? He stared at her to see if anything happened, but he just saw a perfect little baby hungry and crying for her mother's milk.

"Honey, are you going to bring her to me to feed?" Kylie asked sleepily from the bed. "She's crying. I need to feed her."

He convinced himself he had just imagined it and carried the baby over to her mother. Kylie lowered one side of her nightgown exposing her breast for the baby to nurse.

Hope seemed to be looking right at her father as she rooted for her mother's breast. As she was about to take the breast into her mouth he saw a lizard tongue reach out to lick the milk dripping from her mother's breast.

www.ingramcontent.com/pod-product-compliance
Lightning Source LLC
Chambersburg PA
CBHW071105250626
47159CB00002B/602